THE BROKEN PINES

A NOVEL BY

CHRIS RILEY

D1616123

Black Rose Writing | Texas

The author grants the final approval for this literary material.

First printing

This is a work of fiction. Names, characters, businesses, places, events, and incidents are either the products of the author's imagination or used in a fictitious manner. Any resemblance to actual persons, living or dead, or actual events is purely coincidental.

ISBN: 978-1-68513-056-5
PUBLISHED BY BLACK ROSE WRITING
www.blackrosewriting.com

Printed in the United States of America
Suggested Retail Price (SRP) $21.95

The Broken Pines is printed in Georgia

*As a planet-friendly publisher, Black Rose Writing does its best to eliminate unnecessary waste to reduce paper usage and energy costs, while never compromising the reading experience. As a result, the final word count vs. page count may not meet common expectations.

This one's for you, Sherry.

ACKNOWLEDGEMENTS

First, I would like to thank my family—Sherry, Jackson, and Jessica—for putting up with all my writing shenanigans. Much appreciation goes to my fellow Warped Spacers: Steve & Judy Prey, Chris Crowe, Denny Grayson, Jim Czajkowski, Amy Rogers, Tod Todd, Caroline Williams, Lee Garett, Sally Ann Barnes, Jesse Cox, Leonard Little, Chris Smith, Jane O'Riva, and Matthew Bishop.

A special thank you goes to Dr. Elisa Shipon-Blum for her outstanding knowledge and work on Selective Mutism... My interpretation of this disorder is one of fiction (and probably far from accurate), but I have worked with children afflicted with Selective Mutism in the past, and it had a profound effect on me. I'm glad I've had this opportunity to share a bit of my experiences.

I owe a great load of debt to my fellow Humboldt Brothers, Grant Kinkade, and Joe Bressler, for educating me on the unique agricultural world found behind the Redwood Curtain. And of course, for all things Rastafarian.

Finally, speaking of brothers, I should thank one of my oldest and dearest friends, Richard Headley, for showing me so much throughout the years—some of which can be found in the pages of this story.

THE
BROKEN
PINES

CHAPTER 1

Southern Oregon, 1998

The three massive trees outside the kitchen window captured Kenny's attention every morning. As he poured his coffee, he would contemplate their presence. He was quite aware of the daily appeal they had on him, and sometimes he looked forward to this appeal, as lately the trees offered him a sense of something familiar, something grounding.

The trees were some type of old pines, strong and tall, with ancient roots that ran cold and deep, deeper than the history of any living man. Their tall crowns scratched at the sky a hundred feet up, and their wide branches, forever bristling in hunter-green, were like the fingers of some forgotten god, painting the land below with forlorn and shadow, with longing, and commemoration. The bark of these trees was as coarse as pig's hair, yet it looked soft and inviting to the touch, not unlike the fur of Kenny's faithful companion, George. On this morning, the golden retriever sat at Kenny's feet, looking up, tail wagging.

The irony is that Kenny knew this "familiarity" he sensed, lingering in the shadows of those trees, was a false one. But with a stab of longing, it often reminded him of the time when his life was made simple, before his wife and family... before *only* the family. At that time, years ago, Kenny's simple life consisted of only Navy routines.

"You want out, boy?" Kenny caressed George's head, his mind focused on where he was right now, in this moment of his new life, with his new home, those three trees outside, and all the new "circumstances" recently forced onto him with such speed and impact. Like a hinged door, his mind swung back to his latest concern—the insidious one, going on for six months now, which made it not so late after all. Then he wondered about the perpetual wheel of life, and the destinations where that wheel made its last stop, to where it carried, and ultimately deposited, people like him.

Looking at the kitchen window again, Kenny now observed himself, the reflection of a forty-one-year-old man who had recently lost thirty pounds, while gaining two inches of shaggy beard on his face. The scruff matched his hair, which fell just above his shoulder blades, and was still dark amber, lacking a single thread of gray—something he'd inherited from his mother, whose bourbon locks held out well past her fifties. Kenny's eyes, round and bear-like, reflected small pools of molasses, and seemed always to look contemplative and sad. Begrudgingly, this argument, the disposition of his eyes, had clung to him for most of his adult life.

Quietly, he prepared a second cup of coffee, careful not to be so loud as to wake his kids. Most mornings were his, but there was always the odd occasion when one of them got up before he did. It was usually Jolie—short for Jolene Marie Shelton—his seven-year-old box of dynamite. Kenny often imagined his daughter having butterfly wings tucked somewhere behind her back, all but invisible to adults. The girl never could sit still, being like most kids, but what humored him was that it seemed impossible for his daughter to move like any normal person. It was impossible for her to "walk" from point A to point B, ever, as her mode of transportation was a sporadic dance involving a passage through an assortment of byways and hiccups. Which, from afar, reminded Kenny of a butterfly roaming through a flower garden. Sometimes she even pranced around on her tiptoes for no apparent reason.

She'll be up soon, Kenny thought. Their destination today was the beach, to do some fishing. Jolie went out of her skin last night when Kenny announced these plans. She loved going to the beach, loved going anywhere—again, like most kids. She also loved breakfast, lunch, dinner, and all meals in between, and the girl radiated when she had a hand in preparing such meals. His daughter loved furry critters of all sorts, soft blankets, and falling asleep in random places. She loved her family, was loyal as old George. And she was a fighter, born to scrap—which was something else Kenny's mother had passed down. Simply said, Jolene Marie Shelton was a single, unique force in the universe.

Kenny looked out the window again, thinking. In a world of symbolism, his daughter would be the smallest of those three trees, he supposed. The one that stood between the house and the other two, but leaning slightly to the left, peering down the road leading toward the highway. She was the curious tree.

"Alright, George," Kenny said. The dog gave a hop and a twirl as Kenny walked over to the front door. He opened it, and then they both stepped out into the cool, Pacific Northwest morning, with its gray blanket of ocean fog and wet breeze. There was a thin trail of orange fire in the eastern sky, embraced by a thick mantle of indigo. The sun was about to break over the land, like an egg yolk, and Kenny stood on the porch with his coffee cup drawn to his lips, waiting. Another day, another mile down this indeterminable path called life. One more spin on the wheel.

George leaped over the steps and set off to make his rounds across their property, a four-acre spread south of Coos Bay, Oregon, outside the unincorporated town of Millington. Grass covered most of the four acres, but there were a few scattered trees, each of them now intimately aware that a dog had taken up residence on the premises. A flimsy barbed-wire fence sat ragged on the eastern side of the property; behind it loomed a wall of redwood, spruce, and pine. The trees cast gloomy shadows and stood as guardians to the acres and acres of land stretching beyond—land Kenny understood to be owned by the Forest Service.

Included on the new property was the family's new home. Built in the late seventies, the house paled in comparison to the custom home his brother Wayne lived in. Or even Kenny's former residence, an indefinable Mc-Mansion in a similarly vague neighborhood of southern California. But his new home, despite its limited size, was a charming one, quaint and unassuming, with the type of slack atmosphere consistent with a vacation retreat. And as far as Kenny was concerned, the home was hard to beat in terms of location. He had had his eyes on this property for two years, aware of how close it was to his brother— who lived just over an hour away in Roseburg—and how far it was from the rat race of Ventura, California. That was Kenny's home roughly three months ago where, before she died, his wife worked as a District Manager for Sears, and Kenny did whatever construction job came his way, and the kids spent most of their summers indoors sheltering from the heat and the smog. To think; all it took was for his wife to die before Kenny could pull the plug on that place.

Marley was his ruby. He loved his wife dearly, and every morning at the coffeepot, Kenny thought about her. They used to be a family of four, living strong, strong as those pines standing outside the window. At least that's what Kenny had thought. But then Marley's life expired. And like a ball of twine, Kenny's own life unraveled, taking with it every ounce of normality he understood and cherished.

He crossed the front lawn and walked over to his Jeep Wrangler. He set his cup down on the hood and opened the door of the detached, two-car garage, exposing a dozen boxes stacked in the center of the room, still unpacked. Too many things felt like salt rubbing into his eyes when he looked at them. Most of those boxes contained Marley's stuff, which Kenny supposed he would one day get around to. There were many things to get around to, some more worthwhile than others, some that took Kenny's mind off the moment. Yet other things he avoided like the plague—such as those boxes. He had a running list on the fridge that his new home kept adding to: loose light fixtures, a leaking faucet in the kids' bathroom, a haggard shed he planned to tear down and use for firewood. Perhaps he'd build a new one in its place, paint it green and white, to match what he had in mind for the new colors of his house—when he would get around to painting that, too.

Projects such as these were easy for Kenny, given his background in construction. These projects he welcomed, as they came with solutions he understood. They came with problems he knew how to fix, and fix well, unlike what he had been up against since Marley's death. That list on the fridge was Kenny's life-support, a foundation to the unsteady walls of his home.

But none of that mattered for this morning—or so he told himself. The plan for this morning was to take George and the kids fishing.

He retrieved his fishing gear from the garage and put it in the back of the Jeep. The gear included a fishing rod, two miniature rods for the kids, a tackle box, five-gallon plastic bucket, collapsible shovel, and a small seine net he had made from window screen and PVC pipe. The net he used for catching sand crabs along the beach, which turned out to be the perfect bait for catching surfperch. He threw an old army blanket in the back of the Jeep as well, along with a plastic tote full of beach toys for Jolie, and then closed the garage door. He grabbed his coffee mug off the hood and headed back inside, pausing for a minute to study the wideness of the sky.

Coming into the house, he found his daughter standing on a chair in the kitchen, reaching up into a cupboard for a box of cereal.

"I'm making us breakfast, Daddy," she said. "Then we can go to the beach!" Her tiny voice bubbled like soda pop. "What kind of cereal do you want, Daddy?"

"Thanks, Sweet-pea," Kenny replied, "but I already ate." He kissed his daughter on the top of her head before pouring another cup of coffee. Then he glanced out the window. "But hey, we're ready to go. I got the Jeep loaded, and I think I even heard the fish jumping when I was outside. From way out here—can you believe that? They must be starving."

Jolie looked at her dad, her arm half-raised, and into the cupboard. "Oh!" she squealed. "This is going to be so fun!" She jumped off the chair and ran down the hall, her hair a wave of honey glistening in the lamplight. "Wake up, Logan! Wake up! It's time to go fishing!"

Jolie's words brought a smile to Kenny's face. He knew his daughter would spend all of five minutes "fishing," and the rest of the day playing in the sand. She would help her dad catch sand crabs, of course. She would play with the critters while they were trapped in the bucket, and then let half of them go when Kenny wasn't looking, her hand covering an impish grin as she did so. Few of his daughter's shenanigans got past Kenny, which he supposed was what made them even more precious. Life must be like one enormous amusement park for her, he often thought, as the child seemed to let all her troubles roll off her back like the downhill slide of a rollercoaster. His daughter lived for the moment in such a way that would make spiritual leaders envious. She was his butterfly in the garden of life, and damn if she ever needed fixing.

Logan, on the other hand...

His nine-year-old son had been on Kenny's "fix-it list" since Marley's death, and Kenny still did not know what to do with him. He had no idea where to begin.

The boy staggered out of his bedroom and into the hall, rubbing his eyes. Jolie bounced and twirled around him, as

George had done to Kenny just minutes before, until Logan pushed her away irritably.

"Daddy," Jolie complained, sliding away from her brother, "Logan hit me." But her comment was all but hollow, and seconds later she was in the kitchen retrieving a bowl for her brother. "What kind of cereal do you want, Logan?" she asked.

Kenny put his cup to his lips and watched as his son silently wandered into the kitchen and sat at the table. The boy did not say one word—he would not—as he stared at the wooden grains of the tabletop in front of him, blinking the sleep out of his eyes. His hair was a brown mop, and with one hand he clutched his stuffed dinosaur named Solly against his chest.

"We don't have anymore Captain Crunch," Jolie reminded them. "But we have Fruit Loops." She immediately filled a bowl, waving a hand at Kenny. "Don't worry, Daddy, I got this."

A thin smirk crossed Kenny's face. "You guys be sure to dress warm. It'll be cold out there...this morning, at least. And brush your teeth when you're done eating. Brush them well." Kenny walked into the living room, turned on the television, sat on the couch. Quickly, he bypassed the morning news. Everything in the world seemed horrid these days. And was there any point to the madness, anyway? What was the purpose of beginning a day with such grave negativity? Maybe six months ago, but not now, not anymore. Kenny found the cartoon channel and leaned back into the couch.

Minutes later, there was a scraping at the door, and Jolie dropped her spoon onto the table and ran. She opened the door and cooed. "George," she said, catching the dog's explosion into the house with both arms. She guided his head by his ears, made him "look at her" until he licked her face. "Oh, George," she repeated, laughing. "We're going to the beach, George. It'll be so fun. But remember," her voice now authoritative in tone, "when Daddy catches a fish, you can't eat it." She waved her finger in

George's face, and the dog promptly licked it. "Don't eat the fish, George."

Ten more minutes passed, and Kenny felt the onset of a snore. He forced himself off the couch, stood and stretched. He roused the kids away from the television and helped them get ready. No matter how many times he had gone through this exercise of picking out the right clothes to wear, helping them brush their teeth, making sure they had all that they needed in order to get through their day—no matter how many times Kenny did it—it still seemed an impossible task. Always, too many things confused him. Things such as which clothes matched each other, or what exactly the kids *would* need for their day. On more than one occasion, he had taken the kids out of the house ill-prepared, with disarranged outfits and messy hair. Marley had made this kind of stuff look so easy, but for Kenny, even after six months of being on his own, it was still a mountain. He bit his lip as he helped Jolie with her coat and tied her shoes for her. "Did you brush your teeth?" he asked.

Jolie stared back in silence.

"Go on—go brush your teeth," Kenny replied.

Minutes later, they were on the road. The canopy of the Jeep was still off, as it was the month of September—a most beautiful time of year along the southern Oregon coast. But the morning air was still crisp and chilly, and in the Jeep Logan and Jolie sat in the back with the army blanket spread over them. George sat in the passenger front, and Kenny drove a little under the speed limit with the heater cranked. Jolie laughed like a hyena, the rush of wind inside the vehicle blowing her hair into complete disarray. Logan stared into the passing trees, but Kenny caught his son's smile in the rear-view mirror. His daughter had a lot to do with that, he was sure... but not certain. The boy hadn't spoken a single word since shortly after Marley had died. Not one word. He hadn't even laughed. He had become a voluntary mute, and this infuriated Kenny, brought him straight to the cliff of insanity, and left him there, hanging, fingers holding on for dear life. *How the hell am I supposed to fix this problem*, he often thought, *when the kid won't tell me what I need to do?*

The doctors called it Traumatic Mutism. They explained to Kenny that Logan's disorder was severe and pervasive, and obviously brought on by the passing of his mother. They tried just about everything, or so they said, but no form of treatment worked for Logan, and every day it seemed as if the boy fell deeper into his world of silence. At their last appointment, down in Ventura, California, the psychologist told Kenny that Logan's mutism was likely becoming self-reinforcing, profoundly dysfunctional, and that the boy was on a downward spiral from which he may never recover. *Never recover...* Finally, upon pronouncing this, the doctor suggested medication, and that's when Kenny walked out of the office for the last time.

There had to be another way. As absurd as it seemed to him, Kenny could not stomach the idea of forcing a pill down his son's throat to get the kid to talk again. There just had to be another way.

Libby Lane guided them west of Millington for approximately thirty minutes, and then Kenny turned off onto Cape Arago Highway, a short, scenic tour that crossed the South Slough into Charleston, ending shortly at Sunset Bay State Park. The parking lot overlooked the Pacific Ocean. A thick wall of fog sat over the land, obscuring the crashing waves a hundred yards out, and there was a wet, salty tang in the air. Half a dozen surfers milled about, waxing their boards, adjusting wetsuits. As excited as they appeared, even they seemed reluctant to disturb the early morning serenity.

The southern tip of this beach was Kenny's favorite spot, a few hundred yards south of the parking lot. It backed up against a redwood forest and was littered with driftwood that looked like ancient bones left in the sand. The place had also proven to be good for catching perch.

"Carry the toys, Logan," Kenny said as he picked up the last of the gear and led the kids down onto the beach. The three of them trudged through the sand with George dashing past them in intervals, chasing panicked Whimbrels and Sandpipers, and other shorebirds into the surf and air. Jolie howled whenever the dog passed her, and by the time they reached their destination, this had become a game between the two. George would trot ahead of Jolie, make a wide circle into the surf, slink up behind and sprint past the girl, kicking up both sand and laughter. Kenny smiled brightly: George and Jolie and the end of the early morning serenity.

When they reached their destination, Kenny dropped the gear onto a wide rock, inhaled deeply, and surveyed the beach. The tide was out. The fog looked implacable, not likely to burn off until early afternoon. And the waves were a restless snore in the near distance, as if the ocean itself was still asleep, yet on the verge of waking up.

Fifty feet behind Kenny stood the redwood forest, an ominous wall of earthy hues and damp shadows. "Don't get too far, Logan," Kenny said, watching his son mosey toward the trees. That was something Marley would say, and another change Kenny had recognized in himself since his wife had died. He never used to be a helicopter parent, coddling and worrying over his children. He never had to, as that seemed to be Marley's job. That was the job of a mother, was it not? At least, that was how Kenny used to perceive the world of parenting.

He ran a hand through his long hair and watched his son hop from rock to rock, nearing the forest as the boy searched for bugs and other critters. Again, and to Kenny's surprise, there were strange concerns running through his head, unfamiliar words riding the tip of his tongue. "Not too far, Logan," he repeated, and then he forced himself to turn away. He supposed that when this nagging feeling swum inside his gut, it was only because he wasn't sure how Logan would respond to an emergency. The boy was on mute, after all. Would that mean he would fail to cry out for help if something terrible should happen? If a sneaker wave, ever so common along these beaches, were to sweep Logan off the rocks and carry him out to sea, would the kid simply disappear in silence?

The things that change when a loved one dies.

Kenny squatted down and gathered up the shovel, bucket, and seine net, then walked toward the surf. Jolie, spotting her dad, dropped a seashell and ran over.

"Is it time to catch the crabs?" she asked.

"Yep," Kenny replied. "And you stay away from them, you stinker. Don't go turning them loose again. Understand?"

"Okay," Jolie said, in a voice that sounded only moderately sincere. The girl swept little hands across her face, tucking hair behind her ears, looking up at Kenny with a beaming smile. "I won't let them go, Daddy. I promise."

For all that that's worth, he thought. His daughter was notorious for forgetting such promises, and knowing this, he made a point to catch twice as many sand crabs as needed.

Walking down to the waterline, he laid the seine net onto the wet beach and grabbed the shovel. He scooped sand onto the net until a thin wave crept up, and the water rolled over the sand, melting it away like hot wax, leaving several crabs frantically burrowing into a window screen.

"Oh, look at them," Jolie squealed. "They're so cute." She laughed, reaching for the smallest crab.

Kenny never even tried to stop his daughter. "That's a good start," he said, smiling, picking up the remaining crabs and dumping them into a plastic bucket.

Ten minutes and thirty crabs later, he was ready to fish. His rod had a double leader with several ounces of weight and two hooks on it. While baiting those hooks, he stole a glance at his giggling daughter, still cradling the baby crab in her hand, letting it wander the terrain of her fingers. Kenny didn't think too many girls would pick up a crab. Jolie had always had a spontaneous and fearless approach to life, for all her seven years of existence. The girl could not be any more the opposite of her brother, who had always been cautious over so many things. Kenny took a step toward the surf then looked over his shoulder at Logan, still loitering near the forest, now lifting a blanket of dried seaweed.

With a frown, Kenny took several more steps forward and cast his rod. He timed his cast on the outgoing surf, aiming for the backside of an approaching wave. The weighted leader flew high and true, sailing over the water in apparent slow motion, landing far and deep. Kenny let the line go, stepped backwards, and waited. It would not be long now, he knew. Surfperch were voracious eaters, especially in the morning. Within an hour, Kenny reasoned, he would have his limit, more than enough for dinner—which was a planned Surf & Turf at Wayne's house, to celebrate the man's birthday.

With mixed feelings, Kenny looked forward to the upcoming evening, just as much as he was dreading it. Since his wife had died, birthdays had a way of effectively stabbing Kenny from the dark, blindsiding him with a painful depression. A brain aneurysm had killed his wife on the night of February 17, while driving home from work. Logan's ninth birthday was less than a month later, and that had been an emotional disaster. There were a few neighbor kids at the party, and Jolie did her best at entertaining them, while Kenny spent the entire time trying to convince Logan to come out of the bathroom.

Later, in June, came Marley's birthday. Kenny had ordered takeout from his wife's favorite restaurant, and they sat on the floor in front of the television to eat. Except Logan never touched his food, and by the end of the night, Jolie had cried herself to sleep in her daddy's lap.

But they always had a good time at Wayne's house. And if there was just one thing Kenny did *not* regret since they lost Marley, it was moving here to Oregon to be closer to his brother.

He felt a peculiar tug on his fishing rod, something a bit more erratic than the steady pull and release that came with the movement of the Pacific Ocean, and Kenny knew he had a fish on. He waited a few more seconds until he felt an even stronger tug, knowing now that his leader was full, and began reeling them in.

"Caught some fish, Jolie," he said, and watched from the corner of his eye as his daughter turned toward him, absently tossing the baby crab into the sand. She ran over, smiling briefly, before her eyebrows furrowed into a frown.

"I'll make sure George doesn't eat it, okay?" she said.

"You do that," Kenny replied. He dragged his line out of the water and up the beach, pulling two perches as large as his hand onto the sand. Their scales looked like sterling silver, freckled brown and green. The fish flopped and curled and bent their frames into the shape of birch bark, trying desperately to get back to the sea.

Jolie danced and squealed while Kenny carefully unhooked the fish and dropped them into the bucket. The girl stiffened as George came running up, tail wagging. "No, George!" she hollered, jumping in front of the dog. "You can't eat the fish, remember?"

Kenny baited his rod again and cast his line out. Minutes later, he felt another tug and then pulled in two more perches, the same size as the others. He smiled, knowing that this was going to be a good day, and he thought about that and of the birthday party this evening. He turned his shoulder and looked for his son. The boy had moved down toward the surf, and was now squatting in the sand, poking at a mass of seaweed with a stick. *It* will *be a good day*, Kenny said to himself, despite his true feelings.

For the next hour, Jolie guarded the bucket while Kenny steadily added more fish to it. George never got too far away, and the dog barked frequently, which Jolie returned with a holler of laughter and sometimes a shooing of her hands. Logan was playing roughly thirty yards down the beach, and it seemed to Kenny that everyone was having a good time; at least as much as he could tell, given that his son would not express any form of happiness other than a slight smile from time to time.

Kenny looked again at Logan and noticed that the boy was now standing further down the beach. His stance was wide, as if straddling something, an unseen saddle. His head was dropped and his eyes were fixed on something in the sand. From a distance, none of this would necessarily constitute a sense of alarm to an onlooker.

But something inside Kenny's gut told him otherwise. It felt as if he had just swallowed a handful of broken glass, and he laid his rod on the ground and walked toward his son. He heard Jolie giggling in the background, but only in the background, as his full attention was now ahead, and on Logan. *What was the boy looking at?* he wondered—and feared. And as he approached his son, a brief sense of relief swept over him. He realized Logan was staring at something scrawled into the sand. Perhaps words of endearment written the night before, by a couple. Maybe even gibberish from another kid, or even something as mundane as tire tracks. But as Kenny got closer, the coldness in his gut crept back, and his sense of relief gave way to a foreign, unnerving feeling.

"Would you look at that," Kenny muttered, staring at the largest cat prints he had ever seen. Mountain lion tracks, undoubtedly, wide as Kenny's own hand, and apparently— *alarmingly*—still fresh. The tracks led from the forest, and from the surf, as if the cougar that had made them had walked down to the water's edge and then back. Logan was standing over one print, and suddenly the boy squatted and ran his fingers along the inside. He probed the imprints of the pad, and for one aching second, Kenny was sure his son was about to say something.

The second passed in silence, but the chill within Kenny's stomach lingered. It sank deeper, and it spread out and into his bones as he looked into the forest and thought about what had made these tracks. Then: What else was in those woods, lying in wait? Somewhere inside, lurking among the shadows of those trees, was the resounding fear of *uncertainty*—a beast of its own. The same beast that attacked Kenny six months ago.

"Let's go, Logan," he whispered, not taking his eyes off the tree line. "It's time to go home, son."

CHAPTER 2

Rob Boyle's hands shook uncontrollably...

The surrounding sound of idling Harleys was like the roar of a thunderstorm. In the desolated, open field ten miles northeast of Myrtle Creek, Oregon, every bird, bug, and small mammal scrambled for cover. Plumes of dust billowed through the afternoon air, and men hooted and hollered while they opened and closed their motorcycle throttles. A few riders rode wide circles around the field, which smelled of soil and sweat, of gas fumes and grease. The field smelled of crushed sage, savory and oily. And it smelled of chaparral, was slightly intoxicating, an organic mixture of creosote and rain. There was the smell of cracked leather from the black jackets of twenty men, as well as from motorcycle seats, saddlebags, gloves and boots, the occasional pair of chaps. There was also the smell of anger, and hunger, and perhaps even a hint of savage greed.

The eyes of this remote landscape burned with hatred and belonged to hardened individuals, many of whom had regularly witnessed the cooking of drugs, and other nefarious activities. Some of these eyes had watched certain brothers lose their lives against a seventy-mile an hour skid into a guardrail. This was a worthy death, so they all believed. There could be no better way to face one's judgment day than while mounted on a bike. Many of these eyes had observed the inside of a prison cell for long stretches of time—time enough to discover the uncanny intimacy of an institution. And these eyes had witnessed the normal executions of those operations common to an infamous motorcycle club: dope sales, dealings with crooked cops, betrayals, savage beatings and torture, and last but not least, murder.

On the outside, these men carried a bold likeness to one another. They were each branded with leather and patches. They shared the same love for motorcycles, and could spend hours at a time making modifications on their bikes. Their fingers gleamed under the brazen sun, from robust rings of gold or silver, portraying gothic themes such as skulls, fists, battleaxes, crucifixes, and wolves—always the wolves. Some wore their hair long, and all of them had many tattoos. Some had beards, and some were shaven, clean, and bald. Piercings and scars marred their skin, and each of them carried upon their body an assortment of weapons, including guns, chains, and knives. But above all the similarities and differences, each man was identical when it came down to the code—a code built not so much on ethics, as it was on loyalty and reprisal.

Such was the case for what was presently being executed within the field—*a reprisal*—as all eyes, common to the cause, now converged upon the man struggling in the dirt.

Cecil, the club's official Sergeant of Arms, grinned as he clamped an iron shackle onto the prone man's wrist. "Trust me," he said, "this will surely hurt you more than it will me."

There was a sudden burst of energy from the struggling man, followed by a quick attempt to stand, until more bikers jumped down and pinned the man's legs and arms fiercely to the ground.

"But look on the bright side, amigo," added Cecil, "at least this'll be quick and painless... Well, maybe." He laughed. "Actually, now that I think about it, I might be wrong." He grabbed the man's other wrist, clamping a different shackle onto it.

The man on the ground thrashed about, tried vainly to scream through the layer of duct tape sealed over his mouth. But his eyes, blaring and wide, successfully conveyed his mounting terror. He was shirtless. His brown skin, sun-weathered, reminiscent of aged leather, advertised a collage of tattoos. His hair was thick and black, and mangy from his struggle. He was clearly Hispanic, the words "Los Locos Guerreros" tattooed in large Spanish font across his back.

After Cecil effectively shackled irons to the man's wrists and both ankles, he stood and looked up. He drew a long breath of air, exhaled and said, "Chains... you ready, or what?" The man on the ground released another burst of energy, a bold attempt at escape, until Cecil thrust a knee into the small of the man's back, and another biker—named Grover—wrapped his arms around the man's legs, squeezing them like an anaconda. A few other bikers jaunted over to lend a hand, or join the fun, and Cecil hollered again for Chains.

At six-eight, Chains stood as an intimidating figure. He was thirty-nine years old, and had spent twenty miraculously uninjured years working the logging industry. He was well respected, and feared, amongst the men he knew—civilized or otherwise. Chains was known for his skills at dropping timber, whether using modern machinery, or old-fashioned saw and cable methods. He was good, and as a favor, had once dropped a neighbor's hundred and fifty-foot sequoia between two parked cars. But in the MC, his motorcycle club, Chains' talents were now being put to less reputable aims. Presently, he was drawing lengths of one-inch chain out from the back of his pickup truck, when Cecil walked up.

"How long are they, anyway?" Cecil asked.

"Two hundred feet," replied Chains.

"Shit," Cecil said, sniggering. "The suspense alone will kill the guy."

The two men were joined by Hondo, Bones, and Luke—President, Vice President, and Treasurer of the club, respectively. The cadre of men wore leather vests, known as "cuts," indistinguishable from those worn by all the other surrounding bikers, save for the front patches signifying ranks within their Oregon chapter of an international motorcycle club.

Hondo reached out and grasped a length of chain, squeezed it like a handlebar, as if inspecting its integrity. "You sure this is going to work?" he asked. Then, casually, "Not like I care."

"Yeah, it'll work," said Chains.

Hondo chuckled. "Well, alright then." He looked over at the enemy, the man on the ground, and then scanned the roaming crowd of brothers. "Where the hell are the Prospects? Those fuckers need to see this." He pulled heavily on a cigar, exhaled, and laughed again. "They *gotta* see this."

Rob was standing on the other side of the pickup truck, watching and listening. He had seen and heard everything. His hands were still trembling. He was afraid of what was about to happen, and was also coming down off a serious cocaine high. The combined cocktail of narcotics and frayed nerves had his stomach wrenched in a knot. He heard Hondo's comment, but was hesitant to come out from behind the truck. His nickname in the club was "Shits," and not for any reason other than the other men thought it funny, and perhaps because, as a Prospect, Rob was always given shitty chores to do.

His last club assignment had left a vivid imprint inside his head. Cecil had a side-business of breeding bird dogs. He kept the puppies in his garage, and whenever Rob was around, Cecil drove him to his house and made him tidy up, pick up all the crap and piss-stained newspaper. That was Rob's last chore, and he could still remember the foul stench inside that garage: the sour odor of wet dog combined with a week's worth of shit. He hated cleaning up after those pups, and more than once entertained the idea of smothering a few of them with a pillow.

With dread, Rob wondered what his part would be with this late Saturday afternoon event. He wondered what his involvement would be with the man out there wrestling in the dirt. A presumption wasn't too hard for him to reach, as he thought he had a good idea—hence the dread. At the very least, Rob suspected that before the day would end, he would have to dig a shallow grave, and then see that the remains of a human body filled it.

He looked around for Skeeter, the other Prospect. One of them would need to materialize soon, before somebody important got pissed off. Slave-duty was just another part of being a fledgling outlaw, with the ambition of one day receiving his patch and becoming one of these brothers surrounding him. Don't piss anyone off, do as you're told, suck it all up, and keep your mouth shut...

Where the hell is Skeeter? Rob wondered again. His hands were wet and clammy, despite all the dust in the air. And his breath was short and labored, but he couldn't tell if that was because of the drugs, or from plain old fear. Not that it mattered any.

Another scramble in the dirt drew everyone's attention. The Loco Guerrero—The Crazy Warrior—had gotten a leg loose, was kicking Grover in the ribs, as more bikers piled onto the man.

Hondo looked on with idle interest. "Fight all you want, motherfucker," his voice cold as murder. He turned back to the others. "Nobody screws with my family and gets away with it." He hollered again for the Prospects, Shits and Skeeter, then grabbed a length of chain and dragged it through the field, over to the shackled man.

Rob swallowed hard before falling in behind Hondo. He looked forward, his eyes locked onto the ground ahead, his gait stiff as a board. "Right behind you, Sir," he said. Hondo glanced back, but said nothing in return. His face was a canvas of disgust. Rob could see the hatred in the man's eyes: the narrowing of the brows, a watery glaze to his pupils. If there was ever a way to guarantee a person's swift and painful death, it would be to let them victimize a family member of someone from this gang.

Rob knew enough of the details. He knew that the man on the ground was also a biker, from a rival, albeit much "lesser" club. Los Locos Guerreros was a small outfit whose illegal activities had yet to be taken with any real seriousness, even from the Feds. They were nothing like a true Outlaw Motorcycle Club—also known as One-Percenters. Mostly, Los Locos Guerreros were known for larceny and rarely exceeded anything beyond petty theft. They were the guys who smashed windows of parked cars to steal radios and purses. Or who teamed up at stores like Home Depot, where one guy worked to distract employees while another ran out the door with a handful of tools. They were made up of predominantly young bikers who lacked experience, and whose barks were much louder than any of their bites. But for the man presently struggling in the dirt, with Hondo now looming over him like the Reaper incarnate, his bark had attracted the attention, and fierce reprisal from eastern Oregon's most notorious biker gang—The Leather Wolves.

In short, the man had raped Gretchen Sterling—Hondo's twenty-one-year-old niece. Rob was sure the man had no clue who the woman was, and who she was related to, as there were plenty of quicker, less painful ways to commit suicide. Gretchen was a strange number, an intensely gorgeous brunette with a penchant for working on Harleys. A gearhead to the bone, she worked part time at a salvage yard in Bend, Oregon ("the boneyard" as she called it), where she found most of the parts needed to supply her mechanical endeavors. She was widely fluent with the biker scene, and could be spotted at any of their hangouts across central Oregon. Gretchen was known and well-respected for her talents and enthusiasm for working on bikes. She was almost never seen hanging on a man, however, which gave rise to the frivolous rumor that she was a secret member of

Dykes on Bikes—the lesbian Motorcycle Club based out of Chicago.

Rob figured it was simply a matter of ill chance that the young man, whose face was now being squashed into the dirt, had preyed upon Gretchen. Perhaps he had been too drunk to realize who she was, thought only of her as some groupie, or "pass around." Getting raped, being roughed about—these were all too familiar events for women who hung around outlaw biker gangs. And the members of The Leather Wolves certainly owned no exceptions to these particular crimes. But as for Gretchen, she was recognized. And respected. She was an untouchable lady who had not only been raped, but had also been beaten brutally.

Yes, Rob had a damn good idea what he would do this evening. He almost felt sorry for the man in the dirt. If the event soon to unfold was only pure "business," if it was a mere pretext to the transaction of sending a message to a rival gang, or snuffing out a rat, or whacking the source of a financial threat, Rob was sure there'd be a lot less drama. A bullet in the head, perhaps; or, at the very worst, this unfortunate Mexican would get stabbed half a hundred times. And Rob was also sure that Hondo, the chapter's president, would certainly be a little less involved with the matter. At this the Prospect wondered, rather grimly, what exactly the chains were for, as he watched Hondo leer over the pile of limbs on the ground.

With sudden and vibrant interest, it appeared to Rob as if Hondo had transformed into a stone statue, his movements frozen somewhere in time. A subtle curiosity that edged on the verge of morbidity followed this observation, as Rob realized that the entire scene was now absent of motion. Every biker stood in the dirt, or sat on a Harley almost as if they were lost in space; their bodies were locked tight, like ancient gears, frozen against the vagrant misuse of time. The very air around Rob was a coppery, motionless aura. Even his hands stopped shaking.

It was the cocaine. The stimulant was now beginning its descent into the realms of betrayal, where it would ultimately fail him at his high. Rob was coming down, coming down hard. With stark awareness, he knew this to be true. And as soon as he realized what was happening to him, it seemed as if the entire world slowly disengaged from its paralysis and reengaged into orbit. Every frozen gear broke loose, every wheel began once again to spin, and Rob's hands were once more exquisitely vigorous, supremely alive. Again, he scanned the scene for Skeeter. Then he looked back, watching the chapter president go to work.

Hondo crouched down and brought his face six inches from that of the subdued biker. "I'd like to give you a chance to say some last words," he said, before pausing and letting his voice trail off into the dirt. The dramatic effect set something loose on the prone man's face, a mixed rendering of panic and hope, accentuated adequately by the rapid rolling of his eyes. "I'd like to give that to you," continued Hondo, "but that would mean having to take this tape off your mouth. Then I'd have to see what's inside. And that, *I know*, is just a bunch of worms, wriggling and crawling, since that's all there ever is inside the mouth of a dead man... Then I'd lose my appetite, you see? I have it in mind to eat a steak for dinner. Wouldn't that be a pity—to lose my appetite for a juicy steak?"

Hondo left his words hanging in the air as he stared into the man's eyes. It seemed as if he were waiting for an answer, and Rob felt the surrounding silence fall from the sky with such abruptness that he wondered if it wasn't another trick of the cocaine.

The president's choice of words, along with his blasé affect, were all corporeal cogitations stemming from what was profound anger. If his attitude had been anything less dramatic, it wouldn't have struck such a distinct, cruel chord. Rob suspected that Hondo's chosen manner was more a demonstration of disgust for the man in the dirt. In the eyes of the president, the rapist was nothing more than a rodent.

"Hook him up," Hondo said, as he dropped the chain in the dirt and walked away.

There was another intense scramble from the pile of men, and for a minute Rob thought the Mexican just might break free; which, of course, certainly wouldn't mean anything. It's not like the man had any hope of escape. The struggling continued, though, until Chains brought over the remaining lengths of steel and hooked them into the shackles at the man's wrists and ankles. Several bikers moved in and lent a hand, grabbing at the lengths of chain and pulling outward, as if setting up for a complex game of tug of war. The Mexican fought back, but it was useless. They quickly stretched him in four different directions, and his body seemed to hover off the ground. That's when they brought in the motorcycles.

There was no question in Rob's mind now. He knew what was going to happen to this guy, although he couldn't quite believe it. Even as he watched, with subtle, morbid interest, as they secured each chain onto the back of a motorcycle, Rob could hardly believe his eyes. He remembered reading about this form of punishment when he was a kid, while flipping through an illustrated book on medieval history. The ancient captors (and Rob thought that these might have been the Romans) used horses to rip men and women apart, and then sent the bloody remains, as special care packages, to the victim's family members. After remembering these details, Rob hoped to God he wasn't going to be given the task of delivering the mail. The thought of bagging up arms and legs, and then transporting them to Los Locos Guerreros' clubhouse, sent his stomach into a nauseating fit.

The four chosen bikers revved their motorcycle engines. A thin film of dust coated the leather on their backs, but the club's patches, proud displays of "The Leather Wolves," shined like headlights. For the man on the ground, these men must have been The Four Horsemen of the apocalypse. Rob studied them, tried to recognize who they were, but for some odd reason, could not. He knew he must surely know the men, must have partied with them, but that there was perhaps a mental block working behind his eyes—an effect from the drugs, or the fear, he wasn't sure. Like the surrounding air, everything seemed cloudy to him. He gave up on finding Skeeter, kept his stare focused on the man in the dirt. Alice in Chains' *The Man in the Box* suddenly, and inexplicably, entered his mind. He heard the melody in his head, saw the lyrics in the struggling man on the ground before him. Nothing about any of this was going to be good.

The engines revved once more, before opening into a full throttle, and in the corner of his eye Rob saw Hondo's raised hand drop. It was then that a thought suddenly occurred to Rob: a vague notion, really, rooted somewhere in the confines of his own self-preservation. This thought was that he might want to plug his ears.

He was too late. He fumbled with the timing of blocking out the sound, the shakes from the comedown still running its course, still affecting his concentration. *Son of a bitch*, he thought. *I'm too fucked up to plug my damn ears.*

And then he jerked, because the sound was horrifying. Quick, yet ruthlessly unsettling—like the tearing of a canvas tarp, combined with the "pop" of a melon being dropped on the ground, and all of it enhanced by the visceral roar of the Harleys. The irony was that Rob didn't even think to close his eyes. Plug his ears, sure, but close his eyes? Even more ironic was that the image of the man's dismemberment wasn't all that bad— certainly not as bad as the sound. The separation of limbs from torso was too surreal to have an immediate, disturbing effect on Rob. At first, there wasn't even that much blood. It reminded him of something mechanical, such as the dismantling of an engine from a bike frame, or even the simple removal of a pair of handlebars.

But a few seconds later, after many of the bikers had subsequently moved on, becoming specs on the horizon, Rob retched into a bush. He was still alive, what was left of the Mexican—a blinking head on a torso.

"Here you go, Shits," Hondo said, tossing a shovel on the ground next to Rob. "Be sure you make it deep. We don't want coyotes digging up any pieces for some local to find."

Chains stood next to his truck, drinking a beer and smoking a cigarette. He was listening to grunge rock and inspecting a minor dent in the driver's side fender while Rob continued to hurl into the bush. With efficient ease, the biker had recovered the four lengths of chain, coiled and stashed them into the back of his truck. The man was Rob's ride home, and would likely get impatient soon. The full darkness of evening was less than two hours away. Chains would get hungry or thirsty, if he wasn't already. And the prospect of partying it up, getting drunk at the clubhouse, was also a pressing reality. It was what the Leather Wolves did after "taking care of business."

Thinking of business, Rob grabbed the shovel and unfolded his body. He tried not to look at the ruined man, avoiding the blinking eyes and the dazed, pitiful stare, but he couldn't help it. The Devil himself knew what the poor man was thinking, or what he felt. It was unlikely that he felt anything at all—shock and awe replacing the searing pain of being violently quartered. Mercy would have him dead soon. Rob hoped it would happen before he finished digging the man's grave. Or before Chains tired of waiting.

To Rob's relief, the soil was loose, easy to dig. In less than half an hour, he had the start of a deep hole dug. The effects from the cocaine were still stringing him out, like wet laundry, but the anxiousness to get this night done and over kept him busy. To ease his burden, Rob tried thinking of pleasant thoughts: Taco

Bell and a 5th of Jack Daniels; a hot shower and cozy bed; another fat line of coke, maybe some marijuana. Definitely some marijuana. He thought of his plans for the future, of the Harley he was going to buy, once his current "project" got sold. If everything went as planned (and he was damn sure it would), he'd have enough money to get his bike, pay his chapter dues for years to come, and perhaps even help fund an impromptu party—a "run" as it was called—to celebrate getting patched into the club. With the amount of money he was going to hand over to the club, along with the run, there was no way in hell Rob would stay a Prospect for much longer. He'd be done with picking up dog shit, that's for sure... Or pieces of a dead man.

Rob glanced at the torso thirty feet away. He could see that the man's eyes were glazed over, and slightly open, but he didn't seem to be alive anymore. The blinking had ceased for the moment; there was no movement in the chest. Even so, an icy chill ran down Rob's spine as he turned back to the hole he was digging.

"You fucking done yet?" Chains asked. The man glared intensely at Rob, as if studying the Prospect, searching for something to pick fault at. "I could leave you here, you know. Make you fucking walk back."

Chains' words were par for the course, Rob knew. He was so used to getting spit on by patch-holders, used to getting smacked around, and treated like a dirtbag. But also, he was sick of it. Rob let out a cough and said, "Don't worry. I'm almost done."

"Who the fuck said I was worried?" Chains replied.

Rob clamped his mouth shut and dug harder. With amusement, he entertained the thought of cracking Chains over the head with the shovel, then stuffing his body into this hole along with the dead guy.

Fifteen minutes later, he was down to his waist, and he figured that was deep enough. No way in hell that guy was still alive, and this realization offered Rob a bit of comfort. He didn't think he could stomach seeing those blinking eyes again, especially while tossing dirt over them.

He climbed out of the hole and dropped the shovel on the ground, dusted off his pant legs. He looked at Chains; the biker was now grinning, leering at Rob, for reasons the Prospect could only take a wild stab at. Swallowing dust, yet tasting vomit, Rob turned away and started toward what he hoped would be a quick end to this grisly task.

Like a gunshot, some of his pleasant thoughts entered once again into his mind—cheap tacos, fast whiskey, numerous hits of the old "sinsemilla." He'd have all of that once he got this shit done and over with. Or so he hoped. He tried not to think about being given another task this evening, such as spring-cleaning the clubhouse, or running the bar until the last man standing finally fell—all actual possibilities for a Prospect. With a bite of his lip, Rob pushed these thoughts away, and hung the picture of a brand new Harley into his head instead. And after thirty minutes, despite the grueling task of burying the pieces of a dismembered body, or the ongoing assault of a cocaine comedown, Rob was at a sudden loss of all-things-disturbing when he found himself in the cab of Chains' truck, cutting tracks back toward civilization. With exquisite relief, he couldn't even remember which piece of that Mexican he threw into the hole last.

CHAPTER 3

Kenny had caught his daily limit, fifteen perches, and that made for a five-gallon bucket full of fish. The ride home was canine torture, as he and Jolie hooted with laughter, all at George's oblivious expense. The bucket rode on the floor below the passenger seat, inches from their dog's slavering chops, and it was all the poor creature could do not to sink his teeth into the shining, silvery scales.

Kenny played along, teasing George and Jolie for most of the short ride home, saying things like, *What's that, George?*, egging the dog on, until Jolie would scream from the backseat, half in protest, and half in unbridled suspense. Even Logan cracked a smile, and as always, without fail, this had brought Kenny to the point of trembling.

He felt it in his hands and stomach, a jittering sensation, as he stole his glances at his son in the rear-view mirror. He had always believed it would start with a smile; and then the boy would laugh, and finally, for the love of God, he'd say something—just one word, that's all Kenny hoped for. But that's not how the afternoon had unraveled, and sadly, Kenny realized the joke was on him as much as it was on George.

Later that day, Kenny told himself he'd repay his dog for the cruel banter he'd doled out earlier, on the drive home from the beach. For the dinner at Wayne's house, Kenny knew his brother was going to grill a rack of ribs. So in the aftermath, he would see that George would get a nice beef bone, or two.

Kenny thought about this, presently, while filleting the perch in his yard. The table he worked on was made of sawhorses and a scrap of three-quarter inch plywood, which he'd fastened together using a pair of old-fashioned, Bessy wood clamps he had found in the garage. The clamps were just one of the many bygone treasures that came with the new house, things left behind as a buyer's burden; or, in Kenny's case, as an astonishing discovery.

The previous occupant of their new home was a man who, for many long years, had been wallowing in the depths of old age. The man's wife had passed on more than a decade prior to his own death, and his three children had long since grown and moved away. For all intents and purposes, the family had completely disassembled. When they departed, the children even abandoned the entire Pacific Northwest, which had left the old man spending the rest of his days, years even, flailing unprepared through the bitter confines of loneliness.

Kenny hadn't known that these were what the last details had looked like for the old man, but he'd suspected as much. His real estate agent had confided in him the previous owner's history regarding family, and the rest Kenny simply pieced together. The house he'd bought "as-is," and it had come with several unfinished projects, little things that needed fixing, all of which would prove easy enough for Kenny.

In the garage, however, there were boxes and shelves containing many incomplete projects. Woodworking projects such as dollhouses, jewelry cases, and humidors. When observed as a whole, Kenny imagined that the old man had lost the ability to narrow his attention onto any specific task. And that perhaps he too must have seemed lost, aimlessly adrift in his old age.

Aside from the overabundance of projects, the garage also came furnished with heaps of unsorted tools and miscellaneous textiles. Not to mention three dozen coffee cans brimming with fasteners of every kind—nuts and bolts, screws and nails—and a host of other residential gadgets and gizmos undoubtedly deemed trash by the old man's beneficiaries. For Kenny, ever the craftsman that he was, the find was a treasure trove. Almost four months later and these thoughts still made him grin.

Attached onto the filleting table was a scrap of synthetic turf, a two-foot long strip Kenny had cut from a small roll (also discovered in the garage). The turf worked almost as good as having an extra hand, as it applied a modest grip under the fish; and just as well, was easy to clean up, to hose down.

Bending at the waist, Kenny hooked his pinky finger under a fish's gill, pulled the perch from the bucket on the ground and laid it on the pine-green mat. He took his knife and sliced a single crescent at the back of the fish's gills, quick and shallow, to the bone, angling the knife outward and to his right. He followed the spine to the tail, flipped the loose slab of meat over, and made another incision, starting from the tail, under the meat and against the skin. The knife was sharp and flexible, and stripping the perch of half its weight took less than a minute for Kenny. But it also took him roughly half a life away, to the months he'd spent working as a deckhand for an old skipper named Pauli Abito.

The place was three hours west of Kenny's hometown of Redding, California. Pauli had been a college friend of Kenny's dad, and for most of the man's life, he ran a small charter boat from the town of Trinidad, a tourist trap on Humboldt County's northern coast. Pauli named his thirty-two foot Albemarle, *Pauli's Bride*, and for several months Kenny had worked her deck.

He did just about everything there was to do on a sporting vessel, some of which he'd already forgotten about, but more of which he thought he could still manage—in his sleep, even. He'd prepared fishing leaders until he could tie knots with his eyes closed, sharpened hooks and knives, dealt with bait, kept the boat clean, hosed down every square inch of the vessel, and did that same task two more times before the end of a day. And of course, he'd handled fish.

In the heat of a trip, Kenny's chief duty was to help their customers get their fish on the line, and then onboard, but these duties never seemed to tire him out. What did was the filleting, which came afterward. At the end of a good day, there could be several dozen fish in the boxes—king salmon, halibut, rockfish, lingcod—most of which got filleted by Kenny. He remembered that first month, how sometimes the tendons in his wrist would give him a tough time, burning in protest. It was then that his fillets got sloppy, and Pauli would have to take over. The cantankerous skipper had a way of demonstrating his wide disapproval without saying a word. It was in the way he rolled his sleeves up and took his time moving across the deck. The way he casually shouldered past Kenny, the stolid buck who, despite all his youth and all his vigor, still had nothing on the likes of a sixty-two-year-old, third-generation Portuguese mariner.

Kenny slipped another perch fillet into a tray of tap water resting on the table, the memories of his past life masking the moment. Figuring he was halfway done with processing his catch, he laid his knife onto the mat and stretched his neck, working at a kink. He inhaled deeply, and caught the smell of brine from the bucket at his feet, along with the faint presence of burnt cedar—a nearby neighbor's wood-burning stove. George gave three quick barks, rising in pitch respectively; the dog was no doubt trying to flank a squirrel in the cluster of black cottonwoods marking the property's western perimeter. Jolie was somewhere in the house, Kenny reckoned, in her room probably, playing with her dolls, or playing dress up. Or, as he now considered, she was just as likely rooting through the kitchen for something to eat. He knew he never had to worry about his daughter going hungry.

Then there was Logan. Kenny could see the boy, right there in the garage, toiling through those coffee cans that had come with the house. These three—the dog, his kids—they were the sacred spirits of Kenny's life now; three fragile souls who would need every ounce of his shield and guard to make it through every day that followed. But for how long? How long until the combined pressure of becoming a sudden widower and an uncertain father released itself into the gray wilderness of time?

Kenny studied his son. Months ago, he had offered to pay the boy ten dollars if he would sort through and organize all the cans. And from time to time, Logan would take to the task with a certain bravado. But the kid would eventually get bored and distracted, and he'd have to start all over, days later, when he came back to it. Kenny didn't really care, however, and he never once withdrew his offer, never even considered it. In the back of his head, behind that painfully reverberating conversation he'd had regarding medicating his son, and all the heaps of literature surrounding Logan's "disorder," Kenny wondered, hoped even, that something as simple as the sorting of nuts and bolts would be the breakthrough he desperately needed for his kid. Kenny kept that ten-dollar bill under a magnet on the fridge, and he promised Hell would freeze over, or his son would talk again—whichever came first—before that bill would see the opened end of a cash register.

These three... it always came back to them. Daily, the responsibilities yoked around Kenny's neck took his spirit by the shoulders and shook it like a rag-doll. It had been so much different when Marley was around—when his wife was still alive. And often now, Kenny wondered if Marley had ever been aware of all their familial weight. Was there ever a day when she, too, felt so alone and so heavy? Kenny didn't think so, or so he tried to convince himself, as his wife had made everything look so damn easy. But also, subtly, he was aware of just how much he could be wrong on the matter. And this reoccurring worry, it seemed to line his gut with a painful, oppressing layer of guilt.

Kenny finished filleting his last perch and picked up the hose nozzle suspended over the corner of a sawhorse. He sprayed his hands, felt the frigid water sluice away fish slime, sticky blood, and the salty residue of the Pacific Ocean. He felt his hands come clean again, and then he washed off the table, scrubbing it down with a wire brush (also discovered in the garage). He used a dishrag to dry off his hands and began the satisfying process of towel-drying and stuffing the fillets into zip-lock bags.

There were thirty slabs of the pinkish meat, and Kenny thought that this would be enough for the dinner. Then he remembered just how many friends his brother had, and how Wayne was only ever truly satisfied when surrounded by these friends, along with his family. The man thrived in the presence of others. Kenny assumed his brother would die a quick and painful death if ever locked away in solitary confinement.

In this way, Wayne and Kenny were so much different. Unlike his brother, Kenny actively sought his alone time now and then, and would even feel the abrupt onset of suffocation when a spotlight came on him. He worried again when contemplating these known differences between him and his brother, and wondered if he should stop at the store to buy some more fish. In all likelihood, there would be over thirty people at his brother's party.

Moments later, he took comfort knowing that not everyone liked fish, and decided against making a pit stop. Besides, he had too many things juggling through his mind at the moment. The plan was to stay the night at his brother's house, and that meant packing enough things for a sleepover for him and the kids. Extra clothes, toiletries... And it seemed like the list had ended there, even though Kenny knew it did not.

It came back to him, the feeling that he was fighting for his breath along a river that Marley had been so deft at navigating.

In his place, his wife would pilot a kayak, paddling over whitewater, around boulders, through the ebb and flow of a strangling current, while Kenny... Well, he always found himself somewhere near the bottom, fighting at the weights strapped onto his ankles. He felt so lame, so damn pathetic. He thought again of Pauli Abito, the old skipper pushing past him with such casual indifference, and of the anger that resided within Kenny in those vague moments. And how that anger seemed to find its way back to the surface after so many years left down below. Kenny had built entire houses, for crying out loud, from the ground up. He'd spent six years serving as a "boat guy," a special warfare combatant crewman, deploying and retrieving Navy SEALs in parts of the world best left unsaid. And it wasn't often that Kenny doubted himself, or his abilities as a person, except during certain times, such as when he was around his brother. But he was the younger of the two, so even that seemed to be the natural order of things. Even that seemed normal.

What wasn't normal, Kenny often thought, was for a man to raise his children—alone.

He thought about the unfairness of the situation, thought it to be cruel, and not just to him, but to his children. There was also a bitter pang of irony, sitting deep inside Kenny's gut. A lingering pain, as if someone had stabbed his stomach with a bayonet, and then left it there.

The irony came from the fact that Kenny didn't believe he had a right to his feelings. He felt guilty for grieving over the loss of his wife, his life's partner. And he felt guilty for the confusion in his mind, which was ever present, fogging his thoughts. To top it off, he didn't even feel he had the *time* for any of these sentiments. Since her death, his entire world had become such a colossal mess, a scrapheap of emotion, a corn maze with dead ends leading to mental and physical frustrations. Even more frustrating was the fact that Kenny had never been trained on how to deal with all of this. Not from the Navy. And not through the sum of his life.

Then there was Logan. Without a doubt, the boy had only made matters worse for his old man. *Who in the hell was he, to clam up and stop talking? Who gave this kid the right to shut down, like an engine out of gas, and to put everything onto the shoulders of me and his little sister? Christ, didn't Logan know he wasn't the only one suffering here?*

Kenny was quite aware of these ill thoughts he kept for his son, and he felt more guilty for having them. Even though he tried to suppress them as much as he could, they always found a way back.

Finally, Kenny often wondered just where the silver lining was in all of this. Was it the life insurance check (the one that his wife had thought to arrange for, years before), the indemnifying wad of cash, which bought for Kenny his dream house by the sea? Perhaps it was. But that, too, came with a handful of guilt.

Taken as a whole, these thoughts and emotions came down to two simple words: lame and pathetic. That's how Kenny truly felt, how he saw himself now.

He paused in his motions and observed his surroundings. Kenny had forgotten what he was doing, where he was. He felt his heart racing, and his breath had stepped up a notch or two. The fillet table had been broken down, its components strewn over the grass. Of course; he had been cleaning up the mess. George was still in the cottonwood copse, barking at a squirrel up in a tree, and Kenny still heard his son tinkering through the cans in the garage. It occurred to him that maybe he should see how the boy was doing, try for the hundredth time to coax him into saying something. But when Kenny walked into the garage, he just kept his mouth shut and grabbed the ice chest from off the floor in the corner. Logan was sitting cross-legged on the ground beside a workbench, the contents of several coffee cans scattered around him. The kid had gotten nowhere and started all over again. With a bitter twinge of frustration, Kenny noted this, as he put the ice chest on his shoulder and walked past his son, going back outside.

But seconds later, an uncanny reflection struck his mind. Kenny considered the symbolism behind the contents of those coffee cans, behind the heap of metal spread out on the floor. And what he imagined was that heap stood between him and his son. It stood between them like a single, massive wall.

CHAPTER 4

It was Sunday night, a quarter to ten, and Rob Boyle had had less than three hours of sleep in the last thirty-six hours. His mind was on fire. He had tried to watch television, but the flashing lights, the frequent change of pictures, all made his eyes go "buggy." The exercise of reading, for relaxation (or better yet, for falling asleep), had always been a laughable notion to him. Unless it was an auto repair manual, Rob stayed clear of books, as they reminded him too much of school. He'd been a problem child starting at kindergarten, and spent the rest of his education in special day classes for emotionally disturbed children. By the middle of tenth grade, Rob had gone AWOL, and there wasn't a soul on the planet that had shed a tear over that unfortunate decision.

Marijuana was the best option for calming his nerves, but Rob had smoked the last of his weed the night before, immediately after Chains had dropped him off. Getting stoned was something quite needed after burying the pieces of that Mexican. And, unfortunately, there had been no hot shower, no good night's rest waiting in the wings for him, either. Not long after Rob had smoked his last bowl, Cecil was at the door, barking out orders, giving Rob his next set of instructions.

The following twelve hours were a blur of task-oriented misery, beginning with pouring drinks for two dozen speed-injected bikers, and ending with mopping up vomit in the clubhouse bathroom. Skeeter was still MIA, and thus unavailable to share in the glorious duties of a Prospect. (Rob swore, the next time he saw that fucker, he was going to cut his balls off with a Buck knife.) The only bright side was that during this stretch of time, Rob had discreetly gained moderate liberties over the MC's supply of cocaine, reserved only for special occasions—i.e., the complete dismemberment of a rival biker. So, with such liberties, at twenty-nine years of age, Rob was now riding the biggest high of his life.

He celebrated by continuing the domestic cleaning theme he'd started over at the clubhouse. On hands and knees, Rob scoured the floor of his 1992 Scamp trailer—his home—and picked up a host of trash, such as Taco Bell wrappers, cigarette boxes, soda cans, and a dozen stale pizza crusts. When he was done with this, he walked the hundred yards up the dirt driveway of his grandmother's property, grabbed the Shop-Vac from her garage, then lugged it back to his trailer, without once stopping to look at the twinkling stars overhead.

Outside the front of his trailer sat a ratty old couch, a couple of lawn chairs, and a fire pit made from the top half of a fifty-five gallon oil drum. This was Rob's official hang-out spot, on the off chance anybody at all would decide to hang out with him. The couch sat next to the front of the trailer and was sheltered above by a blue tarp, which stretched outward from the top of the Scamp, emulating a built-in awning. Rob vacuumed the couch first, since that's where he liked to sit whenever he sat outside.

He plugged the Shop-Vac into an extension cord running from the inside of the trailer, and began working over the cushions, sucking up leaves and dirt, and whatever else the nozzle came in contact with. There was a desk lamp strapped against the outside wall of the trailer, just under the tarp (it had no lampshade, so Rob had to watch that the bulb didn't get too hot, and catch the whole affair on fire), but the light coming off the lamp was meager, at best. He wasn't exactly sure what the vacuum was picking up. But he *was* sure it wasn't anything to worry about. He kept all of his important shit inside the trailer, knowing that his grandmother would just as soon check herself into an old folk's home as enter her delinquent grandson's questionable lair.

Before Rob completed vacuuming the couch, an impulse overcame him, and he decided at once to make a batch of pancakes. He dropped the vacuum nozzle and stepped up into the trailer, ignoring the high-squeal whine of the Shop-Vac, as it tried to inhale an entire cushion.

He began rummaging through the small kitchen, checking for the ingredients he would need: Aunt Jemima's Complete Pancake and Waffle Mix, a tub of margarine, a bottle of Log Cabin syrup. He gathered the pancake mix and syrup on the counter and found a large mixing bowl. Then he paused...

Rob stared at the ensemble for several minutes, processing his thoughts, his feelings, his rapid breathing, the shaking of his hands and knees. There was a systematic process to making pancakes. He knew this, but damn if he could remember what it was, or even where to begin.

Something told him he now needed the margarine and a skillet, so he took a chance with his memory and went for it.

Because he was so high on dope, his motions in the kitchen appeared disjointed, lacking rhyme or reason, or any sense of fluidity. It was as if his body was part of two different orchestras, playing out two different songs, each in a staccato note duration: open the fridge; get margarine; close the fridge; put margarine on the counter; open the fridge; look inside; close the fridge; turn the stove on; open the fridge; curse softly; open the cupboard; get skillet; close the fridge; put the skillet on the burner—and so on and so forth—until half an hour later, he thought he was ready to start cooking.

He dropped the first dollop of batter onto the smoking pan, and a brown cloud erupted below his eyes. He had left the skillet on the heat for way too long, and now his entire trailer was filling with smoke.

"Oh, fuck!" Rob cried, fanning spastically with his hands. He picked the smoking skillet off the burner, and started for the door, turned back for the spatula, grabbed it, and in a single leap, vaulted outside, coughing and laughing and cursing, all at the same time.

Seconds later, and sensing the sudden presence of another person, Rob paused with his theatrics and looked up. He was greeted by the smiling face of Vance Green.

"Dude, what in the fuck are you doing?" asked Vance. The Shop-Vac was now turned off, and Vance was holding the nozzle in one hand. He had a beer in the other. "You trying to start a fire, or something?"

Rob laughed hard, a real gut-buster, as he sat on the armrest of the couch. "Shit..." he said, coughing, hacking, spitting on the ground. "I'm making my dinner."

"Your dinner?" replied Vance, chuckling. "Alright, then— what's for dinner?"

Rob gestured to the skillet in his hands. "I'm making fucking pancakes, man." His voice raised an octave, at the same time that he stood up and began shifting his weight side-to-side, from one foot to the other.

"Shit, brah, you're high as a kite. Aren't you?" Vance dropped the Shop-Vac nozzle and sat on the couch. From a pocket he dug out a pack of Marlboros and tapped it against his palm, nudging several cigarettes out through the opening. He groped one with his lips, pulled it out, and lit it. Reluctantly, he offered the pack to Rob.

"I might be a little high," Rob said, taking the pack and lighter. There was a pause as both men stared into the quiet night.

"Geez... You're fucking wasted, dude." A look of concern crossed Vance's face. He took three consecutive drags off his cigarette, then blew a plume of smoke at his feet. "I mean, are you gonna be able to function tonight, or what?" He paused, flicked ash off his cigarette. "We had fucking plans, man. You gonna be able to suck it up and head out to the scene?"

"Maybe," replied Rob. With a narrow stare, he lit a cigarette and studied Vance's face. His friend—if one could call him a friend, and that was something Rob had never quite considered—was built similarly to Rob. The young man had a deathly lanky build, as if he'd been running on chemo for three months. And his face was just as slender. But unlike Rob—indeed, very much *unlike* Rob, who was completely bald—Vance's head was crowned with three-foot long, natty dreadlocks.

That was something Rob could never figure out—why a person would go years without washing his hair. Rob often wondered if Vance had lice, or if his hair itches like crazy, day and night, all hours of the day—like the effects of a totally bad trip.

"Yeah," Rob continued, "I'll be able to head out... What the fuck took you so long, anyway?"

"What took me so long?" Vance repeated, a look of irritation stirring in his eyes. "This is the time we agreed on... Don't you remember?"

"I thought we agreed on nine."

"Yeah, well, so I'm a little late—big fucking deal. Had to pick up something to eat, for Christ's sake. At least I'm not tweaking, man."

There was a long pause before Rob said, "I thought it was Jah."

"Say what?" replied Vance.

"Jah's sake. Isn't that how it's supposed to go? You like reggae and shit, right? *Rasta-far-i*, and all."

"Sure," Vance said. "That's it." He made a face, then took a drink from his beer.

"Anyway," Rob continued, "you want some pancakes?"

"No," replied Vance. "I mean, sure. Yeah. I'll have some pancakes." He stood and walked toward the trailer entrance. "But you better lie down and let me do the cooking. You'll just burn this fucking dump to the ground."

Both men went inside, and Vance promptly opened the windows. The night air was still as death; there was no wind to help vent the smoke out of the Scamp. "You got a fan?" Vance asked.

"No," replied Rob. He grabbed a flyswatter off the hook near the door and flailed it vigorously, fanning the inside of the trailer.

Vance was working the kitchen now, bringing the cooking scene back to a functional level. He looked sidelong at Rob and said, "Sit down, brah. I got this."

Slowly, Rob returned the flyswatter and moved to the small wrap-around dining table. Sometimes he hated it when Vance called him "brah," and this was one of those times. It was the way the "Rastaman" would say it, the tone in his voice—always on the verge of condescending. *And what the fuck was a Rastaman, anyway?* Rob wondered. He had always thought it was a person from Jamaica. Not some white boy wannabe, with roots probably somewhere in Southern California.

He glanced sideways at his lanky friend. Rob wasn't too knowledgeable about the whole reggae scene, and he could give a pile of rank shit for all that it mattered. But he had a notion that within the "Irie Culture," with the Jamaicans and their "one-drop" music, the dreadlocks and the ganja, all the peace-loving pussies wearing patchouli and hugging trees, that Vance here was no more than one big poser.

The inside of the Scamp was no bigger than a small bedroom, cramped enough when occupied by a single person. Now, with both men inside, Rob felt like he was being compressed into a tin can. Some of that feeling might have been the effects of the cocaine, he considered, as he sat at the dining table. He watched

Vance at the stove and smoked half his cigarette before he said, in a sobering voice, "Dude, I think I'm really fucked up."

"No shit," Vance replied, without turning away from the stove.

"I'm getting sick of being a Prospect," continued Rob. "I get shit on every day, and that fucker, Skeeter—Skeeter the tweaker—he ain't never around to help with the duties. I swear, next time he's at the clubhouse, I'm claiming him for a rat!" Rob chuckled, and his voice tightened again. His pace quickened. He rambled on in a way that only a coked-out addict could appreciate. "Prospect for a year, that's the fear, bring the fucking gear, don't shed a tear... My mama ain't no Ol' Lady, but your mama is, and I'll be fucking her all night long as soon as I get that patch, but what's the catch? The catch is, I'm gonna be slopping puke, sucking on bloody hooch, scraping shit from the can, gonna be an ass-man... You hear me—*Rasta-boy?*"

Vance looked at Rob, shook his head, and snickered. "That's fucked up, brah. I don't see why you do it—why you put up with all that crap."

Another pause. "You don't get it," said Rob, "because you ain't got the right type of blood running inside your veins." He pulled from his beer. "Warrior blood... *Harley* blood. You ain't got that, and that's the difference. That's why I put up with all that crap."

"Whatever, brah," replied Vance. He dropped a pancake onto a plate and handed it to Rob, along with the syrup.

"Pass the margarine, will you?" Rob said. He leaned to his right and opened the small refrigerator. "You want another beer?"

"Sure," replied Vance, sitting at the table with his own plate. He sliced a wedge of margarine with a knife and began smearing it onto his pancakes, staring at Rob the entire time. "Bullshit, brah," he said. "There's no fucking way you're going out tonight."

"Bullshit to you!" replied Rob. "And quit calling me 'brah'. I ain't your fucking brah... And I'm fine. Just need to eat something, that's all. Just need to eat some pancakes."

Vance shook his head, but kept his mouth shut. He looked at his food, and several minutes passed as both men ate in silence.

A sudden, cold vibe materialized within the trailer, as if something dead had just staggered in from outside. Rob stared at his friend, then chuckled maliciously. "Yesterday..." he said, "I saw a man get pulled apart."

"Huh?" replied Vance. "Like from a car wreck or something?"

"Oh, it was *something*, that's for sure. We pulled some rapist apart, using chains and bikes... Like the Romans, you know? Four different directions." With a fork in one hand and a cigarette in the other, Rob motioned outwards, illustrating the gruesome incident.

Vance set his beer down. "Why the *fuck*...? Dude, I don't want to be hearing any of this shit!" He levered out from the table and went to the stove, poured batter onto the skillet. His movements were now very similar to how Rob's were earlier—disjointed, ambiguous with intent. "Fuck me, man!" he shouted. "I told you, I don't want to hear about you and your fucking biker gang. I'm not into that shit, dammit! Don't tell me anymore! No more, man!"

Rob smiled, then laughed. It pleased him to see Vance squirm like this. Fuck all that peace-loving reggae shit. Life ain't a fairy tale—life's a bitch. And the sooner these faggot potheads learned that, the better this world would be. "Relax, asshole," Rob said, between chuckles. "I'm just shitting you, that's all."

But there was a quality to Rob's voice, a timbre that resonated deceit, and Vance clearly picked up on it, as he seemed more anxious than before. He grabbed the spatula and began flipping hotcakes before they were ready, slopping batter across the counter, muttering words under his breath. "Fuck!" he shouted.

"Shit," Rob said. "Forget it, already." He took a tall pull of his beer, drained the bottle and set it on the table. Then he belched. "Did you bring all your gear?" he asked, changing the subject.

A few minutes passed before Vance said anything. "I got my gear," he finally replied, irritably.

"Good. We'll head out as soon as we're done eating."

"Whatever, man."

"Don't fucking worry. You can drive... I got all my shit in the Bronco—we're taking it, not your crappy van. And I got the camo net in the back, as well."

"Whatever you say, boss," Vance said.

"Your damn right. Anyway... You got any weed?"

•   •   •

Half an hour later, Rob was "couch-locked" outside his trailer, a blanket pulled up to his chin. The world was spinning around him, even with his eyes closed. He kept running his palm over the couch's armrest, as if he were pawing the thigh of some hooker at the clubhouse. His whole body felt like it had been set in concrete, and hisF breathing seemed to have stopped. He could have been dead, for all that he knew—or cared.

It was a ridiculously dumb question, and he knew it before he had asked it. Vance *always* had weed. And that, Rob guessed, was the silver-lining for being called "brah."

"Shit, we aren't going anywhere tonight," Vance said, bringing a small, multi-colored glass pipe to his lips. "I knew I shouldn't have gotten you high," he added, before taking a hit.

"That's cool," Rob said, rubbing the couch. "We'll just go up there tomorrow. That shit ain't going anywhere."

"It sure as hell might," Vance replied. He coughed and exhaled a plume of smoke into the night air. "Shit's about ready for harvest, brah. Rip-off moon is around the corner, and our scene'll be ripe for the picking. We've got us some work to do."

"Whatever," Rob replied. He opened his eyes and glared at Vance. "Hey? You don't need to tell me how to handle my business. I *know* what the fuck I'm doing. Besides, it'll be easier to hide the Bronco in the daytime." He looked away and closed his eyes, then drifted toward sleep, blessed sleep...

But suddenly, in his mind's eye, he saw once again that Mexican getting ripped into pieces. He saw the torso twitching in the dirt, and the man's blinking eyes, not yet dead, only this time... This time, those eyes were the eyes of his partner. They were Vance's eyes.

The unexpected vision hardly fazed the Prospect, and he looked back at the long-haired, dreadlocked Rastaman. "Bet you didn't think of that now, did you?" he added, his voice thin and raspy. "Fucking *Bob Marley*. Everything's easier in the daytime." Then Rob was out cold, cold at last.

CHAPTER 5

Late the next day found Rob parking his Bronco fifty feet off a dirt road, into a stand of Douglas fir, and behind a wide thicket of black hawthorn. They were roughly three hundred yards from the chain-linked entrance and well concealed behind trees and brush. Without comment, he and Vance covered amply the vehicle with the olive-green netting they had brought. Vance even walked deeper into the woods to retrieve fallen limbs and scraps of brush, of which he delicately wormed into the vinyl camouflage.

They had done this job several times in the past, but as the subsequent days brought them closer to the window of their objective, so too did those days increase the need for caution. And at this time of year—well, many things could be observed as clues, by those skilled enough to find them. According to Vance, anything left behind to provide details as to their activities would certainly provoke doom to them. According to Vance, clues were kin to the devil.

As Vance refined his procedures of concealment, Rob took a spot behind the Bronco and stared meticulously at the surrounding forest. He peered into the pockets of sleeping boulders and, like an artist, studied the various leans of wood: the vertical, horizontal, and the angular. He observed patterns in the bark—patterns that seemed to stare back at him. Rob thought he saw grinning cheeks and leering brows, fat jowls rimmed with black sockets that conveyed equal parts, childish imp, and foul demon. These were the true thieves of the shadows, each of them, Rob knew. Above and beyond, and through the trees, the evening approached, and it was warm with its dryness.

In slow measure, Rob turned toward the Bronco. He began rummaging through the contents inside. He retrieved his and Vance's backpacks and placed them outside, on the ground, along with two olive duffle bags. From under a pile of blankets and soiled rags, he found a small cardboard box, crushed almost completely, and stained a dark brown. The box wore the likeness of an old coffee filter, but inside sat a bright orange canvas tool-bag. This was what Rob had been looking for.

"Hey, Vance," Rob called out.

"Yeah." Vance's voice was just a hair above a whisper and carried a tone of irritation.

"Go out to the road... See if you can see the truck." Vance didn't reply, but Rob listened to his footsteps as the man walked away. Quickly, he unzipped the tool-bag and retrieved the handgun inside—a Belgium-made, 9mm Browning High Power. Rob discovered it one day while snooping through his grandmother's garage. He was sure she had forgotten about it; since Gramps had kicked the bucket, there were many things the old woman had forgotten.

Rob held the gun flat in his palm for a long minute, then ejected the magazine. He studied this as well, ran a thumb over the jacketed cartridge that crowned the cold piece of metal. When he heard Vance approaching from a distance, Rob clumsily jammed home the magazine, and then went to his backpack, where he concealed the gun in a side pocket.

Minutes later, the men gathered their backpacks and duffle bags, locked up the Bronco, and headed north. They traveled parallel to the main road, moving like snails through the forest for close to an hour, before they came to another road, a dirt driveway. To their left was the entrance to this driveway, barred from access to the main road by a single length of rusted chain stretched across two poles.

The forest smelled of dried pine, dust, and somewhere in the canopy above, a squirrel skittered across a tree branch. To their right, the dirt road climbed up through a wooded canyon. The men stood at the cornice of these roads and quietly stared into the dimming light, and at the surrounding trees. Convinced by the silence, Rob gave a nod, stepped forward and led the way onto the ascending road. He walked up the hill about thirty feet before Vance made an abrupt stop.

"Hey, man!" Vance said. "Look at this." He was pointing at a rutted-out section on the road. "You remember seeing this? 'Cause I don't."

Both men crouched down to study the impression.

"I'm telling you, that track wasn't here the last time we were." Vance wiped his jacket sleeve across his forehead and looked over his shoulder. He bit a nail and turned back toward the gated entrance, at the main road beyond.

Rob ran his fingers along a six-inch wide gap in the dried mud. "Probably the owner," he muttered. "Definitely a truck."

"The owner?" replied Vance. "Shit... This is fucked up, brah."

"Maybe not," said Rob. He stood, pulled a Marlboro pack out of his coat pocket and lit a cigarette. "But I guess we'll find out, won't we?"

With the encroaching night, the two men disappeared into their surroundings. They wore camouflage clothing, black beanies, and their backpacks sported various shades of green. From afar, Rob's cigarette looked like the embers of a distant campfire. "We'll check out the cabin on our way up," he said.

"But what if the owner's there?" replied Vance. "What if someone sees us?"

"Then we fucking deal with it, you dumb shit." Rob started walking up the road again, and Vance fell in behind. "If we see anyone," Rob added, "just keep your mouth shut and let me do the talking. We're just hikers, remember? Took a wrong turn, that's all."

The cabin was located two miles up the dirt road, which cut through stands of western hemlock, lodgepole pine, and a forest of blackberry thickets. There were three switchbacks along the way, as the road made a steady incline of approximately five hundred feet before dropping into a wide clearing. It took the men over an hour to reach this destination, and when they did, they crept slowly behind a cluster of trees to rest and observe.

They studied the clearing... And the cabin beyond. It was bathed in shadow and a thin veneer of pale gray from the advancing moonlight. Its front door and wide porch faced south, toward the men, as if to stare back at them. The building contained several noticeably unfinished features.

After watching and waiting for close to ten minutes, Rob and Vance quietly stepped away from the trees and back onto the road to get a better look. They observed the clearing ahead, and with careful scrutiny, studied the small cabin some more, along with its surroundings. Their bodies steamed from the climb up the road, but a subtle chill of the converging night hung lightly in the air.

"I'm fucking roasting," said Vance. He pulled off his beanie and his dreadlocks fell with a heavy thud against his jacket. He ran a hand over his forehead again, flinging sweat onto the ground. "No cars, at least. That's a good sign."

"No shit, Sherlock," Rob said. "But that still don't mean a whole lot." He slid off his backpack and set it next to a tree, unzipped the main pocket and retrieved a miniature, pistol-grip crossbow.

"Dude, what in the hell?" Vance turned a shoulder, glanced up and down the road, his eyes white as chalk.

"In case we run into somebody other than the owner," Rob replied. "You know—*rip-offs*." He cocked the crossbow and placed a blunt bolt onto the track. "It's that time of year, *brah*. Isn't that what you keep fucking telling me?"

"I'm not talking about shooting rip-offs," replied Vance. "It's the owners of this cabin I'm worried about. What are they gonna say if they see us now, with you holding that damn thing?"

"The owners aren't even here, asshole. Now shut up already." Rob handed the crossbow to Vance as he picked up his backpack and put it on. He took back the crossbow and crept out of the woods, toward the cabin.

Nothing about the small building seemed different since the last time the two men had been here. The walls and roof were still unfinished, as was the step-up porch, which had several overextended floorboards still needing to be trimmed. Rob checked the front door, which was locked, and after looking into the wide bay window next to the door, he saw the inside was still the same—with a few notable exceptions.

"Son of a bitch," he whispered, staring into the shadowed room. Despite the growing darkness, Rob made out three boxes of nails, a stack of lumber and plywood, and, to the side and against a wall, several sheets of drywall. "Somebody's fixing this place up."

"Shit," replied Vance, stepping onto the porch. Vance's tone was tense, and when he looked into the window, his jaw slackened. "Great. Fucking great, Rob. This shit is getting too deep, man."

Rob ignored his partner and once again slowly slid off his backpack.

Vance went on, his hands quivering. "I knew we shouldn't have come back here. Two years in a row on private property is one year too many. That's what they say, you know." He pulled out a cigarette and quickly lit it, inhaled hard, then blew out a cloud of smoke. "Shit's a fucking no brainer, man."

"What the hell are you doing?" Rob yanked the cigarette out of Vance's hand, then crushed it on the porch with his boot. He cast a malignant stare at Vance. "We're too close to the scene, shithead. If somebody's out here, they're gonna smell that. And we don't need to be leaving any calling cards, either."

"Well, fuck you too," Vance grumbled. He turned and pressed his face against the window, looking deeper into the cabin. A minute passed, and then he checked the door again before stepping off the porch. "So what's the fucking plan then, genius?"

Reaching down, Rob unzipped his backpack and took out a pair of night vision goggles. "The plan is to shut up and get your goggles on."

"I mean, what's the plan about this?" Vance replied, gesturing to the cabin. "What the hell are we gonna do if somebody's up here swinging a fucking hammer in a couple of weeks?"

Rob kicked his backpack to the side and stepped up into Vance's face. His bald head and bearded chin sat firm under a vicious stare. "Look here, you hippie-assed faggot! If somebody's up here, then we will fucking deal with it! You got that?"

Vance stepped back and stared at the ground, a stream of curses drifting under his breath.

"Shit," Rob continued, his tone an octave lower, "and I thought you were the fucking expert with this."

"I am," Vance said. "And like I told you, we should've found a different scene. A fucking expert never operates in the same place two years in a row."

"Well, we did," Rob said, "so *fuck you*."

After donning their goggles, the two men left the porch and headed to the rear of the cabin, where they briefly inspected the area. Finding nothing of interest, they turned and walked to the tree line at the end of the clearing opposite the dirt road. They stopped in front of a narrow footpath that cut through a briar of salmonberry and deer fern before trailing along the mountainside. The ground was soft and moist, and the air was thick with the smell of decaying vegetation.

Both men switched on their goggles before slowly creeping forward along the footpath. They traveled in single file, Rob in the lead, crossbow in hand. Occasionally, he stopped to study the ground, or a nearby bush, checking for tracks. "Tap me on the shoulder if you see anything," he whispered.

"Sure thing, boss," Vance replied sarcastically.

The path led fifty feet up the mountain before sloping downward, and then wrapping around to the southern face. Rob and Vance walked quietly for about fifteen minutes, pausing near a break in the forest. Sedge grass and thin clumps of juniper covered the exposed side of the mountain in front of them. But the fragrance offered by this flora barely concealed the odor that now lingered in the air.

"Shit, that's the smell of money," Rob said, his voice stiff and dry. He looked up and down the mountainside, scanning for distinct outlines or movement of any kind. "Let's check the tanks first. Then we can work our way down and check the patches."

They hiked three hundred feet straight up the mountain, staying inside the tree line, until they reached a long hedge of blackberries. The blackberries spanned the exposed mountainside like an arm reaching for the trees on the other side of the slope. And in the wide open, beginning just below this thorny bramble and stretching down the mountainside, stood the contents of their "scene". Fifty full-grown marijuana plants.

CHAPTER 6

In Kenny's mind, some things never changed. Some things simply remained the same, and were timeless, like Johnny Cash. More than once, Kenny held this perspective about his brother. He knew that the man had long since defined for him this way of thinking. Considering his family's recent trauma, Kenny took comfort knowing his brother could always be taken at face value, and that there wasn't anything complicated about the man. This was one reason Kenny had moved to Oregon. A big reason, in fact. He took comfort in the understanding that no matter how many years would pass, or how much shit life threw at him, that his brother, Wayne Shelton, would always remain the same. The man was a marble slab, indelible in his character, immune to the gravity of it all. Immune to the weight of the world, so it seemed.

As an example of his brother's resounding fortitude, Kenny remembered Wayne's reaction when their father had died. They were both in high school and the old man's battle with cancer was a God-awful short one. Six months had moved in and out like a thick, gray fog, and every day in between left Kenny with an indistinguishable sickness inside his gut. Then the end: how heavy the loss had felt, combined with the sudden presence of a steel anchor strapped over Kenny's shoulders. And Wayne had made jokes with the old man up to that last day. *How did a person manage that?* Kenny still wondered. How did his brother pull that one off, being just the young man that he was back then? It was as if his brother and father had a special bond.

That was something else Kenny could remember, something that left him feeling a little jealous at the time, and a little guilty. All the same, that feeling had been there—was still there: the secret pact; an understanding only ever shared between a father and his oldest son. It was just one more thing that baffled Kenny, and like razor wire, this obscure intuition he'd had about his brother and father, it had torn at his insides and made him feel guilty for even crying over his father's death.

Wayne Shelton, man of stone, *the Marlboro Man*—that's how Kenny understood his brother. But of course, Wayne was family, and that was more important than anything else Kenny would consider, past or present. Family brought with it its own familiar anchor. And this anchor wasn't strapped over Kenny's shoulders, burden-like, but it sat as a claw digging into the sand below, keeping Kenny from careening off-course.

His mind wouldn't quit. He was presently driving to his brother's house, and he looked at the world now in the Jeep's rear-view mirror, observing both Logan and Jolie. His son was awake, the boy's eyes focused on... What, exactly? The road as it passed by, with its coastal redwoods and white pines? The miles and miles of blackberry thickets with their autumn fruits, now ripened, staring back like tiny doll's eyes? At that moment, and like he had done so many other times, Kenny swore he'd give his right arm just to know what his son was thinking.

"Nice view, ain't it, Logan?" he said, expecting (and getting) no response. But a father had to try. Every damn day, he had to try. "Nothing like this in L.A., that's for sure."

Next to Logan, Jolie was a sack of sleep. Somewhere along the past twenty miles, she had weaseled away the wool blanket, and had subsequently fashioned an adequate nest out of the garment, weaving it between the seat belt straps and around her body. Only her head was visible. Her eyelids looked soft and content in their sleep, but her sandy hair seemed quite alive, with a mind of its own, vigilantly whipping at the passing wind.

The music CD Kenny had burned was a compilation mix of country and classic rock songs. Presently, it was playing Ty Herndon's *Living in a Moment*, and Kenny thought this a tad bit depressing, given his circumstances. At the moment, there wasn't much in the song that he could relate to. It didn't seem to match the drive or his current mood. But it was a good song, and George didn't seem to mind, either. As usual, the dog was riding shotgun, hunched on the seat on all fours, sitting upright, relaxed—another happy passenger, George was smiling freely into the wind.

The dog glanced at Kenny and briefly licked his chops, turned back, smiling once again. After he gave away his right arm, Kenny thought he should take the extra step and lop off his left, just to spend a day in George's mind as well, to get a glimpse of what was likely a simple, blissful world.

In his own mind, Kenny reviewed the recent conversations he'd had with his brother's wife, Beth. Sometimes the woman seemed content to be called by her full name, Bethany. Perhaps after a long, hard day, while she was at last motionless and silent, sitting in a chair, or on the porch, a cold beer in hand. But more often than not, she preferred Beth, and Kenny imagined this was because the name was shorter by two syllables. That saved time, and he figured Beth liked that, as it gave her more time to share her opinions.

Something Kenny had yet to shake was the incongruent aspect he'd felt about his brother's wife. Unremittingly, Beth showed a convincing, high level of energy, one that conceivably correlated with her age (somewhere in her mid-thirties). However, the manner in which she spoke, the words she chose, the frequent outbursts of advice she gave to others—*wantonly*—Kenny thought the sum of it all placed Bethany in the category of an octogenarian. Maybe it was the woman's blasé manner to the spins of life, and how she would give a rat's ass what others thought of her. And to complicate Kenny's perspective, whenever Beth opened her mouth, what often came out was stone-cold, epiphany-leveled logic. The woman was strange.

Some might call her an "old soul," but Kenny suspected genetics had something to do with her personality. He'd only met Beth's parents once, at her and Wayne's wedding, but that memory was distant, and clouded with Kenny's inebriation at the event. There were pictures, though, scattered throughout Wayne's house, on the walls and end tables. And in the ones that portrayed Beth's parents, Kenny recognized his sister-in-law's ill-mannered assuredness: the conviction in her mother's eyes; her father's impish smile, as if something about the rest of the world was a joke to which only he knew the punch line. While studying one of these pictures, it had dawned on Kenny that his brother and Bethany were cut from the same cloth, suggesting little surprise as to their steady companionship.

Months before, and not long after Kenny had moved to Oregon, Beth drilled him about Logan. She effectively corralled Kenny into the backyard, had him helping her rope off some tomato plants, while she picked his brain clean with questions about Traumatic Mutism. At first she had it all wrong; she kept calling it "Selective Mutism," and Kenny had to correct her. He didn't blame her, of course, as the first two doctors he'd taken Logan to had both made the same mistake. It was a common misdiagnosis, but one that led to hours of fruitless, counterproductive, even damaging therapy. And the last doctor, as Kenny confessed to Beth: the man had suggested medication for Logan, a cocktail of antidepressants and relaxants— something of that variety.

To his relief—and Kenny wasn't exactly sure why he felt such relief—Beth had given her staunch approval to his decision regarding medicating Logan. The expression of her opinion was less similar to how Kenny handled that appointment, however.

"I would've told the doctor to shove his pills up his ass," Beth had said with a laugh, as she punctuated her words by driving a wooden stake into the ground next to an Early Girl.

Beth had asked questions about Logan's condition only a few more times. Then, oddly, it seemed as if she'd lost interest in the subject—judging by her words, that is. Whenever their families were together, whenever his sister-in-law was within the general vicinity of his son, she had her eyes on the boy. It was as if she was studying a painting, or reading through some notes in a journal, or working away at a puzzle, and Kenny often felt compelled to walk over and say something to her. Something along the order of discouragement; a frank comment that told her how well he knew the road she was traveling down, and that it was a road which led to one big, dead-end. But also, a part of Kenny held on to hope, and that's probably why he never said anything.

He pulled off the highway, just a few miles west of Hillsboro. His brother lived on the outskirts of the city. But it seemed as if that entire city had been invited to Wayne's birthday party, and Kenny wouldn't have been surprised if that wasn't too far from the truth. His brother's charisma reached far back to his childhood, when Wayne had possessed the enduring occupation of being named "team captain" for all of their youthful activities.

As it was, the number of cars parked on and around Wayne's property put the worry of food back into Kenny's brain. He considered dropping the kids off and making a run to the nearest market to pick up some fish, but dismissed the idea, preferring instead to get a better look at just who all had shown up.

Many of his brother's friends were work associates, some of which Kenny had yet to meet—or trust. He felt Marley's cold breath creep back into his lungs, another warning from beyond the grave to watch over her children, to keep them safe, to smother them with that doting attention she had long since mastered, and of which Kenny had long since disliked. But like a vice, it was on him now, his wife's legacy, and Kenny often wondered when it had climbed onto his back. It was never like him to think about all the twisted sickos in the world, the predators who preyed on young children. But lately, these thoughts had plagued him like a shadow—Marley's shadow—and they had built inside of him a hive of paranoia, ceaselessly buzzing, and whispering thoughts into his ear.

Just where exactly had this voice come from? Was it perhaps an echo of his wife, from all the times he'd overheard her warning the kids not to talk to strangers? More hauntingly, was it his son's voice—Logan's lost voice, as the boy now apparently could not cry for help—was that the voice that had taken up sudden residence in a part of Kenny's mind?

He realized his hands had grown white over the steering wheel, so he looked for a place to park. His brother's home was on a five-and-a-half acre parcel sprawling with native shrubs and berry thickets, oak and pine tree groves, all of which made for a landscape of wilderness inviting to the imagination. Centered within these acres was a skirt of green lawn, along with a four-thousand square foot log cabin home, custom-built out of lodge-pole pines harvested from the Bitterroot Mountains of Montana.

It was never a surprise to Kenny that his brother had made a small fortune selling insurance and other related securities. He certainly possessed the hallmark personality for success. It was this—a good job, a happy family, the money—or the reigning seat behind some organized crime racket. Either way, Wayne would have found success.

The driveway onto the property was a gentle curving strip of asphalt defined by sandstone pavers, which led to a circular roundabout at the front of the house. For a central island, the roundabout featured a big leaf maple tree, the base of which was exquisitely decorated with the signs of children at play: an assortment of toys and household miscellanea; trodden pathways around the tree trunk; a capsized birdbath. Kenny shook his head and made a lap around the roundabout, wondering if his own daughter had engineered much of that mess days before.

The parking arrangement was a hodgepodge affair, with cars and trucks parked in an unruly, first-come, first-halt fashion, owing that there simply wasn't enough space to account for all the guests. Giving up, Kenny put his Jeep in reverse and backed into the central island, wedging his vehicle with perfect precision under a low-hanging branch and the trunk of the maple. The precision was almost too perfect, as if the space had been planned one hundred years prior, to account for the exact dimensions of a Jeep Wrangler, with inches to spare. Kenny laughed at the irony as he stepped out of the vehicle, walked around the front. George was already out and gone, the dog trailing a path toward any or all of Wayne's three Labradors.

"Take this into the house, Logan," Kenny said, retrieving the ice chest from the back. "Make sure you give it to Aunt Beth." For a minute he watched his son climb out from the backseat, then pick up the cooler and stroll away. Logan was wearing denim jeans and a charcoal sweatshirt, its hood drawn tightly over his head. Kenny studied the boy, observing that his son had grown a few inches since his mother had died. *At least some things hadn't frozen in time*, he thought.

He looked at his daughter then, who was still asleep. "Jolie— time to wake up," he said, giving her a shake. His watch read a quarter to six, and Kenny could already feel the approach of an evening chill. He caught the passing smell of briquettes and lighter fluid, along with the damp loam under his feet. "Jolie," he repeated, "wake up."

Yawning and rubbing her eyes, his daughter climbed out of the Jeep. She seemed wide-awake, though, by the time her feet were planted firmly on the ground. And she howled with delight, suddenly aware of where she was. Like George, she trailed her own path toward the house, in search of her cousins, or perhaps food, or maybe just the fun of it all.

From the back of the Jeep, Kenny pulled a large duffle bag containing an assortment of clothing and toiletries. Earlier, when he had packed the bag, he actually felt a bloom of pride, thinking that he nailed it, gathering everything he and the kids would need for a sleepover. But now, with his recent thoughts clinging to Marley, Kenny wondered what he'd forgotten.

He slung the bag over his shoulder and walked toward the house, hearing adult voices coming from the backyard, loud and jovial. At the front door was Beth, and she was holding an opened bottle of Sierra Nevada Pale Ale. Her eyes were squinting into the dark, despite the apricot aura bleeding from a porch light.

"Thought you could use one of these," she said, sucking on a tooth as if working at a piece of lodged food. Beth had on a red and white checkered-apron, and was playfully twirling a kitchen towel in her other hand. Her hair was pulled back into a ponytail. The woman rarely wore makeup. She didn't have any on now, and Kenny was reminded of how much Wayne and his family valued a casual approach to life. This approach wasn't necessarily a traditional one when considering Wayne's line of work. But Kenny knew that most of his brother's clientele were blue-collared business owners, individuals who believed in Levi jeans and Carhartt jackets, and who likely felt uncomfortable, even threatened, while in the presence of a man wearing a three-piece-suit.

"Thanks," Kenny replied, accepting the beer. "I can definitely use one of these."

"I got the cooler from Logan," Beth said. "He set it on the kitchen table, just before going out back."

They walked into the house, where Kenny dropped the duffle bag onto the floor of a side room, an office containing a pullout bed. "Did he run off to his spot?" he asked, following Beth into the kitchen.

"Probably," she replied. "Logan's spot" was a patio swing in the backyard, a place that he frequented often. More than once, Kenny had observed his son sit there for hours on end, his toe gently pushing at the ground, causing a subtle sway, the perfect tempo for lulling a baby to sleep. Sometimes Jolie or one of Wayne's kids would vigorously clamber onto the structure, get it to move fast, and then Logan would step off and quietly retreat into the woods behind the house.

"Did you see Jolie come through here?" Kenny asked.

"No. But I heard her down the hall. The kids are in Laney's room. Someone brought over a giant stuffed kitten. Laney confiscated it—you know how she loves her cats." Laney was Beth and Wayne's middle child and only daughter, a girl of eight who loved kittens and ponies, and who believed that one day her and Jolie were going to live on a farm with hundreds of animals, huge gardens, and where trees and bushes produced every kind of candy imaginable.

By two years, Laney followed her older brother, Aiden, who often rolled his eyes at his sister's grandiose plans. His preference now was skateboards and video games. Oliver was the youngest, pulling up the rear at two years of age. A good sport for a toddler, Oliver was up for anything his siblings offered: kittens, candy, skateboards and video games—all the above.

There were other children running throughout the house and outside, none of whom Kenny recognized. Two women (strangers to him also) were presently leaning against the kitchen counter, conversing; one was chopping cabbage, while the other was wrapping aluminum foil over ears of corn.

Beth followed Kenny's glance, stared, and took a step forward. "Not like that, hun," she said, taking the corn from the woman's hand. "You're forgetting the best part."

Kenny watched as Bethany—nay, *Beth*—showed a woman twenty years her senior how to apply the correct amount of cayenne powder to an ear of corn, before rolling it up in foil, all with the speed and adroitness of a stage performer. "There," she said, handing the finished product back. "Now it's ready for the grill."

"Thanks," the woman replied, her tone sounding somewhat ruffled.

Minutes later, after Beth had made introductions, Kenny learned that this woman's name wasn't "hun," and that she was the fiftyish year old wife of Stan Milton, general contractor and proprietor of Milton Builders. The woman's name was Barbara, in fact, and Kenny assumed she probably hadn't been too keen on being called "hun" by a much younger woman. With comical insight, Kenny wondered just how many wrinkles his brother was used to ironing out.

He peeled away from the conversation with tactful ease and stepped outside onto the back deck. The backside of the house began with a redwood deck comprising three levels, each of which led further down to a wide patio, an inviting courtyard built out of stone pavers, scattered with lawn chairs of various sizes and comfort, and featuring a robust fire pit.

On the first level of the deck, Kenny's brother stood guard over a restaurant-grade charcoal grill, and was surrounded by acquaintances. His voice was loud, his laughter louder yet, but his smile, as described by the twinkle in his eyes, was the loudest of all.

"Fifty bucks says he was a virgin!" Wayne hollered, and this was followed by a roar of laughter from everyone present. The meaning behind the comment eluded Kenny, but he smiled nonetheless. "Hey!" Wayne suddenly announced, effectively stopping the present conversation. "It's my baby brother! Come over here, you." He grabbed Kenny and pulled him in for a hug, bringing him further into a surrounding air inundated with an acrid smell of alcohol, cigar smoke, and seared meat.

"Some things never change, eh?" Kenny said. His brother gave him a quizzical look, and then Kenny followed with, "The life of the party, as always."

Wayne laughed, said, "What can I say?" He produced a cigar from a pocket inside his leather jacket and handed it to Kenny before introducing him to half a dozen men. Kenny forgot most of their names within minutes, but what followed was a long evening of amiable conversation, a time in which Kenny blissfully forgot about his role as a full-time father, and of his ceaseless inadequacies inherent to this occupation. The kids were supposed to start school soon, but their worthless dad kept forgetting to pick up the enrollment papers. Perhaps this was because he was toying with the notion of home-schooling them, as that would be the best course of action, considering the recent death of their mother. It's what Marley would have wanted, what she had unknowingly planned for, wasn't it?

But then, the very thought of home-schooling: the required organizational skills, the proper school work (she called it "curriculum," Kenny remembered, that's what his daughter's teacher had said), where to even begin, how many hours a day he would teach the kids, and whatever the hell he would need to instruct his son. How in God's name would he accomplish that? he wondered. *Could* he accomplish it?

Who was he kidding?

Once again, Marley's advent for proper financial planning was a stain that bled in the back of Kenny's mind. The foresight of putting into place an instrument designed to offset the risk of financial devastation by a terminal event had given Kenny the opportunity to ease the pain of it all... Yet half the time he still felt severely helpless, and paralyzed with uncertainty.

But not tonight.

Kenny drank three beers as he dismissed the nagging urge to check on his kids (something Marley would have taken care of by now, like the life insurance). Using a butcher knife, he helped his brother dismantle a rack of ribs, the first of six other slabs of meat presently cooked and lying on a long wooden table. And as he did this, he also forgot about Logan; he figured the boy was in his spot, swinging the hours away, present in body, absent all the same. There was an alabaster platter made from fired clay, something Beth had crafted and Kenny held onto the dish with two firm hands while his brother piled on the ready-to-eat ribs, and while Stan Milton, in the background, hee-hawed endlessly with his comparisons between being a husband and a business owner, and throughout this moment, Kenny was reminded once again of the warm comfort, the familiar anchor.

"Did I tell you I got the materials up in the cabin?" Wayne said at one point, brushing secret sauce onto another rack of ribs. The grill was hot, and Kenny felt the rising heat pull at his beard, a feeling that was strangely placating against the growing chill of the night. "You should have enough to keep working," his brother added. "There's a generator inside, and a can of fuel in the back."

"Sounds good," Kenny replied. "I'll get on it this week."

Later that night, he ate a plateful of beef, sided by a mound of coleslaw and two ears of corn lathered in butter, along with a quarter-sized nugget of breaded perch. He washed it all down with six knuckles of Jack Daniels, four more beers, and laughed modestly when he thought about the amount of fish he'd brought, how little it was.

"Whatever else you need, just put it on the Home Depot card," Wayne reminded him, and there it was again, with all its weight: *the anchor*. Kenny felt it dig deep as the night rolled on. His brother's cabin, he remembered, was another thing Kenny understood. This was a project he could stand behind, something he didn't have to think too hard about. Like the broken pieces of his new house, it was a problem with a solution that he could forge with his bare hands, and was nothing as complicated as homeschooling. Or worse: fixing his messed up son.

Into the small hours of the night, Kenny ate until he was stuffed, and drank until he couldn't see straight, and in his mind he mapped out his plans on how he was going to fix up his brother's hunting cabin. Then, somewhere in those dark hours lingered a vague recollection of Bethany's voice, unusually slow and mild, a mere echo, announcing that, "Yes, Logan *was* in his spot."

CHAPTER 7

The morning brought with it a dull pain in both of Kenny's temples. The last time he'd had a hangover like this was the morning after he and Marley had gone to a brewery in Oxnard, having dropped the kids off at a coworker's house. Blue Oyster Cult played that night, on a cramped stage set too high under an alarmingly low ceiling, adorned with low-hanging, white Christmas lights. It was a sad affair, Kenny recalled, watching world-renowned rockers having to duck and navigate their way through such a precarious set-up.

His temples throbbed, and a sharp pain grazed the back of his eyes after he peered out through the window blinds. There was a gray, pallid morning slowly losing itself to the brilliance below the horizon. He'd slept on the twin bed in the study, with Jolie curled up next to him. Most of the covers were twisted around her—not entirely unusual—but the fact that she had slept in here, with her dad, and not in Laney's room, struck Kenny as remarkably curious. He wondered if she had gotten into a tiff with her cousin. Or maybe she was missing her mom.

Thinking only made his head hurt worse. The pain in his temples fluctuated; there was a rhythm to the pulsing. Kenny debated whether to get up and go see Beth (he thought he heard her in the kitchen), suspecting that she would have an excellent remedy for a hangover, or to just stay in bed and try to sleep it off.

He turned from the window and stared at his daughter's sleeping face. This seven-year-old child had her mother's thick eyebrows. She had the woman's flaxen hair and prominent cheekbones. She had the same early morning lay against-the-pillow stillness. And this stark, miniature version of Marley left Kenny feeling uneasy. He suddenly remembered a conversation he'd had with his wife many years before, a passing joke more or less, when she said children were the shrapnel of love's explosion—and the fragments carried were pieces of the parents.

As for the uneasy feeling, Kenny now understood what that was about. It was the illness brought on by his loss, and all the symptomatic shit that came with it, trying to fill the cosmic-sized hole left behind. He was nervous about getting pushed back into that gloom—he'd been there enough times already. But also, he didn't want to take his eyes off his daughter, because he knew he was staring at a piece of his wife.

A shift of his foot and Kenny realized that there was sand in the bed. Lots of sand. This discovery forced him through a mental survey of the day before: the morning at the beach; an afternoon of filleting the fish and packing the overnight gear; the drive here, to his brother's house; the celebration that followed. His daughter hadn't bathed since the night before last. She hadn't even changed her clothes since coming home from the beach—because Kenny never told her to. And with this, he had a sudden sense that there was something not entirely suitable for this oversight he'd made. The subtle sounds of cleaning from the kitchen only heightened his feelings, as he imagined Beth lecturing him—very soon now—over proper parenting techniques. She had done it before, bold as a bull, and would do it again, Kenny knew.

He crept out of bed and staggered into the hall. His lower back ached; he had to piss something fierce, so he went straight to the bathroom. The hardwood floor felt cold as the sea, and an archipelago of toys and various children's clothes provided a small obstacle course for Kenny. A moment later, after a long piss, he splashed water on his face three times before sitting on the edge of the bathtub. It felt as if metal gears were slowly grinding down sand and rubble between his ears.

"Good morning, Jolie." It was Beth's voice he'd heard. Jolene was now awake, in the kitchen, undoubtedly looking for food, or hinting at her aunt to make pancakes, while dragging a beach's worth of sand across the floor. That sand was in the cuff of his daughter's pant legs, he realized, as she had rolled them up before chasing George into the surf. With a sigh, Kenny pushed against the tub and forced himself out of the bathroom.

In the kitchen now, Beth was wearing green sweatpants and a white, long-sleeved t-shirt with a picture of a tow truck, and the words "Frank's Garage," on the back. Pink fuzzy slippers covered her feet. She was presently engaged in organizing various objects into categories across the counter and kitchen table. She dragged her feet while she moved, spiriting laughter from Jolene. The girl was crouched on a chair, pointing at Beth's slippers, calling them "little pink bunnies."

Kenny entered from the hall and leaned his shoulder against a pantry door. He heard the coffee pot percolating on the counter, caught the sweet aroma of Arabica, Sumatra, or some such blend, which made his mouth water. Red and blue party cups spotted the room, along with a substantial amount of beer bottles and bottle caps, dinner plates and utensils, crumpled napkins. The kitchen windows faced east, and a fan of orange light was just coming through, painting the back cupboards and cluttered counters with the colors of autumn. There were half-a-dozen whiskey bottles crowded near the sink, some opened, some not yet empty. Beth grabbed one and offered it to Kenny. "Hair of the dog?" she asked.

"Sheesh," Kenny replied, mechanically running a hand across the side of his face. "Seriously, though... What'cha got?"

She gave him a surprised look, pulled a glass from a cupboard. "Here," she said, "start with a glass of water." She motioned toward the refrigerator. "There's filtered water in there... It tastes better. I'm making huevos rancheros as soon as I put a dent in this mess. That should clear your head—it's what works for your brother. He's still in bed, by the way."

"I figured as much," Kenny replied. In steady motion, he poured and drank two glasses of water before placing the Britta container back into the refrigerator. In that time, Beth had cleared a spot at the table, and had Jolene sitting with a bowl of cereal. There was also bread dropped in the toaster.

"Will you get some butter and jam?" Beth asked, motioning to the refrigerator. "In the door."

"Sure thing." The throbbing in Kenny's head subsided. He placed the butter and jam on the table, then went to the patio door and looked outside, thinking about his son.

"Logan's on the couch," Beth announced, as if she had just read Kenny's mind. "That's where he fell asleep. But don't worry—I made sure he had plenty of blankets."

And there it was.

"Thanks," Kenny replied. He thought his words sounded infinitely lame, and the following length of silence, the grotesque pause, only confirmed his thoughts. "I'm really grateful, Beth... Truly. I'm not sure what I'd do without you and my brother."

"Oh, you'd be fine." But there was a hollowness in her voice, as if to allow for an echo's response: *Though, I'm not so sure about your kids.*

Somehow, all the guests had made it home. None of them required a place to crash for the night in order to sleep off their inebriated states. Kenny discovered this as he paced throughout the house, coffee cup in hand. He passed his son on the couch and stopped to observe the sleeping boy. Logan had his head pushed against the armrest, his neck craned down, chin resting on his chest. There was a rattling sound to the boy's breathing, so Kenny placed his cup on the floor and gathered his son by the legs and pulled him further down the couch. Logan rustled his shoulders and snorted in response, but did not wake up.

Minutes later, Kenny found his way back into the kitchen. He was about to volunteer his services at cleaning up the night's aftermath, knowing that Beth would likely rebuke him with a customary, ardent protest. He thought of the plastic cups and looked under the sink for a trash bag, glancing out the window momentarily. In the backyard, George and one of the Labradors were sniffing busily in the grass, their tails swatting heavily, side-to-side. Somewhere underground, a gopher scurried.

"Can I have some more, Auntie Beth?" Jolene asked.

"Tell you what," Beth began, "let's go run you a hot bath—a *bubble bath*—and when you're all done, I'll make some blueberry waffles."

Jolene squealed and pranced down the hall, just as Kenny found a box of plastic bags in the pantry. "I got the trash," he said aloud.

"Thanks," replied Beth. "You know you don't have to."

"Oh, I'm sure I do," Kenny said.

He was almost finished with picking up in the kitchen when Beth returned. She brought with her an unnatural silence, a characteristic he hadn't observed in her before, didn't think she was capable of, for that matter. It left him feeling alarmed, and he braced himself as he asked, "Is there something wrong?"

"How long has it been, Kenny?" Beth replied. "Six—seven months, now?"

He knew where this was going, and at once Kenny avoided any illusions to the matter. "About half a year since Marley died."

"Right. Half a year." She paused for a minute, leaving her statement hanging in the air like a dead stare. "So what exactly is the plan, then?" As she said this, Beth set herself back in the motions of cleaning. "Did you get them enrolled in school yet? That starts in two weeks. You know that, right?"

"Look, Beth, I know I've got a lot—"

"No more excuses, Kenny. If you need help, then I can help you, but you need to pick up all this *shit* of yours. You're a father, for Christ's sake. Your kids need you."

Kenny dropped his head and continued to comb the kitchen for trash, his body now on auto-pilot. "Yeah, I know, Beth. I know what I need to do."

"No, I don't think you do," she replied. She paused again and gave Kenny a sharp look. "Your son, for example. Are you just going to let him wither away in his world of silence?"

Her words struck a nerve, and Kenny felt his face flush, felt the fire of anger, like a rush of whiskey. "Hey!" he said, with command. "I've been doing the best I can with my son. I don't know what else the fuck I *can* do!"

Beth didn't waver. "Spend some time with him, for once!"

Her response was both shattering and confusing. *Spend some time with him?* Kenny thought. *What in the hell have I been doing?* "I do spend time with him," he replied. "I've been with that kid every damn second since Marley died—half a year. Just what are you talking about?"

Beth shook her head, as if in disgust. "I've seen how you are with your son. Put yourself in his shoes, Kenny. Get down to his level. That's what you need to do. Logan's lost the only person who ever knew him... The only person who knew what it was like to be him—what he liked, or what he thought... What made him smile."

Kenny quietly stared back.

"Yes," Beth continued, "you've been there for him—but you're never *with* him. And that's the difference, Kenny. It's a big difference. It's *all* the difference."

The ensuing silence was heavy; it fell between the two of them like the drop of an anchor. As his thoughts raced and he scoured the kitchen corners for litter, Kenny observed his daughter's playful sounds coming from the bathroom. He heard other sounds as well: a cough from down the hall, dogs barking outside, the ticking from the clock on the wall behind him. He pondered Beth's words, tried to wrap his mind around a meaning—any meaning.

At last, he buried his pride. "I guess it's just not something that comes easy for me."

Beth scoffed. "No, it sure isn't."

At that moment, Wayne stumbled into the kitchen, rubbing the palms of his hands into his eyes. He was wearing a brown bathrobe and brown slippers. His shoulders and belly lacked the celebration from the night before, were drooped and pronounced, respectively. He went straight for the coffee.

"Well, good morning, birthday boy," Beth said.

Wayne grunted a reply, poured a cup, drank it black. He looked at Beth. "I'm starving."

"Right," she replied. "As soon as I make some room to cook."

Wayne kissed his wife on the cheek—she smiled curtly in response—then he turned toward Kenny. "Hey, come with me," he said, as he went to the patio door, opened it, and stepped outside.

Kenny followed his brother into the backyard, instantly grateful to be relieved of Beth's presence. He spotted George and the other dogs running wildly through the trees, fifty yards away; he figured they had moved on from the gopher to a squirrel. The morning was as cold as it looked. A thin surface of fog was still holding out, along the western front—the trees, and a patch of blackberries being its last stand against the imminent fire of an autumn sun.

They walked to the southern end of the property, to the fenced garden Wayne had methodically constructed the year he took the keys to his home. The garden patch itself was approximately fifty-foot by fifty-foot square, and was surrounded by an eight-foot tall fence. Kenny recognized the tomato plants he'd helped stake into the ground, the largest of the branches now as thick as his thumb. Many more vegetables sprouted neatly from individual planter boxes of different shapes and sizes. There were salad greens, squash and turnips, and cucumber vines that stretched across latticework made of cedar. The surrounding fence was a structural icon, leaning thirty degrees away from the garden. This architectural characteristic— the "leaning fence"—was not only appealing to the eye, but served as an adequate animal deterrent, as it kept out the many deer that happened upon the property.

Next to the garden's entrance was another looming construct—a six-foot tall abstract sculpture made completely out of redwood lumber scraps. Mounted on top was a portable, all-weather radio, plugged into an outdoor socket at the base of the wooden structure. According to Wayne, the radio (forever tuned to a classical music station) had been playing non-stop since he built the backyard statue and plugged it in roughly five years ago. This was one of the property's unforgettable details, and every time Kenny heard the notes coming from the black box, it reminded him of his brother's inimitable personality.

They talked more about the hunting cabin, with Wayne adding further specifics, such as the type of insulation to be used, what kind of lighting he wanted, and the dimensions for the proposed, extended porch. As Kenny and his brother walked the perimeter of the garden, inspecting the integrity of the fence and searching for various animal tracks (this, being the presiding reason Wayne had ventured into the backyard), Wayne also steered the conversation to the additional amenities he had in mind for the hunting cabin—such as a hot-tub, and a detached, three-car garage, to store all his hunting equipment.

Some details were mere ideas, simple notions designed to propagate excitement (which, coming from Wayne, almost always had the intended effect). But as it was, Kenny had already been champing at the bit to get up there and begin the work. He knew what manual labor did for him, how it cut the edge off his never-ending problems. He knew how relaxing it was. And none of this work would prove difficult for Kenny. It would hardly prove difficult for Wayne, who had a proficient enough level of carpentry skills, but who lacked the time needed for the job. The goal—after all—was to have the cabin completed within a year, before the following deer hunting season.

However, as his brother continued on with the many details, and despite Kenny's overall excitement, he couldn't stop his mind from drifting back to what his sister-in-law had said. The concept of spending more time with his son—quality time, he presumed—baffled him. He thought about how much more he could do for Logan. Or how his wife was apparently the only person on the planet who understood their son—again, a baffling notion, but one in which he felt he had no other choice to accept as being true.

In his head, he damned Beth. She was right; he knew. Right about so many things: from how to wrap an ear of corn, to perhaps fixing a broken kid. Kenny had observed how the woman irritated people, and at the moment, it was all he could do not to feel this way as well. *Is the offspring of wisdom and youth pretentiousness?* he wondered. It was a harsh thought, yet adequate all the same, as it brought with it a cold lining adding to an already chilled morning. Sure, Kenny might have loathed that woman, but damn if she hadn't nailed him to the wall.

They walked through the gate and into the perimeter of the garden, where Wayne stooped to pull a few weeds. He ran his hand over a ripe tomato, plucked it, brought it to his nose. "So what do you think?" he asked.

"About what?" replied Kenny.

"About the cabin." Wayne stood erect and craned his elbow outward, cradling the tomato against his midriff. His face adopted an incredulous smile. "Shit, brother. Haven't you been listening to me?"

CHAPTER 8

From afar, the plants looked like a wall of errant weeds, randomly placed and capped by the dark shadow coming from a stretch of blackberry thickets. They sat on the ground in thirty-pound plastic garden bags, the black variety commonly found at nurseries. An exception was that each bag had been spray-painted a collage of matte greens and yellows, to mask their shiny black exterior—which would be a dead giveaway to any patrolling helicopter.

These ten plants made up the first of five patches spread out along the hillside, and they gave off an aroma of musk and skunk. In the dry and dusty air, the stink was thick enough to taste, and ironically, Rob found it mouthwatering. The other patches each contained the same number of plants, and sat further down on the hillside, roughly thirty yards away. Fifty plants in the crop made for a good number, and whenever Rob thought about it, he couldn't help himself from doing the math.

In the previous spring, a year and a half ago, when Rob had first partnered up with Vance to begin this agricultural endeavor, he was quickly put-off by the number of arduous tasks it involved. He had to make several trips up to the scene, hauling in fertilizer and extra equipment, such as plastic bottles, irrigation tubes, and several trash bags full of crushed madrone leaves. "Why can't we just plant them in the ground?" he had asked Vance, irritably. With impatient eyes, the veteran grower looked at Rob, replied only with, "It's good to be mobile, brah."

Now, many months later, Rob knew all the answers to that first question, as well as many more. He knew that regardless of the indigenous soil quality, their crop required mobility to compensate for the ridgeline half a mile away—which, because of its position and altitude, cast an early shadow on their scene by mid-September, and therefore cut into the much needed hours of sunlight.

Also, portable plants made for a quick and easy post-harvest cleanup. Rob understood that such a convenience allowed for the increased possibilities of returning to the same spot in future years, regardless of Vance's vehement objections on the matter. As for the madrone leaves, he learned that even though the resident soil, which they had used to fill the grower bags, was adequate enough, the added leaves were crucial for the development of "killer buds." He wasn't sure about this last detail, but Vance's insistence seemed plausible enough, so Rob had held his tongue as he churned the many pounds of leaves into the many bags of soil.

What made the most sense to Rob, however, and thus offered his greatest vessel of knowledge to date, was Vance's explanation on the three key components for successfully growing marijuana—sun, water, and soil—with soil being the easiest of the three to control. That is why they hauled in the extra materials, and why Rob endured the hours of hard labor. And that was also why, despite Vance's stout protests, Rob would use this same place next year, the year after, and the year after that. The site allowed for good sun exposure, and had an excellent water source. And besides, what the hell did Rob care about Vance's opinion, anyway? Once this season was over, and Rob learned everything there was to know about growing and trimming pot, he wouldn't need the reeking Rastaman around anymore.

The shortest of their plants reached Rob's chin, over five feet tall, and had a girth that was easily the same in size. The buds on this plant, fondly referred to as "colas," were already reaching toward the ground. Rob observed this detail with mild excitement as he cracked his knuckles and walked past the plant, up the hill, and toward the concealed water tanks.

"Check for clogs," Vance reminded him, as he trailed close behind. "That's first on the list, man."

"No fucking shit," Rob replied. It seemed now that whenever his partner opened his hippie mouth, all it did was piss Rob off.

"Dude, I'm just saying."

"Well quit saying, already." Rob stopped when he reached the top of the blackberry hedge. He glanced back at Vance, the night vision goggles and long dreadlocks making the young man look like a gangly insectoid out of a science fiction nightmare. "You know what, fucker? I'm gonna start calling you Mom."

"Brah, you need to relax," replied Vance. "And keep your voice down."

"Whatever you say, Mom." Rob turned away and walked toward their water stash: five fifty-five gallon drums stationed above the blackberry thicket, and covered with the same type of camouflage netting they had used on the Bronco hours earlier. With modest care, Rob peeled the camo fabric away from the water tanks while Vance inspected them. They had sealed each of the tanks with a plastic lid containing a half-inch feeder tube running out of its center, like a flexible straw.

The feeder tubes traced a slow incline along the hillside, away from the scene, for approximately two hundred yards, where they attached to the bottom of a large collection tank sitting at the base of a precipice. At this juncture dripped a steady, year-round trickle of spring water. Albeit crude, the gravity-fed irrigation system brought enough water to supply all fifty of their plants with five gallons of water per day.

After five minutes of inspection, Vance said, "Water looks good." Rob grunted in reply, and both men carefully sealed up the lids, then replaced the camouflage netting. They moved slowly back down the hillside, where Rob checked the individual drip lines.

The drip lines fed water to each plant, and were connected to a series of tubes, all of which ran from main lines coming out of the water tanks above. This was another one of those long and arduous jobs, which the Prospect had little patience for. He almost complained about having to be the one to do all this "shit-work," as he called it, but knew that Vance's talents were better applied with the inspection and early harvesting of the plants.

And that was the rub. Some plants already had fully formed, sticky buds on them, which were ready to be picked, and only Vance was skilled enough to know which ones they were. After watching Rob for a few minutes, he skittered off with a duffle bag and a pair of pruning shears. "Okay, me bitches," he said, cackling as he slipped off into the shadows. "Here cometh the Rastaman." Rob cringed at the hippie's words and secretly hoped his partner would twist his ankle on his way down the mountainside.

It took Rob over an hour to check all fifty drip lines. He found three tubes that had almost been pulled out of their respective bags and repositioned them. Vance came by anyway, to see if any of the plants had suffered from a lack of water. He said that the culprit was likely a raccoon, but Rob wasn't so sure.

He examined the general area for human tracks, thinking about the cabin just a few hundred yards away. And he thought about his conversation with his partner on their drive up here. Vance had been dead serious about keeping an eye out for "rip-offs" casing their scene, since "Rip-off Moon" was only two weeks away. That conversation had sent bolts of adrenaline racing through Rob's chest, and for good reason. "Rip-off Moon," also known as "Hunter's Moon," was the last full moon before harvest. Rumored to be abnormally brilliant, the fullness of the moon allowed for a person to walk through a dark forest using no form of light. It was common for growers to get their crops pinched by thieves on this night, and Rob was damn certain it would not happen to him. But if it did...

Absently, he checked the side pocket of his backpack, making sure the zipper was still closed, then scoured the area for footprints, or cigarette butts—anything that showed somebody else had been here.

At the outer limit of the patch he was presently working, Rob crouched below a transparent length of high-test fishing line, which formed a perimeter around the marijuana patch. The line had been wrapped around trees and wooden stakes, and it sat approximately three feet off the ground. Its purpose was to serve as a deterrence against deer, which would otherwise happily devour their naked cash crop. Several plastic bleach bottles filled with urine and plugged with cotton rags sat along the perimeter as well, adding as an additional defense against various critters. But if Vance was correct about raccoons getting into those three plants, then just how successful were the bottles of piss? Again, Rob wondered if somebody had tampered with their scene.

Later, he met up with Vance, who had finished with his inspections and harvesting. They filled both of the duffle bags they had brought up from the truck with ripe buds, and this proved to be a tremendous relief for Rob. He released a deep sigh, wondering how much money sat in the bags.

Before they packed up to leave, the two of them crept through the entire scene once more, looking for clues whether anyone had visited them. They checked the integrity of the surrounding fishing lines, tightening them up at certain points as needed, and studied the ground for footprints or other telltale signs. With soapy water, they sprayed for aphids, and then they checked for mold, inspecting stem crotches on some of the larger plants. And with suppressive laughter, Vance pointed out some beauties of the crop. Many of the colas, or buds, were a foot long, or more. Adding to these were numerous acorn-sized nuggets called "popcorn buds".

"Shit just keeps getting bigger," Vance said in a low whisper. "Shit is multiplying, too." He wore a huge smile, and seemed relaxed—almost too relaxed, Rob suddenly observed.

"Hey, are you fucking stoned or something?" Rob asked. The thought of Vance being half-baked and stumbling carelessly through the scene, causing a racket, sent Rob's blood to boil.

"No way, brah," replied Vance. "Not me—I ain't stoned. Not now, and not ever... Not here, or there... Or in a box, with a fox..." Then he burst into laughter, until Rob smacked him viciously across the head.

Vance fell into an ugly sprawl on the ground, his laughter quickly replaced by a hard, dry gasp for air. "Dude, what the fuck!" he said, struggling to pick himself up.

"Shut up, asshole!" Rob hissed, kicking Vance in the ribs. "Shut the fuck up, I said!"

Vance threw his hand to his side and sucked air. He fell silent and motionless as Rob hovered over him, a tightly wound coil ready to spring. "When the fuck did you get high? Were you smoking out here while I was busting my hump? We're supposed to keep a low profile, shithead. *Remember?*"

"Dude," Vance began, between breaths, "I only ate some cookies—down by that cabin." He pulled himself up, held his ribs and stepped away from Rob. "That's all, man."

"I don't fucking care," Rob said. "And all your laughing and shit—people can hear that."

"There ain't nobody out here, brah," Vance said, and Rob made a move toward him. "Okay, okay!" Vance quickly added. "I'll shut up, man." He backed away and removed his night vision goggles and backpack, craned his neck and inhaled deeply the night air. "Fuck," he whispered.

Rob backed off and leaned heavily against a nearby tree. He too took off his goggles, then he studied the sheet of blackness spread out before him... The cash crop. He took a deep breath and waited, listening to the night. Once again, his thoughts played with the math behind their operation. Fifty plants. On average, half a pound of smokable product per plant. Two thousand dollars for each of those half-pounders... Two thousand times fifty added up to one hundred thousand dollars. And those were conservative numbers, Rob knew. If they were lucky, they'd make more money than that. Much more.

The calculations were always a catch-22 for Rob. Thinking of money made him giddy with excitement, but also paranoid beyond control. He noticed his hands were shaking when he put his goggles back on. "Come on," he said, "get your shit together. Time for us to bail." He shifted his stance and looked beyond the clearing, into the tree line, before abruptly raising a hand. "Hold up, Vance."

"What?" Vance whispered. "What is it?"

"I thought I saw something. Over there, in the trees."

Vance swung around and fumbled with his night vision goggles. Rob studied the near distance, dropped to a crouch, and began a slow walk across the hillside. He felt a shiver run through his spine, electric, like a flash of lightning. He adjusted his goggles and scanned the opposite tree line. Nothing. Nothing but a few swaying branches, and the sound of Vance's footsteps rustling through dried brush behind him. A soft updraft of wind stroked the hillside, as subtle as a touch from a child's hand, but bringing with it a pungent odor.

"What the hell is that smell?" Rob whispered. The stink was strong, and it fell over the men with the thickness of a wool blanket. Rob felt the stench find a pocket in the back of his throat, a place to sit and loiter, and he pulled his goggles off and gagged, almost retching.

But just then, a sudden rustle in the bushes twenty feet away broke the silence of the night. A coyote had jumped out from its hide and was now sprinting through the trees, away from Rob and Vance.

"Son of a bitch!" Rob cried, fumbling for some kind of weapon—any weapon. His gun and crossbow were both inside the backpack, but he had a K-Bar strapped to his side. He remembered that and went for it until he heard Vance snickering.

"Relax, dude," Vance said, smiling at Rob with what looked like small triumph. "It's just a fucking coyote. He ain't gonna hurt you."

Rob clenched his jaw and squeezed his fists. Snuffing out this wannabe Rastafarian might have entered his mind, initially, as pure fantasy. But now, after being called "dude" and "brah" for the ten-thousandth time, after seeing the asshole's smarmy smile when Rob nearly panicked at the sight of a coyote, he now had zero reservations over the prospect of killing his beatnik partner.

Rob's thoughts went to the mutilated biker he'd buried a few days earlier. If only he could exact the same form of torture on the dumb tree-hugger. But dead was dead; and in this case, that would have to do.

Rob ran the final math equation in his head, making sure to include Vance's bullet-riddled body stashed inside a dumpster, and he released the tension from his fists. A hundred thousand dollars was a lot of money—especially after being divided one way.

CHAPTER 9

In the absence of direction, life had suddenly become a frantic whirlpool for Kenny. Despite his many years of living, and the mass multitude of experience embedded behind his eyes, at once, every context seemed to have slipped away. Also, the focal point of his life now appeared to be the same mechanism that was drawing his world into oblivion... And that focal point was his family.

As he drove his kids home from his brother's house, Kenny's mind toiled over these thoughts. They had formed themselves into the mental equivalent of a cerebral rat's nest, and working through the various knots and snags had caused his knuckles to whiten, his eyes to ache.

Kenny did not know how to act on Beth's suggestions of being there for his son. And damn if he was ready enough to ask the woman. One thing was for certain: Monday morning would bring with it the paperwork to enroll his kids in school. That and everything following it should be an easy decision, or so Kenny had hoped.

But then he pictured his son going through his entire fourth-grade year without speaking to anyone. Without a doubt, Logan would become the school's sideshow freak, and without mercy, the kid would get picked on daily. Kenny's stomach roiled itself into its own knot at this thought. Deep down, he knew what he must do—what he *would* do—about his son. In some ways, this knowledge delivered a layer of relief to Kenny. But in other ways, the knowledge brought with it genuine terror. A terror in which he had no answer for dispelling.

Less than an hour down the road, Kenny found temporary salvation once again, none other than by thinking about the list taped to his refrigerator. He thought about what he wrote on the list, and what he would add as soon as he got home. His brother had given him plenty to work with, bless his wealthy soul, but Beth was still the thorn in Kenny's side. Completing those school papers would be a good first step. Perhaps he'd call the woman afterward, just to brag.

Like willow branches, the passing wind snapped at the Jeep's interior, and this time it whirled Kenny's long hair as much as Jolene's. His beanie and gloves he'd stashed in the glove compartment, as the day had grown warm, the afternoon sun a lonely ball of brass, high in the sky. More than an hour yet from home, and Kenny thought he caught the scent of brine. An ocean's breeze, perhaps, though it could have easily been from his vehicle, the beach sand on the floorboards kicked up from all the wind.

The smell had a sudden and powerful effect on him, as, for whatever reason, it placed Kenny back on the *Pauli's Bride*, with the boat's skipper standing next to the wheel, prepping tackle. It was Kenny's first day, and on that day the old man had never said a damn thing beyond *Hello*, and then, *You watch me.* That was it. And, as it now dawned on Kenny, that was more than enough. On that first day, he observed much more than what he could have possibly understood.

Ironically, it was the simple act of watching the old man that Kenny learned best the unique language of the fishing profession. He observed the casual nuances in how Pauli moved about the boat, or in his timing with setting leaders, or reeling in fish (some quicker than others, depending on the species). Pauli performed everything on the boat in only the fewest of verbal directions.

Considering this recollection, it dawned on Kenny that the old skipper—man of paltry words as he was—seemed most comfortable when not pressed into conversation, of any sorts. The Portuguese sailor seemed perfectly content when simply left to his silence.

It was an odd memory, yet perhaps not so odd in its timing. His speechless son was always on Kenny's mind, and his current situation had dredged up memories of his past. Was there something about Pauli he had yet to learn? A missing lesson, perhaps? Another part of the fishing language: one more noun, verb, or adjective left to describe the solution to an intricate problem. Or was there something Kenny could apply to his current situation—to Logan, that is—something regarding, and surrounding, the mysterious power of silence?

He drove south along highway 42, was presently well into the Camas Valley. The highway divided a seemingly endless meadow combed vastly with sedge and slough grass, brushing the near horizon a deep, pastel green. An occasional pond inhabited with waterfowl, and often braced by tall clumps of leaning, white alder, broke lightly the long stretches of monotony. To his right, in the far distance, Kenny spotted a tan barn accompanied by half-a-dozen grazing cattle. At his side, George chomped saliva and the passing wind, smiling happily like any good retriever would.

"You kids getting hungry yet?" Kenny asked, casting a quick glance over his shoulder.

"Yeah!" Jolie replied. "I'm starving."

Kenny doubted his daughter's response, typical as it was. She had been finishing up on a second serving of fruit salad she'd helped Beth make when it was time for them to leave. But as for Logan, the boy had only eaten a single pancake. Mostly he'd picked at it, like a sick bird. It's how the kid ate nowadays—and how could that not worry Kenny? He remembered nostalgically of the time when Logan would tear into a plate of beef ribs, all caution thrown to the wind. *Where was that kid now?* Kenny wondered. *Where was his blossoming football star, or home run hitter?*

The image of Logan trudging through an indefinite length of time with what some would now consider a *disability* left Kenny feeling cold and bleak. More so, it left him feeling cheated, which, of course, was how he often felt since Marley's death.

His thoughts went again to Beth and her astounding gall. 'Spend more time with your son,' she had said. And by this she meant quality time, Kenny assumed. Also, there was her eloquent exclamation that it was high time for Kenny to pull his shit together. That he had *no more excuses*.

Despite Beth's renowned boldness, given a bit of distance and time, Kenny was now beginning to appreciate her advice. To some degree, at least. And, as he drove through the length of the Camas Valley, the great expanse of land before him, the wideness of the sky above, these troubled thoughts of his seemed to carry less weight to them. It was as if he was catching his breath at last, but for reasons he could not yet explain.

He looked at his kids in the rear-view mirror, his gaze settling briefly on Logan's profile as the boy was staring outside the vehicle. *Put yourself in his shoes...* That was something else Beth had said. Kenny wondered what his son would appreciate most. What was it he needed? The doctors had been vague regarding therapy, but more explicit about the use of medication, to treat Logan—none of which offered any help for Kenny. To the contrary, it caused him to mistrust the professional world of medicine, a result that left him feeling remote, even bleak.

For the rest of the drive home, Kenny's mind juggled between Beth, Pauli, Logan's schooling, and the apparent hopelessness of his overall situation. Though in his gut, he believed there was something to this circus of thoughts. That he was perhaps knee-deep inside a riddle, the answer of which, although surely profound, was as vague as the very question with which he was wrestling.

After arriving in Coos Bay and picking up food at the local Taco Bell, Kenny drove them north along the Pacific Coast Scenic Byway. He pulled over on a side street, which overlooked the Isthmus Slough. The tide was in and there was a casual wind, the water gray and choppy.

"Look at those seagulls, Daddy," Jolie said. She was standing on the backseat, pointing up into the sky. Above the slough, a massive flock of gulls was circling en masse, their bodies sculpting a great, rotating wheel below the clouds. Jolie hopped three times on the seat, slapping the Jeep's roll bar before Kenny told her to get down. "I want my rice, Daddy. And my taco—did they get me my taco?"

"Yeah, yeah, it's all here," Kenny said. He dug through the bags and began dispersing the food to his kids. "Probably a fishing vessel," he said. "You think?"

"Think about what?" Jolie replied.

"Those seagulls. They're probably up there scouting for fish scraps." Kenny looked at his daughter, as if begging a question, but she just replied with a smile and a shrug.

"Daddy, I need a spoon," she said.

"For—oh yeah, the rice." Kenny searched through the bags, soon realizing that they'd forgotten to include a spoon for his daughter's side of rice. "Son of a..." he mumbled.

"They forgot my spoon, didn't they?" Jolie said. She crossed her arms in a pout and slowly said, "*Not again.*"

Kenny searched the bags one more time, checked the glove compartment and door pockets for a plastic fork or spoon. He even looked under the seats, hoping to find an old utensil.

"How am I supposed to eat?" Jolie asked. "With my hands? Little ladies don't eat with their hands."

"Just relax," Kenny said, half chuckling at his daughter's comment. "I've got this." Honestly, he couldn't remember a meal that Jolie *didn't* eat with her hands. Giving up his search, he retrieved a pocketknife from the glove compartment, took an empty plastic Mountain Dew bottle from a cup holder, and carved away. In less than a minute, he handed Jolie a finely crafted, translucent green spoon.

"What?" Jolie said, incredulously. She took the spoon and studied it, smiling. "Why, this is perfect. It's a rectangle, Daddy. A rectangle spoon."

Kenny gave her a smile and then looked at George. The retriever seemed embarrassed about something, but Kenny knew that this was his dog's "patiently hopeful face". Kenny ran his hand over the dog's neck. "You can relax too, George. We'll be home shortly—then you can eat. But no more Taco Bell for you." He looked in the rear-view mirror as he said this. "You guys understand that? Logan, don't be giving your food to the dog—it makes him sick."

"Logan understands, Daddy," Jolie replied.

Under the pressure of his daughter's continued request, Kenny made a pass through McDonald's for sundaes. They were minutes from home, and after pulling into their driveway, George apparently lost all hope for scraps, and jumped down and ran off toward the yard. Grinning, Kenny grabbed the sundaes and stepped out of the Jeep, his kids trailing close behind. "Life is short, George!" he shouted. "Go get you some!"

Jolie laughed, and they watched the dog run headlong for the cottonwoods behind the house.

"Yeah, he'll be back soon enough," Kenny said. An alabaster veil sat thinly upon the sky above; the common, late-afternoon fog had rolled in.

The family ate their sundaes on the back porch while Kenny studied the property. His first big project would be to scrap the old shed and build a new one. Then maybe he'd construct some garden beds; but he wasn't sure what vegetables would grow best out here, being so near to the coast. As he thought this, the afternoon fog settled above the house like a heavy winter coat, effectively blocking out the sun. His brother would have the answer, Kenny was sure. Perhaps he'd even build an elaborate garden the same as Wayne's, with the fancy, angled-out deer fence. Maybe even add the radio, as well.

Jolie was as silent as her brother now, and the only sound that came from both of them was the occasional slurp of their sundaes. This made Kenny smile, for it was good to see Logan eat more than a handful of food, for once. The kid had eaten one taco, and was now half done with his dessert.

"I've always liked these sundaes," Kenny said. He observed the ice cream on his spoon, then glanced at the garage, freezing momentarily. The garage seemed to stare back. It seemed to Kenny that there was something in there. His mind had been weeding through a quagmire of thoughts since the minute he'd woken up. But right now, as he looked at that building, where inside, his son had failed so completely with performing what should have been the simplest of tasks...

Suddenly, Kenny was back on *Pauli's Bride*, learning how to speak. This was it, he realized. This was perhaps the answer to his riddle. All those months working the deck next to an old man, absorbing the language of the mariner by simply watching, and doing, and rarely, if ever, talking.

The revelation was uncanny. It brought with it the image of those Portuguese hands, leathered and wrinkled, working deftly as they untangled a rat's nest of line. As they untangled a rat's nest of worries and thoughts.

Casually, Kenny finished his sundae, then dropped it in the Taco Bell bag designated for trash. He moved off the porch and stood straight, eyes sharp as an eagle's beak. "Logan," he said, "when you're finished with that, you come and meet me in the garage." Kenny walked over to the building, cranked the handle counter-clockwise, pulled the door open. He turned and looked again at his son. The kid was staring back, a curious look spread across his face, his spoon sticking out of his mouth.

"You hear me?" Kenny said, and Logan nodded in reply. "You and I, we've got some work to do."

CHAPTER 10

All things considered, Vance Green had tremendous patience—for he was a patient man. Patience was a trait owned by him, was widely recognized and admired by both his friends and family. Growing up, it took endurance to withstand the poverty and instability Vance had been up against, moving from one low-income rental to another in the rough neighborhoods of southern California; and later, as a teenager, in the San Francisco Bay Area, in and around Oakland. To save enough money for the dreaded first and last month's rent, as well as deposit, his mother (single parent was she) regularly moved the family into the car for the duration of the summer, while the kids were out of school. Occasionally, they roamed the campgrounds of the Sierra Nevada on these stints, and this Vance had loved the most, a total, refreshing dream. To be so close to the sights and smells of nature, the earth-toned landscapes, and the tranquility of open space—it was always such a relief for him. He cherished being away from the black and gray surfaces of the inner city. And he prized the absence of the inhospitable din of society, with its crime and materialism, its pollution and rampant suffering. These things—these grim faces of humanity—Vance knew all too well. But as much as he recognized and despised them, he had a vague understanding that these were also the very things that had forged his inner strength. They were the things that had cultivated his patience.

There was nothing ambiguous about Vance's destiny, however. It did not surprise him when, once old enough to drop out of high school, he left home and found himself in southern Humboldt County—beginning a new life, one built on the foundation of massive redwoods, and the peaceful subcultures of the hippies and the Rastafarians. Reggae music, and the lazy summer days down at the river. And last but certainly not least— all that wonderful, organic, homegrown ganja.

Humboldt seemed to be Vance's saving grace. No more city ghettos. No more of the hand-to-mouth reality he'd grown accustomed to. And as for the marijuana, well, he took to growing that weed like it was second nature (and perhaps it was, as eventually he developed the reputation of having quite the green thumb). Working the good earth, and being surrounded by Mother Nature, had left Vance feeling needed, and complete. For once in his life, his life seemed to have meaning, and it was all because of pot.

Oh, and what a beautiful drug he'd found. So befitting to a man of sophisticated patience. To submerge his hands into the rich, dark soil, to cultivate something so alive and so green... And at the end of the day, to have his mind clouded over in an herbal fogbank of pure spiritual bliss. Pure epic-ness. After a childhood of being subjected to the quagmires of poverty, Vance was convinced he had finally found the Promised Land.

But eventually, disillusionment reared its ugly head, as *yes*, the agricultural world of southern Humboldt came with hardships of its own. Not owning his own piece of land, the only option Vance had in the way of proprietorship, was guerrilla growing. And Vance quickly learned what that option entailed.

Working on a guerrilla growing crew was backbreaking work; literally, every step of the way. At times, Vance was expected to haul soil, fertilizer, and even water up to the various scenes he'd worked on. Then there was the constant toil of crop maintenance, followed by the hundred miles an hour rush of the harvest, and all that came with that—cutting, trimming, manicuring, drying, packaging, and sometimes selling. Of course, these challenges also included the many superfluous dangers inherent to the job. Hazards such as angry property owners, gun-toting rip-offs, local law enforcement, CAMP (officially recognized as Campaign Against Marijuana Production, and unofficially as Cocksuckers After My Pot), and eventually, as Vance branched out on his own projects... unscrupulous buyers.

For ten years Vance put up with all of this, as he trudged through the rugged hills surrounding little-known towns, such as Garberville, Briceland, Whitethorn, and Redway, busting his ass from early April to late October. Then he'd take his paycheck—in the neighborhood of several thousand dollars—and smoke the winter away. Always, during this part of the year, Vance would shack up with some girlfriend, and spend the cold, rainy months in a blurry, couch-locked haze, with his beer and his bong, Grateful Dead music, and countless runs to the local pizza joint. Soon enough April would roll back around, the clouds would part slightly for the sun, and Vance would crawl out of his winter den and get back to work, to begin the marijuana season all over again.

Yes, it took patience, Vance told himself, to deal with this lifestyle, and the personalities he'd subjected himself to as an adult. Astounding patience. A lesser man, for instance, would have probably murdered Rob Boyle a long time ago. At the very least, said man would have beaten the crap out of the wannabe biker. Yet for all his patience, Vance also considered himself a peaceful man who abhorred violence. The thought of hurting another human being rarely, if ever, crossed his mind. Occasionally, perhaps, when a driver cut him off on the road; or, worse yet, tailgated him. But that was rare, or so it seemed.

So why was he still working with this maniac, this Rob Boyle?

Presently, Vance asked himself this very question, as he sat on a couch in his living room and methodically rolled a joint. His "partner" (and Vance always felt like he'd swallowed bong water when he thought of Rob as being his partner) had been gone for over an hour, which seemed exceedingly long for a trip to Lucky Pete's liquor store, just three blocks away. Running his tongue across the joint's edge, and then twisting it light and tight, Vance's thoughts shaped themselves around the fantastic hope that Rob ran into a pack of biker thugs from a rival gang. What if they'd cornered him in an alley, pulled out a chainsaw, and cut the asshole into forty pieces? For thirty long seconds Vance sat motionless and stared at a stain on the carpet five feet in front of him, a thin grin spread across his face. Then he blinked and snapped out of it, lit the joint and whispered a humble prayer to Jah, asking to be relieved of his "partner"—in one way or another.

Probably, the suspicious bastard got another case of the jitters, and turned his quick jaunt into a two-hour tour of southern Oregon, just in case he was being followed by someone—anyone. That alone was one problem with working alongside Rob. The guy was a stone-cold tweaker. And tweakers, as Vance realized, were sketchy as shit. They were always looking over their shoulders, even during those measly hours of sleep they got each week.

But Vance had to admit, such paranoia lent itself well to the process of guerilla growing. Tweakers were always on full alert. They were always keeping an eye out for the smallest of clues, and were absolutely convinced that the entire world was lined up behind a nearby tree, waiting to snatch their shit just as soon as they dropped their guard. Such "talent" mixed well with the illegal-in-three-ways (State, Federal, and Civilian) growing of weed. But often Vance wondered if the tradeoff was worth the hassle. Was the asset of having a paranoid partner worth the risk of being in the company of a druggy—and all that came with that?

Vance found that hanging around someone who was constantly paranoid made *him* paranoid. The shit was contagious. Whenever Rob's forehead showed beads of sweat, or his hands shook, Vance's heartbeat sped up. And the more Rob made suspicious comments, or stared for whole minutes at a time at sights unseen, the more Vance asked himself, *What if?*

To add to the complications of working with a coke fiend, with Rob, there was the whole outlaw biker thing. Vance had never been comfortable with that association. He'd seen his share of One-Percenters in his Southern Humboldt days, riding through the hills with their guns and their meth, scaring the shit out of the locals as they muled weed out for the big-time growers. Typically, these bikers would show up incognito, under a "charitable guise," such as to attend the annual, three-day long Redwood Run, held in early June. Although still months before the end of the marijuana season, certain hills of the area remained populated with certain bikers, until the end of the harvest. And these were the same bikers who had long histories with Johnny Law. Vance, blissfully ignorant to the original foundations that supported the annual biker event, swore to everything Rastafarian that the big growers devised "The Run" to propagate fear amongst their own pot crews. What better way to stop your guys from ripping you off than to hang above their heads the constant, unnerving threat of biker-violence?

So, yes, why was Vance working with Rob? Once again, it went back to his history—his teenage years, and to Humboldt. A friend of a friend's friend, whom he'd hung out with in high school, and who still lived in Oakland, had connections with the local street gangs, which ultimately distributed the methamphetamines that Rob's biker associates had cooked up in southern Oregon. It was a weak connection, and Vance couldn't even remember who had first introduced him to Rob. But the green, sticky nugget in Vance's eye was the prospect that came with working with the fledgling biker—and that was money. Rob said he knew of a place to grow marijuana in Oregon, a big place, and Vance had all the skills required to deal with weed, from seed to sale, and Rob *seemed* like he would be a willing participant—a good enough "partner." There was that word again.

In theory, working with Rob gave Vance the opportunity to earn tens of thousands of dollars (more money than he had ever had at one time), which meant that he could buy some land of his own, somewhere back in Humboldt. And that would cause his dream to come true.

Also, *in theory*, Vance only needed to suck it up for a single season. According to Rob, there had been enough land to grow five hundred plants. They'd hire Mexicans to do most of the manual labor, and Rob's nefarious connections to the underworld would take care of all the dangerous distribution work. In theory, Vance was only supposed to be a "consultant" of sorts, who would rake in fifty percent of crop yield just to teach Rob and his crew how to grow killer weed. Christ, who on Earth doesn't take a consulting gig, especially one of this magnitude? The plan seemed bulletproof—in theory.

But in reality, Vance soon discovered that Rob was a first-class, five-star fuckup. The property was, at best, a few acres large, and had only one access point, which cut straight past the landowner's cabin. They were screwed if that landowner spent any of his summer days lounging in the great outdoors.

Furthermore, there was no Mexican labor force. None at all. Not so much as a single man. The reasons for this Rob had never fully explained, but Vance gathered it lay somewhere between Rob's paranoia and a falling-out with another biker gang.

And speaking of bikers: as it turned out, Rob himself fell quite short from being the real deal. He didn't even own a motorcycle, for Pete's sake. The asshole just drove around in his dead granddad's rusty Ford Bronco, wearing a denim vest embroidered with the word "PROSPECT" on the back. *What the fuck is a Prospect?* Vance had so clearly wondered. And the definition for that, he soon learned, which opened up and dumped out another can of rancid worms onto Vance's lap.

Rob, as a "Prospect," meant that he was rarely available, rarely clean and sober (if ever, now that Vance thought about that), and rarely in a good mood. In fact, the guy was chronically miserable—a characteristic that never failed to spill over into Vance's life.

But of course, no part of this "reality" became visible until it was apparently too late. Before Vance figured out just how fucked the prospect of working for a fucked-up "Prospect" would become, he was knee-deep in the shit, living in a one-bedroom duplex on the outskirts of town, where he had already set up shop for the processing of weed. He'd also made several trips to various nurseries and hardware stores, to purchase supplies, and to gather information about the area, such as local weather, soil content, and indigenous plant life, all of which might prove pertinent to growing.

In short, within days, Vance had invested way too much of his time and money to simply walk away from this gig. Knowing this, he called on his tremendous patience, and he called on Jah and reggae, he called on daily tokes of weed, and he buried his nose into the grindstone and went to work, hoping to get the fuck out of Oregon, and back to Humboldt, as soon as he earned enough money.

That was over a year ago.

Despite all his patience, Vance was on the brink of losing his shit. Their first season of growing proved disastrous in terms of production; they got their plants in the ground way too late and lost many of their precious buds to varmints. Then the rains came two weeks sooner than expected, which nearly wiped out the rest of the harvest. In the end, Vance made barely enough to cover his rent for the next several months—hardly enough to buy him a piece of land in Northern California. With grand puissance, wannabe biker-boy assured Vance that next year would be "the year," and that carried Vance through the following months in a weed-induced fog to the here and now.

And right now, half-baked and reflecting at random on these ruminations, Vance jumped out of his skin when there came a sudden knock at the door. A loud, repetitive banging, to be precise.

Heart six inches out of his chest, he snuffed his joint and fanned the lingering smoke with his hands. He stood and froze in place, like a terrified cat, scanning his tiny living room for any damning evidence.

His vision roamed through the standard bachelor debris with scrutiny. That Rob would have simply walked through the front door without knocking meant that whoever was out there right now was a complete stranger. And strangers—they weren't good. Strangers were bad. Terrible, in fact.

Spotting his dime bag of weed on the coffee table, Vance grabbed it and shoved it in his front pocket. He glanced at the door down the hall, the one that opened up into the bedroom, which was full of last night's haul from the scene. Currently, several thousand dollars of untrimmed cannabis was hanging from a metal wire in that room. *Strangers... very, very bad.*

The banging repeated, only this time it was louder.

"*Shit*," Vance whispered. Then he shouted, "Just a minute!" He fought back a rasping cough, tip-toed over to the door, looked through the peephole. "Oh—*fuck me*," he mouthed, silently.

"Come on!" said the man on the other side. "Open the goddamn door already!"

Vance took a step back and slowly opened the door, and then a leather-clad, greasy-looking biker entered the room, pushing him to the side. "Where's Shits?" the man demanded.

"Dude," Vance began, "what the hell? This is my apartment, brah. You can't just—"

"Can it, douchebag!" The tone of the man's voice carried a threat of certain violence, which rendered Vance speechless. In slow measure the biker studied the room, with its cluttered array of litter—food wrappers, Pabst Blue Ribbon beer cans, ashtrays, records and CDs, various magazines, and in one corner, on top of a speaker, a statue of Buddha presently burning incense. The biker inhaled deeply, *distinctly*, then smiled. "Right," he said, shaking his head. "Incense." Casually, he turned and walked into the kitchenette, opened the fridge, grabbed a can of beer, and returned to the living room, where he sat down on the couch. He popped the beer can and began guzzling it.

Vance stood against the wall near the front door, staring at the biker, half-terrified, half-incredulous, and still unable to form any words.

"Just so you know," said the biker, "I prefer Coors over this Kentucky pisswater."

"What?" Vance stuttered, flabbergasted.

The biker gave Vance a serious look. "Are you asking me to repeat myself?" He took another drink. "I hope you're not asking me to repeat myself. Another thing you should know is that's the one thing that just gets me thinking about... oh, I don't know—*homicide*."

Vance suddenly felt very cold, and very hot. He noticed his hands were clammy, his breathing short and rapid. "No, man," he replied, "I'm not asking you to repeat yourself."

"Swell," replied the biker.

"But dude, who are you? And why are you in my apartment?"

"Where the fuck is Shits?" the biker replied. "And notice," he added, offhandedly picking a thread from the couch, "I believe I've just repeated myself."

"Dude, I don't know who you're talking about. I don't know anybody named 'Shits'."

The biker stared up at the ceiling, as if searching his memory. "Oh, that's right, he has another name. *Boyle*. Where the fuck's Boyle?"

The cold and the heat both grew with intensity, and Vance now felt acutely uncomfortable. "You mean Rob?" he asked, lamely.

"Sure," replied the biker. "Let's call him, 'Rob'."

"I don't know where he is," said Vance. "He took off for the store about an hour ago. Haven't seen him since."

The biker closed his eyes and slowly dropped his head. He sat like that for what seemed to Vance like an infinite length of time. And each passing second was a terminal sentence spelled out in red bloody letters within Vance's mind. *Was this really happening?* He thought. *Was this biker really here, in his living room, not twenty feet away from a room full of pot?*

As far as Vance knew (and prayed), Rob's biker friends were still in the dark about his and Vance's agricultural endeavors. More than once, Rob had made a big deal about this, how he was going to surprise everyone by showing up at "church" (a term used for an official motorcycle club meeting) with a fat wad of cash. 'That'll get me my full patch,' Rob had bragged.

But Vance knew the whole game would change if Rob's biker friends found out about their minor operation. They'd certainly take things over. And in the end, Vance might wind up with a bullet in his head, just for knowing too much. *Shit... I might be totally screwed right now*, he thought.

"So, Mr. Vance Green," the biker said, suddenly looking up, suddenly smiling wickedly. "Aren't you going to offer me a joint?"

CHAPTER 11

From the small window in his kitchenette, Vance studied the biker (the man had said his name was Cecil) as he rode off on his Harley and into the sunset, a thin veil of dust and gravel lurching up from the parking lot. Ironically, it was only then that Vance had first noticed the embroidered patch on the back of the biker's leather vest, the words THE LEATHER WOLVES proudly advertising the name of Southern Oregon's most infamous Outlaw motorcycle club. He had heard Rob say those very words many times before, but this was the first time Vance had seen them in print... And upon doing so, he felt absolute dread.

As Vance watched the biker, without apparent explanation, his mind toured him through a vivid entourage of sights and sounds: the snap and crunch of a deer's legs under the chomping jaws of a black timber wolf; the unnerving rip and tear off some indistinct fabric; a high-pitched shriek, visceral growls, and then a massive splattering of blood. An icy shiver crawled down Vance's spine, absorbing the length of an entire minute before settling like wet clay in his shoes.

When the biker faded to a dark spot on the horizon, Vance closed the curtain with a jerk. He stepped away from the window and leaned against the kitchen counter. He took a deep breath, a *real* deep breath, his thoughts pinging between the multitude of implications and potential future hassles he would likely face, now that The Leather Wolves had apparently sniffed him out.

It hit him then; he needed a drink. Perhaps something strong, something in the neighborhood of a few shots of whiskey. *Jack Daniels—the perfect medicine right about now,* he thought. *Just what the mental doctor would order.*

Sadly, such an option was not available, considering the fact that Vance only had beer (and buds), and hadn't so much as thought about hard liquor since perhaps his twenty-first birthday. Drinking beyond a slight buzz had never been his thing, but now... Yes, now things were different.

He opened the fridge and settled for "pisswater," popped a can of PBR and began pacing the confines of his apartment. In less than a minute he had finished the beer, and was now standing in the hallway, staring dumbly at the bedroom door, wondering just how deep this quagmire of shit he'd stumbled into was.

He thought about what he was going to say to Rob once the loser finally made it back to the apartment. Without pause, Vance's mind went to work on those questions, framing them like the walls of a new housing project.

Then, almost as if it were the natural course of the universe, he thought about "getting out," and what that would entail. What if he packed his shit right now, this instant? What if he packed everything, including the drying buds in the other room, threw it all in his car and simply bailed? Vance's mind simmered over this option, and the two words that clung like spiders onto his brain were, *simply,* and *bailed.*

Simply put, he knew there would be nothing *simple* about taking off right now—especially with last night's haul. Rob and his "friends" would come looking for him, and they knew exactly where to begin their search. For all its charm and beauty, and isolation, Humboldt County was not exactly the easiest place to hide out in if your pursuers had particular connections to the area. Vance knew that there were plenty of seasonal laborers in the area who, for a small pittance of cash or bag of dope, would be more than happy to point Rob and his friends toward where they had last seen Vance. In the interest of survival, Vance would have to go *way* off the grid—Grizzly Adams style—and that was something he wasn't prepared to do.

No, simply bailing was not an option, not even a close one, unless he left the weed behind.

That thought gave Vance pause—a brief pause—and ended up being just as viable as the previous option. Returning to Humboldt broke and busted was the last thing he intended on doing.

With that in mind, it seemed he had only one choice left: to confront Rob about his friends. He would need to have a sit-down with his *partner* and weasel him for answers, because if the Leather Wolves were conspiring to relieve Vance and Rob of their harvest, well, that would be the same as returning home empty-handed, assuming he returned at all.

It all seemed so confusing, reminding Vance of algebra, and quickly his head ached. He needed another beer, and then he would get started on the trimming, an activity that never failed to bring Vance to a state of mild euphoria.

He went to the fridge, pulled out another PBR, and popped the top. He looked out the window once again, wondering when Rob would finally get back, and also fearing that Cecil would return.

Briefly, Vance replayed his short time with the biker and pondered what, if anything, the hangout session had meant. He had gotten the man stoned, as requested, but that was all. There weren't any more questions from Cecil, and certainly no conversation to speak of, other than the occasional remark regarding the benefits of smoking stellar ganja. Once more, thinking about the incident left Vance feeling confused, not to mention creeped out, so he finished his beer and got to work.

The first step was to put on some reggae, which was an absolute must when preparing weed for the marketplace. Vance went to the milk crate next to the couch and fingered through his stack of vinyl records. Black Uhuru's *Sinsemilla* album could've spoken actual words to him. It was that perfect of a choice.

He pulled the album out of its sleeve and set it on the turntable, feeling the positive vibes already beat a drum inside his chest, pushing away the echoing howls left behind by the lone Leather Wolf. Vance cut to the chase; he placed the needle on track six, and the title song filled his cramped home with the rhythms of old school, Jamaican roots reggae.

Next, he cleared a spot on the coffee table, retrieved a shoe box from behind the couch, and placed it on the table and opened it. Inside the box were his paraphernalia needed for manicuring weed: a Ziploc bag full of rubber gloves, pruning shears, and two different surgical scissors.

There were several ways to prepare marijuana for the sale, and Vance was a master with all of them. But for the sake of expediting this harvest (and thus, making his cash and then getting the fuck out of Oregon), Vance decided there would be no sense in keeping the parts of the plant known as "trim," which comprised all the leaves cut from the branches, and surrounding the buds—more or less, everything other than the bud. Trim could be used for a variety of products, such as hash oil, or marijuana butter, or even smoked for an inferior quality high, assuming one was desperate enough. Vance was desperate alright—desperate to end his partnership with Rob, so all the trim was heading for the dumpster. And that's what the cardboard box was for; the one Vance had also retrieved from behind the couch, opened up, and placed on the floor next to the table.

The scene now set, he slid his gloves on and headed for the bedroom. He opened the door and stepped into a gloomy room strung from end to end with four lengths of thin metal wire. Several dozen marijuana branches hung by their large leaf stems on the wire, and were already in the early stages of drying. Most of them were from last night's haul, but those weren't the ones Vance was after. They still had at least a week's worth of drying left before he could begin the manicuring process on them.

Instead, he went to the far corner of the room, where he had a separate, smaller stash of buds, ones he'd picked from the two plants he'd grown in this very room.

It wasn't a big deal, as the two plants had yielded little. Vance had harvested them early, to give Rob something to practice with, before they tackled the *bigger* load from the main crop. He was afraid Rob would botch too much of their product with his poor trimming experience (something else last year's worthless endeavor had yielded). But in all likelihood, even if Rob were a master gardener, Vance probably would've still grown *something* indoors. He wouldn't have been able to help himself, bored sick as he was in this Oregon town. His daily check-ins of his "little ladies" were, on most days, the only thing Vance had to look forward to.

There were three rotating fans buzzing like insects in various corners, circulating the heavy pall of ripened ganja throughout the room. That smell always brought a glistening tear to Vance's eyes, as it filled his head with profound nostalgia. If he could have but one request for his funeral, it would be a simple one: to be buried in a coffin stuffed with sticky, green colas.

He inhaled deeply before gracefully plucking four branches off the wire. He returned to the living room and settled in on the couch. And within five minutes, Vance was in the zone. He took his time with the scissors, clipping buds off stems, and trimming away at leaves, both actions he performed in slow measure, unrushed, each step of the process congruent with the brush strokes of a master painter.

It was uncanny; every time Vance began the laborious, time-consuming job of manicuring weed, his mind went to that scene in *The Karate Kid*, where Mr. Miyagi taught Daniel-san the techniques of sculpting bonsai trees. *Bonzai!* Vance would recall, reminiscing over the movie; and then he'd apply Mr. Miyagi's lessons to the art of shaping the perfect bud.

Yes, it was uncanny, and more than once, Vance wondered what the old karate instructor would think about his interpretation of the ancient Japanese ritual. With a glorious smile, Vance often pictured himself sharing a joint with Mr. Miyagi.

All the same, manicuring weed—manicuring it *well*—could easily be considered an art form. To do it correctly, it took hours upon hours of motivated concentration, not to mention a considerable amount of patience. Vance had banked thousands of hours with this activity. And within a matter of minutes, he could deftly slip himself into a meditative state—with the addition of a smooth high and good reggae music being certain to expedite his trip to Nirvana.

Within five minutes of snipping leaves, Vance had forgotten all about Cecil. He'd forgotten about The Leather Wolves, and his druggy partner, Rob Boyle, and he was sitting on a sunlit strand of sand along the South Fork of the Eel River, somewhere near Garberville, scoping the hills for a piece of land to buy—*to fucking buy!*

"Keep your eye on the prize," he mumbled to himself, more than once, as he continued with his snipping and shaping. Instinctively, he assessed the quality of the marijuana while he worked it, judging it against what was his standard baseline for the "perfect bud." But wasn't this "standard" nebulous, in all honesty? The marijuana-growing subculture, which Vance considered himself to be fluent with, was an ever-changing world. The external pressures coming from law enforcement and market conditions, as well as the environmental factors inherent to the process of guerilla growing, kept that "baseline" of the perfect bud in a state of constant flux, because that baseline was always shifting. There were hundreds, if not thousands, of different strains of marijuana throughout the world; and that number, as Vance figured, was also in a state of constant motion. Each of these different plant strains was likely born from the result of some type of external pressure (and yes, the search for THE PERFECT BUD was also pressure, perhaps the oldest one of all). But with each of these different strains came a different type of product. So what again, Vance asked himself, as he clipped away, *was* the perfect bud?

His head hurt; he'd slipped out of the zone, was thinking too hard about the qualities of weed. In short, the crop he and Rob were dealing with was Indica dominant in variety, which Vance considered a perfect enough strain for their absolute need of discretion.

The Indica was a shorter, bushier plant (as opposed to its cousin, the Sativa), and this allowed it to blend in easier along the side of a hill, and with the various native shrubs of Southern Oregon.

Because of their short size, Indica plants were also easier to manage during early harvest runs, when the desire was to trim just part of the plant. With the taller Sativa, early harvesting often required the use of a ladder, and that would mean just one more thing they'd have to haul up to the scene. But best of all, Indica was faster-growing. And that, in Vance's mind, was the clinching factor for growing weed on someone else's property.

The buds formed on the Indica weren't as thin as the Sativa, however. They were more compact, denser, and often more difficult to manicure. But this detail weighed little on Vance's conscience (except for when he thought about Rob doing the work), because Vance was a master with the scissors. And once he was in the zone, the laborious aspects of trimming weed, along with the time it took, would often fade into the distant shadows of his consciousness. While manicuring weed, the hours simply passed by for Vance.

The hours *had* passed, in fact, as he sat on the couch and snipped away. He'd taken a few breaks to use the pisser, or change the music, or smoke a bowl, but before he stopped to consider his world outside of all-things-marijuana related, Vance discovered that almost three hours had passed, since Cecil had left.

Where in the fuck was *Rob?*

He wondered, seriously now. Half a dozen scenarios regarding his partner raced through Vance's head as he stood and walked to the kitchen window. He looked outside, saw nothing but the gravel parking lot bathed in shadow, and an old man standing under a street lamp, walking his lap dog. The night had long since awakened. Vance's stomach growled with hunger, which had the effect of irritating him; Rob had said he'd bring back some snacks.

"Dude, what the fuck?" he mumbled to himself, wondering if the wannabe biker actually went on a tour of Southern Oregon. "Either that, or Cecil found you and put a knife in your gut for being *stupid*."

He thought more about that scenario, and specifically, about the prospect of Rob being out there right now, lying dead in a ditch, for whatever reason. It seemed... well... plausible enough, didn't it? Shit, tweakers die every day, or so Vance presumed. Probably by the droves. And wouldn't that be the perfect solution? If Rob were suddenly out of the picture, Vance could reap all the pot for himself. He could harvest the rest of the crop on his own—or most of it, at least, time permitting. He could definitely harvest enough to cash out, move back home, and buy that property he'd always wanted.

And, of course, Vance certainly wouldn't need Rob's connections for unloading the weed. In Humboldt, he could do that himself, no problem.

But what if The Leather Wolves were on to the growing operation? That question still lingered in Vance's mind. He didn't think they knew where the scene was, however. (Although they now knew where Vance lived, and that was a main part of the operation, considering that this was where all the post-harvest production would occur.)

Once again, Vance's head hurt. His stomach growled. And his hands were slightly shaking, his heartbeat slightly increased, and his nerves just slightly frayed. Shit... Vance was *way* out of the zone.

He turned away from the window and walked back toward the couch. He decided he'd finish manicuring the remaining buds on the table, and then take a drive to Taco Bell, or Little Caesar's. Maybe he'd stop and get some hard liquor while he was out, kill that lingering crave. It was a serious thought, and he was riding heavily on it as he fell frustrated onto the couch. And then, at that exact moment, Rob Boyle walked through the front door.

CHAPTER 12

The boy had placed the coffee cans randomly about, filling corners and pockets of the garage with no apparent rhyme or reason. Logan's latest attempt at organizing them had been all but fruitless in its results. On the long wooden workbench that ran the length of the garage's back wall, a pyramid of these cans sat haphazardly, one of which had been previously tipped on its side. The contents of this can were spread out on the table in gray heaps, both sharp and blunt, an assortment of galvanized nails and washers. A shower of dim-gray light from the window above bathed the workbench in milky shadow. This spectacle of the cans and the hardware and the aged wooden bench reminded Kenny of something from which Norman Rockwell could have drawn inspiration. Adding to the atmosphere was a dank, musty smell that hovered in the air, a combination of engine oil and mold, the vague aroma of rotting plant matter.

"At first, I just want you to watch me." After Kenny said this, he went to the workbench and pushed the cans and loose hardware to the side. "Just watch how I do this, Logan. Watch me... And learn."

Kenny took the tipped coffee can and dumped its remaining contents into a pile. He placed the empty can in the center of the workbench and grabbed a roll of masking tape hanging from a nail against the back wall. Then he tore a piece of tape off, smoothed it over the front of the can, found a black Sharpie resting on the windowsill, started to write on the tape, but then paused. He handed the pen and can to Logan. "You should do this," he said.

Slowly, the boy took the items, and then he looked at his dad. There was a brief concoction of uncertainty and excitement in his eyes.

"Now," Kenny began, "I know that there are a lot of washers in this garage,"—he glanced around—"I've seen them." Running a finger through the pile of hardware, he retrieved three different washers and placed them on the table in front of Logan. "Three types. That's all we need to know right now. Stainless," he said, pointing to one washer, "metal—of some sort—and then galvanized. You see how they look different? Those three are all we're looking for. That's all we need to worry about."

Kenny went and got two more cans, dumped them out onto the table, and gave them to Logan. "Now put some tape on these. And label them with the names I just told you—Stainless, metal, and galvanized. And don't worry about the spelling—close enough is fine with me."

Logan did as he was told while Kenny sorted through the piles of hardware. The variety within the few cans Kenny had emptied astounded him, and he blinked his eyes in wonderment. The dysfunctional organization of such capable hardware, in Kenny's opinion, bordered the edge of a crime. He wasn't sure if his son was solely responsible for the disarray, but he didn't think so. All in all, Logan had spent little time with this project his dad had initially given him, and from what Kenny could remember, it seemed the kid mostly tinkered with a handful of pieces, or picked a particular item out to study for a few minutes, before eventually giving up.

The assortment of hardware was impressive though, as Kenny suddenly realized. Even after living in the house for a few months, this was the first time he'd inspected the contents of the cans with any real scrutiny. And these contents, spread out on the table before him, were from only four of the coffee cans... a mere fraction of what the old garage held.

In a quick, mechanical motion, Kenny began sorting through the hardware, picking out washers of various sizes and types. He moved his fingers through what he estimated to be ten pounds' worth of fasteners, which included nuts and bolts, roofing nails, small brackets and brass hinges; and the occasional, randomly (and wildly) misplaced item, such as a padlock or motor bearing. And there were washers, many types of washers: flat washers, finishing, split lock, both internal and external tooth lock washers, square washers, and even a few specialized washers, which, at first glance, eluded Kenny as to their applications.

He looked for washers only, and when he had an example of each of the three material types, he placed them on the table, and in front of the cans that Logan had labeled, respectively.

"Galvanized," Kenny said again, picking up a washer. "There's poor light in here, but see how it looks? Gray... Like dishwater, or something." He offered it to Logan, and the boy took it. "Brackish," Kenny added. "Maybe that's what it looks like—brackish. But see how it feels? Feels like sandpaper. That's galvanized."

Then he picked up the stainless steel washer and gave it to Logan. "This one here is stainless," he said. "Feel it—it's smooth. Maybe a little heavier than the metal ones, but about the same as galvanized. Very hard. Looks like the other one, but shinier. Used on boats. And *expensive*."

He handed the third washer to Logan. "And that's a plain old metal washer—probably zinc. Looks like a silver coin. Used, well, just about everywhere. On everything.

"Okay, put 'em back down," he said. "And get ready to sort."

Then Kenny went to work on the pile, picking through the hardware as if he were working an assembly line job. His hands moved efficiently, sifting out washers and lightly tossing them on the table in front of Logan. Occasionally he isolated a small pile of hardware, studied the assortment briefly, before sweeping it off the edge of the table, and dumping it into a separate coffee can. When he first did this, the temptation to speak was strong. He wanted to explain his reasoning to his son, wanted to "teach" the boy the prudence of, at all times, keeping a clean work station. And this feeling seemed to recur, intensify even, when Kenny ran across a specialty washer, such as a split lock. As a father, he must have been hard-wired to pass his knowledge down to his son. But then Kenny would think about that old Portuguese angler, and he'd bite his tongue.

Several minutes in, and father and son had found their rhythm. Logan kept pace with his dad, and it seemed the boy was enjoying himself for all that Kenny could infer. It occurred to Kenny, at that moment, that by the time Logan should ever speak again, he and Jolie would become masters at the reading of body language. The thought brought little consolation, however, in consideration of the gravity from which such a skill-set would evolve.

There was a sliver of pleasure for Kenny, though, knowing— or suspecting, rather—that his son was having a good time. Kenny had guessed that most days, Logan didn't feel so much as an ounce of joy in his life. All the kid ever seemed to do was shuffle silently and blankly throughout his day. The most exciting thing he'd do was chew his nails. Sometimes his son's condition drove Kenny nuts, such that he ached to shake the kid violently, commanding him to say something, even if all he would say was, "Stop, Dad, please stop!" After all, how many kids could resist the will of an angry father? What stopped Kenny from doing this, from shaking his son, wasn't the knowledge that such an action was morally wrong. Not entirely. But that deep down, he knew it would only make matters worse. That it would stack trauma upon more trauma, which might send his son further down his rabbit hole of silence.

"Stainless, galvanized, and metal," Kenny repeated. "That's all we need to know for now."

Again, the depth to the variety within the cans was staggering, and Kenny considered that the level of organization could easily expand beyond his current plan. Briefly, his thoughts carried him to the previous owner, the lonely old man with an obvious penchant for collecting things. A tinkerer, for certain, and perhaps a retired mechanic or engineer who had invested forty years of his life at a nearby logging mill, keeping the plant up and running. Or maybe the old man worked down at the docks, fixing fishing vessels and tugboats alike, along with all other sorts of maritime machinery. He was certainly a handyman, the jack-of-all-trades type, who was an expert with his hands, but perhaps quite the amateur with his relations, as apparently no one had come to his rescue with organizing this mess. They took the bigger tools, though—the table saw and drill press, and the metal lathe—whoever they were. Probably sold those pieces at a garage sale for a penny on the dime. Kenny had seen the outlines of such machines on the garage floor, stenciled with wood dust and metal flakes, left gummy from oil as old as Oregon.

It was pleasant for Kenny to think that whoever had lived here before him had inadvertently paved the way for the widower with the broken family. And that all the things left behind, the contents of every coffee can, the discombobulated fragments of one man's entire life, would somehow carry forward and serve as some type of legacy. It was a nice thought, if even a bit too much on the spiritual side of the meter for Kenny; the slap of Fate came from quite a heavy hand, after all. More than likely, Kenny had gained the habit of imprinting his life too much onto that of the previous owner. But whatever the case, it was now Kenny's belief that something was there, inside that garage, within those coffee cans. Something which was meant to be. Perhaps a tool of some kind. A specialized "fastener" of sorts.

He kept thinking this as he sorted through the barrage of metal, tossing washers of all kinds his son's way. Logan kept pace, and whether or not he was having fun, the course of this activity proved exciting enough for Kenny. At last, he was getting something done, was on the path of fixing something, with Logan at his side, moving faster now than Kenny had seen the boy move in six months. The moment was invigorating—a methodical exercise of "cleaning things up". A simple act of organizing the contents of three dozen coffee cans; restoring the meanings for such banal hardware; putting right to a mess of wrong...

"I need to take a short break," Kenny said. He slid a pile of steel into a can, placed the can on the table, then stepped away. They'd been sorting for what must have been an hour, and the back of his eyeballs had begun to hurt. The light from outside had turned a shade of blue as afternoon approached evening. "Don't mess with any of this. Just leave it be. I'm gonna go check on your sister." He stepped out of the garage, then turned back toward his son. "You hungry?" he asked. But Logan didn't look at him. He wouldn't take his eyes off the table.

CHAPTER 13

"Dude, where the fuck have you been?" As Vance said this, he immediately noticed the watery ripple in Rob's eyes, immediately smelled the distinct odor of whiskey. "Don't tell me... Shit, you're fucking drunk."

Rob stumbled into the living room carrying a brown grocery bag and then sat on the couch next to Vance. He placed the bag on his lap and started fishing through it, pulling out a bag of chips, a bag of beef jerky, and a two liter bottle of 7-UP—but then he froze. Looking over, his cheeks now red and flushed, he said, "Look, asshole, last I checked, *you're not my fucking mother.*"

Vance stood up and began pacing the room. His heart was pounding, threatening to exit out of his chest. His hands were sifting aimlessly through the air. No reason, just in need of moving. "I can't believe you," he said. "This is fucked up, man. *You're* fucked up!"

"Do we have to listen to this crap?" Rob asked, looking now at the turntable. "How do you expect me to concentrate under these... under this... duress... *Fuck*, I can't focus with that hippie shit on!"

"Christ!" Vance replied. He walked over and cut the power to the turntable. The room fell into a state of silence as both men stared at one another.

"Don't you mean Jah?"

"What?"

"I thought you—"

"Dude!" Vance interrupted. "Will you shut up and listen to me? We've got some big problems, brah. *Real* big problems, other than you getting drunk at the worst possible time." He walked over and sat back on the couch. "I met Cecil..."

Rob's eyelids split a quarter of an inch. "You met Cecil? How did you know his name?"

"Because he told me, you idiot. I *met* him. He came knocking at the door when you were out. Sat right fucking here and made me get him high."

Rob turned and slowly picked up the bag of jerky, tore it open with deliberate ease. Vance could tell he now had his partner's attention, that the dumb asshole was wading through his quagmire of a brain, and this insight proffered a glimmer of relief for the young Rastafarian. Hassles aside, Vance thought he could stomach the many and more deficiencies that came with Rob Boyle, as long as it was just him. "How the hell did he find out where I live?" he asked. "You didn't tell him, did you?"

"Fuck no."

"Then how'd he find out?"

"I don't know." Rob tore at a piece of jerky with his teeth, then rubbed his chin. "It's what he does, I guess. He's Cecil: the Sarg. He knows shit—finds shit out." Rob stopped talking and started chewing. He was looking at something across the room, and his stare slowly turned suspicious. "They're following me, I bet."

"Who?" Vance said. "Your biker friends? Why would they be following you?"

"Probably just keeping an eye on me, that's all. Making sure I'm not a fucking narc. Hey," he said, and a sliver of hope entered his eyes, "maybe this means they're gonna patch me in soon. Now *that*... I could live with that, man."

No matter how many times Vance had cultivated the promise of redemption for this dirt bag, Rob Boyle always wound up disappointing him.

"You still don't get it, do you?" Vance said. "Whatever Cecil finds out, your club finds out. And what do you think your club is going to do after they find out about our little operation here? You think they'll just sit on their Harleys and drink beer?"

Rob looked down the hallway. "He didn't go in there, did he?"

"Yeah, right. You think he would've left if he did?"

"No," Rob said. And then he laughed. "No, he certainly would not."

"Hey man, this ain't funny. I'm serious. If those fuckers keep coming around here—*following you*—then they'll sure as shit find things out."

"Relax, man. I'll fucking take care of things."

"How?"

"What do you mean, 'how'?"

"I mean, how the fuck are you going to take care of things, Rob? You can't even take care of yourself. Getting drunk, when we've got work to do. Always jacked up on crank. I don't think you get it, brah."

"Oh, will you get off my ass already? I *get* it." Rob threw the bag of jerky across the room, then fished out a pack of cigarettes from a pocket. He had a cigarette lit and in his mouth in ten seconds flat. His eyes were seething, glaring back at Vance through a veil of smoke. "You want me to be your *bitch*, that's what I get. You want me to be your bitch so you can make your money, and then you're fucking outta here! That's exactly what I get."

There was a deafening pause as Vance processed Rob's accusation. He couldn't remember how much he'd openly expressed his frustrations about this gig, or if he had ever mentioned to Rob his desire to move back to Humboldt. But Vance had grumbled more often than not, and it suddenly occurred to him that the wannabe biker was at least smart enough to read between those particular lines.

Smart enough... Or paranoid enough.

And that was the real rub. Fear eased its cold hand across Vance's chest as he thought about what was now transpiring. Rob's paranoia had finally bled through and into Vance. *The hazards of working with a tweaker...*

"Look, man," Vance said, words coming out like footsteps across ice, "you're not my bitch. It's just that I don't want your club getting into our shit."

"Yeah," Rob replied, "don't worry about my club. I'll keep them in line, and you'll get your money, and we'll all live happily fucking ever after."

"Fine then," Vance said. He moved off the couch and went into the other room, then came back carrying four large branches of weed. "Let's just get to work," he said, laying the branches on the coffee table before sitting back down.

"Yeah, let's do that," Rob replied.

"Here, take these," Vance said, holding out a pair of clippers. "Trim the larger leaves. I'll take care of the smaller ones. I'll take care of the shaping."

"Why can't I do that?"

"*Dude...* It takes a bit of skill to shape a bud properly. And here, put these on." He handed Rob a pair of rubber gloves, then went to work.

"What the fuck?" Rob said, laughing. "How hard can it be to shape a bud?"

Vance held his tongue, but he felt that uncomfortable feeling creep in once again: the urge of violence. So much for getting back into the zone. Certainly not with this clown sitting next to him.

And then there was that freshly minted, staggering worry of the Leather Wolves breathing down his neck. Vance truly doubted Rob's ability to keep those feral dogs at bay. Once they found out about their Prospect's side job—and they *would* find out, Vance was sure of it—they would be all over the scene. Vance could kiss away any of his profits. He could forget about the reasons he came to this shithole in the first place.

Time was of the essence. That was Vance's only hope, if there was one. Whatever he could do to get this job done as quickly as possible, he had to do it.

Briefly, he glanced over at Rob. The guy was taking his time, so it seemed, his fingers spending more time on beef jerky and his cigarette than the task at hand. Time *was* of the essence, and Vance considered just taking over the job. He could move much faster and more efficiently if he were in "the zone," listening to reggae, and not having to fester over Rob and his attitude.

"We need to think about getting back up to the scene," Vance said, glancing again at his partner.

"Sure, man, whatever you say. *You're the expert.*"

"I'm thinking in a day or two. Three days, tops." A few days may be a few days too soon, but Vance had to get things done. He also had to think about stashing the current harvest after the drying and trimming was finished, just in case Cecil showed up again. He thought more about that, weighing his options. "Also," he said, glancing sideways at Rob, "we should hide this stuff, brah. I mean, if your friend comes back. You know?"

Rob gave Vance a look. "Fine by me."

"I'm thinking we should rent a storage unit... For a few months. And," Vance continued, his clippers working a slow rhythm over a thick bud, "you better let me rent it—you being followed, and all."

Rob stopped what he was doing and looked at Vance. "You sure have a lot of plans, don't you?"

"I'm just saying, brah. We need to keep this shit on the down-low. Sorry, but I don't trust your biker friends."

"Yeah, okay," Rob said, "but what if I don't trust *you*?"

Vance looked at the scissors in his hand, wondering how much damage they would likely do.

Rob continued, "I'm thinking, perhaps there won't be a storage unit after all. Maybe you have some other place in mind. Someplace I don't know about."

"You are way too paranoid, brah," Vance said.

"Whatever, man. I don't care if I'm being followed; I want to see where the stash is going to be. And I want a key, dammit. I want a key to this storage unit you're talking about."

He had gotten worse, Vance realized. Much worse. The obsessive paranoia, the drinking, and the drugs. The ever-increasing oppositional defiance. Certain ingredients and certain machinations that formed the parcel of Rob Boyle had, over the course of a few months, worked themselves into a dark malignancy. Whereas, moments ago, when the prospect of cleverly excusing Rob from the business at hand so that Vance could work more efficiently seemed promising enough—was entertaining, at least—now Vance worried his partner would never leave.

Vance's hands began to sweat. His fingers stiffened, went clumsy with the scissors, threatening to botch the trimming job; which, as he knew, was the single, most crucial process of adding aesthetic value to their product, and thus preparing it for a higher asking price amongst a judgmental market. *The things that asshole would never know.*

Still, the fact remained: Vance's doubts had now traveled further than their previous point—the point where Rob might keep his friends from finding out about everything, in which case they would then rape Vance both figuratively, and (God help him), literally. That point also included Vance's confidence in dealing with Rob's shenanigans.

In a nutshell, and with a sudden unnerving alarm, Vance now doubted *everything.* He doubted his ability to finish up with harvesting the scene, or getting their product ready to sell—let alone selling it. And he had no faith in the hope of driving out of Oregon burdened with his share of the profits. Instead, what sat heavy on his mind was Cecil kicking in the door and planting a gun on Vance's head, for the sake of finding out about how much pot they had, and where they kept it. And then, ultimately, watching as Rob—his partner—snickered on the sidelines. That would happen too, Vance was sure of it.

So what then were Vance's options? Did he have any, for that matter?

At the very least, he would need to get his hands on a portable CD player with headphones and some more selections of reggae music. That would cover him for the short term, for working beside Rob. It would buy him some time, help him get somewhat into the zone. Then he could strategize. Vance wondered if, and where, he could find such musical components in and around Myrtle Creek. In his mind, the place was an ass-backwards, one-horse farming community. He swore he felt the stare of a thousand righteous souls every time he and his long dreadlocks appeared in town.

But again, a CD player was only a short-term fix. And all the bigger problems, which mounted Vance's conscience with heavier and more profound consequences, had resolutions that eluded him at every fucking turn. He thought about the unthinkable: the horrific, yet (God help him *again*) tantalizing prospect of murdering Rob. Then he pushed that thought out of his head, quickly, and pondered his ever-decreasing options—a mental exercise which had become akin to searching through a pile of coal for bong ash.

It all seemed so hopeless. Vance was stuck, *truly stuck*, and any option for action on his part will come with terrible consequences. If he took what they had already harvested, took all the buds in the house, and then bailed, Rob and his pack of wolves would no doubt come looking for him. But if he stuck it out to the end of the season, he would certainly become "involved" with Rob's friends, and there was nothing remotely appealing, or safe, about that option. He could drop everything, pack up and split... Which, of course, also meant kissing everything goodbye: his own piece of land, and the rest of his life spent lounging in the shade of a cannabis grove.

Truly, truly, stuck.

But then again...

"They call me 'Shits', which I think is fucked up, so I figure I need to pass that one on down. Know what I mean—*Shits*?" Rob was looking at Vance, a mischievous grin clamped over his cigarette. Cords of gray smoke rose steadily, halting under the ceiling, anchoring the room. "And yeah, I'm pretty damn sure I can trim these buds as good as you."

... with a most dreadful appeal, there was that other, horrific option.

CHAPTER 14

On Monday morning, Kenny drove to the Coos Bay School District to pick up the enrollment forms for his kids. The woman in the office, after Kenny had told her he was a single father, pointed out *twice* that school starts in two weeks. Then she wrote the date on a piece of paper and handed it to him. She offered her name—Barbara—and inquired as to the ages of his children. It was at this point that Kenny felt compelled to tell the woman about Logan's current state of "incommunicado".

"What do you mean he doesn't talk?" the woman asked. Her eyes were the color of strong coffee, and gauging by the coarseness of her voice, Kenny thought she might be a smoker. Closer inspection and he noticed a yellowing on her hands, a color that vaguely matched the woman's hair. She stood behind the counter with a certain self-confidence, a durable bearing that suggested she knew every angle and corner hidden within the inner workings of a school district.

"I mean, he stopped talking," Kenny replied.

"Sounds like a behavior problem to me." Barbara said this matter-of-factly, as if an old-fashioned tanning of the hide would solve the boy's problem. Her eyes skipped up and down Kenny's frame, the weight of judgment landing at intervals.

"Well," Kenny said, "I'm not the expert, but I don't think so. He stopped talking about six months ago, just after his mother passed away."

Barbara stared brightly at Kenny, and awkwardness fell down from the ceiling like thunder. From a back office, Kenny heard the tin overtones of a radio, the shuffling of paper, and then someone coughing. "I'm sorry to hear that," Barbara said, her words coming out clumsy.

"It's called traumatic mutism. That's what my son has. But he might start talking again, someday. Sooner than later, I hope." The look in the woman's eyes suggested to Kenny that she may have never heard of the condition.

"Perhaps you should talk to Mister Donahue, then—Floyd Donahue. He's our program manager for special education. He's not in right now, but let me give you his phone number." She took another piece of paper from her desk, wrote Donahue's name and number on it, and handed it to Kenny. "Floyd is a good man. He'll help you out."

"Thanks," Kenny said, taking the paper. "One other thing, though—I'd like to consider homeschooling my son. Actually, I'm thinking I'll do that, just so you know."

"You want to homeschool him?"

"That's right."

"Well, then... you should still give Mister Donahue a call. He can help you with that, too. There are certain procedures you'll need to follow regarding it, though—homeschooling, that is."

When Kenny walked out of the office, he was in a state of dull shock. Remotely, his conscience was aware of this sudden paralysis, which had gracefully closed over him, not unlike the hand of God. His body had gone into autopilot as he made his way out of the building and toward the parking lot, where his kids sat waiting for him in the Jeep. Kenny opened the door and climbed in. He glanced briefly at the enrollment forms, the extra slips of paper he'd received from the woman, his gaze processing nothing beyond Donahue's name and number. Then Kenny folded the stack in half and shoved it in the glove compartment, before turning the ignition.

"Where are we going now?" Jolie asked, a childish thrill of the unknown resonating in her voice. Kenny heard his daughter's request, but still could not get past what the woman had said. Those two words—special education—and Kenny was out of his mind and in a dark place. Sure, he'd formed the words in his mind before, wondering how and when Logan would get aligned to such a condition, such a stigma. Over the last few months, Kenny had mapped this reality out, albeit halfheartedly, and with the thinnest of ink. But all it took was a hint of reality coming from the likes of Barbara—queen of all things school-related—before Kenny now felt surrounded by a tower of concrete. He felt claustrophobic, boxed in, incapable of climbing out, with no handholds to pull himself up.

"Daddy," Jolie continued, "where to?"

"Gotta run some errands." The sentence came out short, clipped with sentiment, as Kenny seemed lost inside himself. For certain, he had underestimated the weight behind those two simple words. A train of emotions was now running inside him, making speed and heavy with momentum. A first thought came in the form of denial: the unequivocal exception allowed for his son. But then this verdict hit an angle, bent sideways, and was followed by a dampening effect. Sure, Logan might need special education, but only for a little while. It's what Kenny told himself, his last ditch effort to keep from sliding.

"Can we go to Denny's?" Jolie asked. "I'm hungry."

"No," Kenny replied. "You just ate."

"I ate—like a thousand hours ago," Jolie said.

"I said no! We're not eating out. Not today." The stress of facing a reality he did not want to accept brought a cramped pressure to the back of Kenny's eyes, as if someone's thumb was pushing into existence the start of a migraine.

But it was only seconds later that Kenny felt guilty for raising his voice. Just why couldn't they go out to eat today? It's not like the family was hurting for money. The half a million dollar tax-free indemnity was still going strong. And the sale of the house in Ventura came with a profit three times as much as Kenny made in any year. The life insurance check, the capital gains from the former home, and an indefinite length of time off work—wonderful benefits, contingent upon the death of one's spouse.

But what about the costs incurred? Kenny didn't want to think anymore about those particular expenses. He felt he'd been doing better lately and was afraid to fall backward.

He lowered his voice and said, "Maybe we'll get dinner somewhere... As long as you two are good."

They spent the next three hours in town, picking up supplies Kenny needed for work up at his brother's cabin, along with a few things for the house. For a treat, he bought cupcakes for the kids in Coos Bay, and a package of smoked salmon for him and George, as suggested by his daughter. Kenny had left George at home for this outing, and Jolie thought it was only fair to bring him some kind of treat, since he had to miss out on all the fun. Kenny didn't feel like arguing with her anymore. Most of his energy was now consumed with processing Logan's future, as well as piecing together the logistics of working on the cabin. And that homeschooling thing, which was causing a low echo somewhere inside his gut.

A sudden conflict percolated within Kenny's mind, as he thought about teaching his son academics. Would it be anything like sorting washers in the garage? He wondered about that. His first step about homeschooling would be to find out where to begin.

It was mid-afternoon by the time he pulled to a stop in the driveway. There was a sudden flurry of commotion as he reached forward and opened the glove compartment. George was inside the house barking at their arrival, and Jolie, tittering brightly, clambered expertly out of the Jeep. Even Logan seemed eager to move on to something else.

"Hey," Kenny said, glancing back at his son. Logan stopped halfway out of the vehicle and met his dad's stare. "Don't run off—understand? We've got more sorting to do." The kid nodded before hopping out. "And I want you to help me get things ready for tomorrow." As he ran toward the house, Logan looked briefly back, a sudden curiosity playing off his eyes.

Thirty minutes later, Kenny was in the garage, setting up for another sorting session. Logan stood limply at his side. The boy now had his favorite sweatshirt on, the charcoal-colored one, and he had his hands tucked into the front pocket, hood drawn over his head. A damp, sea-born fog had found its way into town, coating the land with a deep chill. Kenny knew that the bank of gray moisture would settle in for the rest of the day. But he pulled his son's hood down nonetheless, and gave the boy a faint smile. "Can't see your eyes, kid," he said. "I like to know that you're at least watching me."

Just outside the garage, Jolie was putting together a "setup," a random combination of Barbie dolls and My Little Pony figurines. For her age, the girl was sharp. Kenny suspected that she may have already understood what this "moment" might be about—perhaps more so than Kenny did. He figured she would play with her toys quietly enough, and close enough, to observe, yet not distract her brother and father.

He handed the roll of masking tape and black Sharpie to his son and then placed two coffee cans on the table in front of him. "Now write 'stainless screws', and 'metal screws'," he said. "I haven't seen too many galvanized ones—nothing loose, anyway. But there are four boxes of roofing screws over there on the floor." He pointed to a corner of the garage. "And roofing screws are usually galvanized. If we find some, we'll set them aside. Maybe put them over there with the others." Logan gave a subtle nod as he labeled the tape.

Kenny began sifting through the pile of steel he'd dumped onto the table, examining the contents, searching for screws.

Although his recent worrying continued to plague his thoughts, he was conscious now of the power of redirection, and considered that this activity, for a time, would put his mind at ease. He picked out various sized screws, with a mixture of lengths and diameters, and different heads. There were panheads and flat, countersunk heads. Most of the fasteners were of the standard metal variety, with only a few stainless; and upon noticing this, Kenny told Logan to label another can "metal".

At this request, Logan gave another nod and did as he was told. Then the minutes ticked away until whole chunks of time had passed. Within an hour, they had gone through the contents of half a dozen coffee cans, separating out only the screws, and they did this without speaking. It was a peaceful affair, identical in Kenny's mind to the last sorting session, but one that would ultimately become interrupted by Jolie's request for something to eat.

"I suppose we should have dinner now," Kenny agreed, looking at his watch. He stepped away from the table and placed his hand on the back of his neck, arched his head toward the ceiling to work away the stiffness. "Come on, let's go see what's in the kitchen." In what looked like a relaxed, noncommittal fashion, Logan gently placed a handful of screws onto the table before leading the way out of the garage.

"So what's for dinner?" Jolie asked. She was at her father's heels before they had reached the front door. "I'll help make it... Oh! But you said we could go to Denny's, remember?"

Kenny stopped at the front door and turned toward his daughter, who was standing beside him. Not standing, really, just moving in place. Presently, she was engaged in some sort of ritualistic-looking dance, her waist and knees swaying from side to side, arms waving up and down, her eyes fixed on her dad's nose. She met his stare and smiled. "You said that, you know? If we were good. Remember?"

Kenny let out a sigh. "Jolie," he said, "why are you the way that you are?"

His daughter maintained the stare, the dance, the impish grin, and said, "Because I can be?"

With a shrug, Kenny turned and walked toward the Jeep. "Fine," he said. "Put George inside the house."

They ate their dinner at Denny's and ordered a whole cherry pie to go. When they got home, Kenny served each of them hot slices with a scoop of vanilla ice cream, and they ate their dessert on the couch in front of the television. They watched *The Great Muppet Caper*, and Jolie laughed easily, sometimes without apparent cause, which added to the overall entertainment for Kenny.

When he was finished with his dessert, he looked at the clock above the mantle, saw that it was a quarter to nine. Jolie was lying on the floor surrounded by a heap of pillows, blankets, and stuffed animals, while Logan sat in a distant corner of the couch. It was likely that both kids would fall asleep in these very places, and Kenny put his mind into the order of deciding whether he would leave them here, or carry the children down the hall and into their rooms.

As he thought this, it surprised him when Logan moved unhurriedly across the couch, taking position next to him. The incident struck Kenny as unexpected, and perplexing, as the boy hadn't voluntarily closed a distance with anyone since shortly after his mother had died. For as much as he was unavailable for conversation, Logan was also unavailable, or incapable, of providing any kind of emotional proximity. His very presence had become almost a moot point; he was a shadow, commonplace, and inconsequential.

Seconds later, and Kenny stopped thinking about the incident entirely, his thoughts now solely on the moment, solely on personal restraint. Miraculously, the boy had twisted to the side and cuddled his dad. It took all of Kenny's strength not to clutch his son in response, to boil over with tears, and to holler toward the ceiling at this single, fractional step back toward normalcy.

CHAPTER 15

In the musty, dim confines of the "clubhouse," where Rob spent the last half-hour picking up empty bottles and cans of beer, an old man sat on a barstool against a wall, staring intently at the Prospect. The man's face was a weathered map of wrinkles and gray whiskers, and he had gray, rheumy eyes that, without relent, stabbed vicious holes into Rob's ego.

Rob had never seen the geezer before. In fact, he didn't know who the old man was, or why he was there, and couldn't for the life of him figure out why the man kept staring at him. He wasn't wearing a cut, so Rob didn't think he was in the club, but he looked... Yes, he looked mean enough.

Eventually, Rob lost his patience. "What the hell you looking at then, old man?" he said. "You got a problem or something?"

The old man remained silent, while his eyes remained steadfast on Rob. He was vigilant, Rob gave him that. The Prospect shook his head and went back to work.

Architecturally speaking, the clubhouse was a nightmare. It consisted of two single-wide trailers merged onto opposite ends of a two-bedroom house that had been built in the late 60s. This entire construct was connected on the inside, but one of the trailers was designated off-limits, reserved only for patch-holders. It was there that the club held its official meetings—meetings known as "church"—to discuss business-related topics. Rob had never been inside that trailer, and he wondered what it looked like. Supposedly, the outer walls had been reinforced with sheets of quarter-inch steel, to ward against assassination attempts from rival gangs. This rumor had yet to provide for Rob any evidence, but it fascinated him, nonetheless. At the very least, he thought it sounded cool.

The rest of the clubhouse was within his domain, relatively speaking. He went where he was told, cleaned up that which was pointed out to him. And, on the rarest of occasions, was allowed enough time to drink a beer in the "den," as the bikers called it, usually when there was a ball game on the television, or when everyone was too passed out to notice Rob.

That's when Rob did his sneaking around. When he pocketed loose cash, and loose drugs, half-emptied bottles of whiskey, or the remnants of an eight ball of coke. *What good was a Prospect who didn't prospect?* he regularly told himself.

His biggest score yet was only a few nights ago, just before he and Vance went up to the scene to collect the first of their harvest. Rob had swiped, and then quickly "blew" almost four grams of coke. That was only his best estimate, of course, taken from the number of baggies he'd pilfered through, and the several lines he'd snorted, left unattended on a table top here, or mirror there. That was one hell of a night. And one that left Rob with absolutely zero regrets.

But there was no pilfering going on right now, much to Rob's dismay. The old man was still staring at him, and the scowl on his face seemed to have broadened, if that were possible.

"You can help me, you know," Rob said, gesturing to his surroundings. The clubhouse had endured another night of celebratory activity, but the resulting mess, in Rob's semi-professional opinion, wasn't all that bad. He had seen much worse. Still, having some stranger stare ceaselessly at him while he picked up trash had quickly become an agitating affair. "Go on, grandpa," Rob continued, "there's some bleach in the bathroom. Get a sponge, already... Shit don't clean itself."

The night before, while at Vance's house, Rob thought he was going to lose his mind. He had to hear that tree-hugger bitch and moan about the proper way to trim pot for almost two hours, before Rob finally threw in the towel and left. No worries, though. He had the feeling that Vance didn't want him there anymore than Rob did; and so be it, as he let the shithead do all the work. As long as he didn't run off with the product, Rob could not care less.

When Rob finally went home that night, sometime around two in the morning, he found a note on the front door of his trailer. Cecil had written it (or so Rob presumed), and it said only two words: CLUBHOUSE, MORNING. And those two words were more than enough to spell out for Rob what the next day would hold. A day loaded with what he knew as "shit duty".

But now, despite his appointed cleaning and various other errands, the biggest thing on his mind was that old man. He kept staring at Rob, a face wrapped in age, and bitter with judgment.

"Can't you do anything other than stare?" Rob said, all but losing his temper. "Say something, grandpa! For fuck's sake, are you dead? That's it, huh? I'm looking at a dead man, aren't I? Fucking geezer up and croaked over there in the corner." Rob laughed. But then he felt another person in the room, before he heard the sound. He turned and looked over his shoulder, his eyes fixing onto the leathered, black silhouette of the chapter's president.

Hondo.

Fear, in the truest sense of the word, enveloped Rob. It was asphyxiating, as if two massive hands had wrapped tightly around his throat. And this fear sped up as Hondo spoke. "Hey, Shits, is there a reason you're talking like that to Leroy?"

"I ahh..." Rob stammered.

"Don't you know this man's my uncle?" Hondo said. "Patch-holder or not, you treat him with respect—always."

Fragments of a few nights ago replayed within Rob's mind: the gruesome sights, the horrendous sounds, and then the gut-churning shakes coming from handling a dismembered man.

"Are you hearing me, Shits?" Hondo said, irritably.

"Yes I am, sir. I hear you, sir."

"Good," Hondo added. He turned and walked over to the old man—to Leroy—and, simultaneously, spontaneously, *unnervingly*, the entire room filled with a crowd of bikers. The sudden movement of men into the room, being so close in time to the scary incident with Hondo, pushed Rob into flight mode. He looked around, watched as bikers gathered here and there, faces coughing up morning phlegm, heads shaking off hangovers. The scene was over-stimulating for Rob. At once, he wanted to leave. Or, at the very least, disappear into a corner of the room.

"I don't like him!" Leroy announced bitterly. The old man's words were icicles stabbing into Rob's eyes. "You sure he ain't a rat?"

Fuck you, Leroy... Rob thought. *Fuck off, already.*

"Nah, he's no rat." That was Cecil, leaning against a wall, lighting a cigarette. "He's too damn dirty to be a rat."

"Bullshit!" replied Leroy. "Ain't no such thing as a clean rat. They're all fucking dirty. Dirty with something."

Rob swiveled his head nervously about from side to side. He quickly realized that this obvious display of theatrics was centered on him. The sudden import of men into the room, the chapter president, the sergeant at arms—*Uncle Leroy*—they were all there on behalf of Rob. *And why was that?* he wondered. It might mean that they were considering patching him in! Or, it could mean just the opposite...

"Nope," Cecil repeated. "I'm positive he ain't connected."

"Not now, but maybe someday," Leroy said, without hesitation. Rob looked at the old man. His lips contorted into a scowl, his eyes cold and furious. Somehow Rob had found himself on this man's bad side, and everything about that left Rob feeling hollow, very hollow.

"You all know I hold a lot of weight in what my uncle says," Hondo said. And with those words, Rob felt as if a sack of concrete had been placed on his shoulders. His knees slipped, almost buckled.

Cecil shook his head. "How long has he been a Prospect? Fifteen months or so. Over a year, at least."

"That don't mean shit!" Leroy snapped. But Rob had already caught the looks on some of the other bikers. Cecil was on the Prospect's side, and apparently so were a few others.

"One thing I would like to know," Hondo said, turning his shoulders and moving closer to Rob. "Who's this Vance character?"

The climate of the room transformed. Rob's hands had become damp, and his arms were now itching fiercely. A bead of sweat drew a path down his cheek. "Vance?" Rob said, pathetically.

"Yeah," Hondo replied. "Who's this guy you've been hanging out with? And why are you spending so much time with him?"

"Ah, no reason. He's just a friend, that's all." Sporadically, Rob searched the room, scanning the many faces. "He's just someone I hang out with."

"Cecil tells me he's a fucking hippie," Hondo said. "Is that right?"

"Yeah, I guess so. But he's cool and all." Rob laughed nervously, trying to play the topic down, while trying desperately to think fast. "That's the best part, you see. The guy knows how to roll a killer joint." As he said this, he looked at Cecil for affirmation.

A lengthy pause hit the room, accentuated by the antics of gross men deep in thought. In what Rob assumed was the last stretch toward the deciding factor of his fate, they subjected him to the sounds of passing gas and hasty coughs, the scratch and shift of leather, an abrupt belch, and lazy laughter.

Leroy broke the lingering spell. "I don't trust him," he said, shaking his head in apparent disgust. "Don't think I ever will. He's crooked—I can tell. I bet he's a *thieving bastard.*"

Rob could have walked over and decked the old man. He would have, in fact, if the consequences for such an action were anything less than what he knew they would be. "I'm not crooked," he protested, but his voice sounded weak and flaccid. At once, he regretted speaking out.

In response, Leroy simply glowered back at Rob, his eyes gleaming with knowledge and triumph.

"Maybe Leroy's right about the Prospect," Hondo said. "Seems like ever since he's been hanging around the clubhouse, shit's gone missing."

"Damn straight!" Leroy added.

"Oh, what do you know about it, old man?" Cecil stepped away from the wall. "You've been here what—once, in the last year? Never even seen the guy before today."

A rush of elation caused by Cecil's defense felt exhilarating to Rob. It was almost as good as a coke high. He wasn't sure why the sergeant of arms was so adamant at backing him up, but Rob wasn't about to think too hard on the matter. He made a mental note to buy the biker a beer one day and tried pushing his mind three steps into the future. Where was the club going with all of this? Was there a point to having Leroy there, other than to stir up trouble? And, most of all, was this the beginning of the young Prospect's indoctrination into the club? If so, he would receive a good pummeling any second now. Such was the tradition for patching members into the family. Maybe that was the reason for the old fossil in the corner—to ignite the flames of a good beating.

He glanced at Leroy, tried to find out the writing on his face. The old man sat quietly on a bar stool, his mouth set on autopilot, empty gums chewing on empty words. He reminded Rob of a pouting child.

"Even so, there's a reason we haven't patched this fucker in yet," Hondo said. "Am I right?" Casually flipping open a pocket knife, the club's president surveyed the room. "Maybe Leroy's on to something." He looked then at his fingertips and worked the blade under one of them. "Maybe we just need to take a closer look at things."

A general murmur stirred throughout the room. Rob felt the onset of queasiness once again. He could hurl at any moment.

"We'll give it more time," Hondo said, closing his blade and walking out of the room. Then, like the drop of the curtain at the end of an act, it was all over. The tension in the room collapsed suddenly as everyone dissipated. Cecil walked past Rob and slapped him on the shoulder. "Don't sweat it, man," he whispered, winking. "By the way—get me some more of that smoke your friend has."

When Cecil left, Rob felt only a bit less shaky, less frazzled. He scanned the room, which was now as vacant as it was several minutes ago. It seemed, however, that an extra layer of dust and debris had found its way in and onto the various surfaces. And of course, the biggest piece of trash—Uncle Leroy—he was still there, sitting in the corner. The old man, with his infinite stare, looked smug, appeared to be gloating. If only Rob had his gun right now.

Rob turned away. He didn't dare say anything, still unsure what had just transpired. And still fearful of what yet may come. No, Rob was done with speaking his mind to the old man, despite how much it damaged his pride. He stuck his nose back into the grindstone and recommenced with his cleaning duties.

But like a dog at a bone, Rob's mind worried over the recent moment, as well as the impending future. Too many questions clung to his brain, pulling him closer to some type of edge, a drop-off leading to a nebulous void. Were they going to patch him in soon? Or would they decide he was a rat and slit his throat? Would they pry further into his affairs, where they would ultimately discover his side business? And was Leroy gunning for him?

As much as Rob couldn't answer the many questions swimming in his head, he could still put together a shell of a plan. A few ideas, at least. Topping the list, he had to finish up with the harvest, and then offload all the weed, as he desperately needed the money. Without a doubt, that cash would not only buy his way into the club, but it would also cement his reputation. *Fuck you, Leroy*, he thought again.

But what if his share of the take wasn't enough? What if he needed more? Shit, what if he *wanted* more? After all, how much of his allegiance sat with his pothead friend, Vance? None, really. More than once, Rob had entertained the idea of offing his "partner." And more than once, he'd promised himself he'd do it. At this point, wouldn't anything less than following through with that idea be an act of cowardice?

Without thinking, Rob caught himself glancing at the old man in the corner, and that man was quick to meet his stare.

"Thieving bastard," Leroy said, under his breath.

And because he was so untouchable, so damning, or perhaps so *conniving*, Rob looked the other way and whispered into the dry air his promise to run a knife under the chin of not one worthless sack of shit, but two.

CHAPTER 16

The following morning, Kenny was up before the sun, organizing the tools he needed to work on his brother's hunting cabin. He packed power saws and power drills, hammer and nails, plumb bobs, chalk and string, and a variety of measuring instruments into a heavy canvas work bag. He tossed the bag into the back of the Jeep, then drank his coffee in the kitchen and listened to the wake of the day.

There was warmness in the morning air, what seemed like the whisper of grace circling around him. He thought of Marley, and for once, in a long time, the thought brought a smile to his face. Of course, he wished his wife was here, wished she could have seen her son the night before, opening up through the smallest of acts—a seamless, natural act owned by every child. As cautious as he told himself to be, Kenny was still overpowered with joy. And relief.

The kids were still asleep, and that was a bright blessing. Kenny was in no real rush. He would let them sleep as long as they needed, knowing that there was powerful medicine to be found in slumber.

George seemed to be on the same channel as the kids. He was lying on the couch, his chin wedged between his two front paws, glancing frequently at Kenny, but with eyelids that were sinking fast. As tired as he was, Kenny knew the dog would be up and at his side as soon as Kenny made a move toward the door. He thought George always knew when the family was about to leave.

Despite his unhurried, relaxed demeanor, Kenny still had a long day ahead of him. The plan was to drive to his brother's house, leave Jolie there, and then take Logan with him up to the cabin. But he knew there'd be distractions along the way. He wanted to stay up at the cabin for a few days, so that would mean he would need to get Jolie settled in at Wayne's house. She would want to bring half a dozen stuffies, her favorite clothes, a bag full of toys, and whatever else she'd feel was necessary. Kenny would have to reel his daughter in, he realized, or he would never get out of the house and on the road.

He considered there might also be some required time spent with his brother, which he looked forward to. Beth would be there, most likely, and Kenny knew he'd have to make a stab at convincing the woman of his measly accomplishments, that he was on the proper track of success with his kids. Why Kenny even cared about what Beth thought was beyond him. *Why was she so damn annoying?* he wondered.

Considering these distractions, it would take the better part of the day just to get up to the cabin. But Kenny was prepared for that, too. He'd packed the sleeping bags and lantern, as well as an ice chest of food and a bag of canned goods—enough supplies for a few days. The remoteness of the cabin was such that too much time would be spent driving to the nearest store if he had to. So Kenny planned to avoid such an event. He even remembered to include ingredients for S'mores.

Admittedly, his plan for the following days fell right in line with his current strategy for dealing with his son: to have Logan at his side as he finished projects—or put things back in order. While he made things right again... like the coffee cans in the garage. Nothing about any of this was a planned effort on Kenny's part; it just sort of fell together conveniently. And nothing about Logan's current state made this difficult, the quiet shadow that the boy ever was.

Kenny moved quietly about the house, still content to let his kids rest. He noticed that the place needed Marley's touch, was too dark, too cluttered. Even on the brightest of days, not enough light made it into the living room. In this part of the house, only the kitchen window faced south, and the largest window, in the living room, faced north, and had thick, tan curtains that Kenny almost never opened; Jolie made a point of doing that.

His home was too damn dark, Kenny realized.

"I'm tired," he suddenly said, sinking onto the couch next to George. He rubbed the dog's ears. "Just like you, boy. I'm tired." As he said this, he thought of Logan and Jolie, and wondered what they may be tired of, as well.

Suddenly, Kenny felt a mass of guilt settle at the back of his throat. Perhaps he was on the path to correcting his family's trauma (if that were ever possible). But now, more than ever, he needed to remain on this path. He needed endurance, if only for the sake of his kids. Frankly, he couldn't afford to be tired.

He stood and walked over to the large window, and with a quick jerk, yanked the curtains open. The room filled with gray ambiance, was brighter than Kenny expected. In two beats, George was off the couch and pacing the room, wagging his tail. He paused before Kenny, licked his hand, then went over and sat patiently near the front door.

Three cooked pancakes later, and both Logan and Jolie were awake and at the kitchen table. A certain bubbly energy flowed effortlessly throughout the room, thanks to his daughter. But as for his son, it disappointed Kenny to observe that the night before had little effect on the beginning of this day. The promise was still there, though. And it was a strong promise, he was sure. A promise that any parent would cling stubbornly to.

After breakfast, Kenny told Jolie that if she was ready to go within the hour, he'd leave some ingredients for S'mores at his brother's house, for later that night. His daughter was in the Jeep and ready to go in less than thirty minutes. Fully loaded with gear and passengers, Kenny left the house and drove George and the kids toward the familiar highway that led to his brother's house.

It was a tedious drive. Kenny passed the time by mapping out his plans for the cabin. It was difficult to assign a systematic approach to the project, given the condition of the cabin and the lack of laborers to help him with the many tasks involved. Although the cabin was small, there was still a considerable amount of framing to complete, which was Kenny's hope for this trip. He would certainly do his best to solicit Logan's help, but Kenny thought it was unlikely that the kid would be of much use. At the very least, he hoped the boy wouldn't get in the way.

But then again, wasn't that the plan? Kenny reminded himself of this idea, this *strategy* of his, and that this trip meant more for the repairing of his son than it did for the building of a cabin. Undoubtedly, a conscious decision would be necessary on Kenny's part. As busy as he got with the cabin, he couldn't forget about including Logan.

The drive to his brother's house took longer than expected. There was construction on the road, a repaving project, and the smell of hot tar reminded Kenny of his former life in southern California. Years ago, he had worked on a few commercial roofing jobs—a blistering pain-in-the-ass-stint if ever there was one. The memory left him feeling both bitter and sweet. It was of a time before Marley, before the kids, a time laden with freedom, and of few responsibilities. But now, for Kenny, it was a crisis to imagine once again living that kind of life—a life without his kids. Even though he sometimes felt overburdened with the responsibilities, the *impossibilities*, his kids still meant the world to him. Given the smallest of reflections, he knew he'd have things no other way—except for losing Marley.

They arrived almost an hour overdue. At Wayne's house, Jolie wasted no time "moving in". She had packed everything into one suitcase and, shortly after hopping out of the Jeep, had everything unpacked and scattered across her cousin's bed.

Kenny attempted to organize her stuff, but Beth dismissed him with a wave of her hand. "I got this," she said. "Go see your brother. He's in the kitchen."

"I got them enrolled," Kenny announced lamely, almost as an afterthought. "In school, that is. But Logan..." he coughed, clearing his throat, "I think I'm going to homeschool him."

Beth gave him a skeptical look. "Really?" she said, pausing amid tidying up. "You're going to homeschool?" A gesture of impracticality crossed her face, and Kenny felt his shoulders tense in response. "You really think you can do that?" Beth added.

"That's what I'm figuring," Kenny replied. "Not talking and all... I think he'll be better off with me. He'll get picked on too much. You know how kids are."

"Yeah, but, *homeschooling*... That's a lot of work, Kenny. It takes a tremendous amount of organization." She crossed her arms and looked frankly at him. "You know, you really need to think about what you're planning here. I don't mean to pry all that much, but this is your kid's education we're talking about." She went back to sorting the various articles on the bed, adding, "Don't you think you should let someone who knows what they're doing take care of that? I mean, there's already a lot on your plate, Kenny."

Kenny scratched his chin, felt a band of heat tighten across the back of his neck. "And what's that supposed to mean?" he said.

Beth's shoulders rose to her ears. "Well, you can't even take care of the basic things for your children. I've seen you—you just *can't* do it. You're unable to." Her tone was both blunt and demeaning. "Christ, Kenny, half the time they're not even dressed properly. Your house is cold and depressing. And Logan... Well, how the hell do you expect he'll ever break out of his silence without a mother around to help him?" She shook her head. "And now you want to homeschool the boy. *Really?*"

Her accusations stabbed Kenny painfully, were oddly debilitating, and yet... provoking. At once, he felt the urge to buckle, but also to fight back. Briefly, his mind searched for a logical retort, but then, inexplicably, the words came right out of him. "I've heard enough out of you, Bethany. I love my children. And dammit, they *know* I do. That's worth more than all this other shit you keep running on about. In the end, that's what'll keep my family going." He paused, feeling the full weight of his words.

Beth said nothing in response. She stared absently at the bedspread, seemingly at a loss for words. "So yeah," Kenny continued, his tone now more subdued. "I sure as hell *will* homeschool Logan—in our cold and depressing home—and my son will be all the better for it."

He said no more as he left the room. He walked down the hall, taking deep breaths, and almost regretted half of what he'd just said—almost, but not entirely. In the kitchen, he found his brother at the table reading the morning paper. Wayne was dressed in his normal office attire, a pair of jeans and a long-sleeved corduroy shirt—a rugged individual pulled from the pages of an L.L. Bean catalog. The smell of coffee and bacon sat heavy in the air, even though it was nearing noontime.

"Morning, little brother," Wayne said, looking up from the paper. "Get yourself some coffee. You have breakfast yet?"

"I'm good," Kenny replied. He went to the counter and poured himself a cup, then sat at the table across from his brother. "Skipping work today?" he asked, conversationally.

"I've got a meeting up in Sutherlin tonight," Wayne replied. "Thought I'd sleep in to make up for it."

Kenny nodded and sipped his coffee. "By the way, I just had some words with your wife."

Wayne glanced up from the paper again, a sharp look in his eyes. "Oh yeah? And what about?"

"She keeps riding me about my kids."

Wayne laughed, then looked back at the paper. "That woman never knows when to quit," he said.

"Well," Kenny replied, "I think she might quit now. At least I hope she will."

Wayne chuckled in response. He flipped the paper over and changed the subject. "You got everything you need—tools and all?"

"Yeah, I think so," Kenny said. "What about up there? Is there anything I need to pick up on the way?"

"There shouldn't be," Wayne said. "I put up a Honda generator with some fuel. Two truck-loads of lumber... Several sheets of drywall." He took a bite of toast, chewed for a minute. "But I doubt you'll need any of that on this trip. There's still a lot of framing to be done."

"What about insulation?" Kenny asked.

Wayne nodded his head. "It's there. Probably got a family of mice living in it by now."

They talked further about the cabin, hashing over specific details. Then Kenny told Wayne about his plans for Logan, how he hoped the boy would be of some help. Wayne seemed mildly interested in the idea, but Kenny thought there was something else there permeating from his brother.

"As long as he doesn't hurt himself," Wayne finally said.

"He's not going to get hurt," Kenny replied. "The boy hardly does anything on his own."

"Still, the area has its dangers. Rattlers and cougars—I'd keep an eye out, if I were you." Wayne folded the paper and set it to the side. "You got a gun with you?"

"No," Kenny replied. "I guess I didn't think to bring one."

"Shit, take one of mine. At least a twenty-two... Hell, why not? You guys can have fun plinking cans."

Kenny sipped his coffee as he mulled the idea over. He had never taught Logan how to use a gun, and didn't think the boy would even care for it. Logan had always been "atypical". He wasn't interested in sports or weapons of any kind. Still, every boy should at one point learn how to shoot a gun, or so Kenny believed. And who knew? Perhaps the fun of shooting cans together would offer a higher degree of quality time between the two of them.

He considered the idea. It seemed like a good one. But ultimately, Kenny passed on it. He figured that by working on the job, and possibly exploring the area, they'd have enough to fill their time. Besides, shooting a gun might put the thought of killing something in a person's mind. And with that, there came the prospect of death, which was the last thing Kenny wanted his son to be thinking about right now. "Maybe next time," he finally said.

"You sure?" Wayne said. "In case you run across a snake or something."

"Don't worry. I'll be fine, big brother."

Before Kenny left, he reminded Wayne of when to expect him back. Then he went outside to the swinging bench—to Logan's spot—and told the boy it was time to go.

• • •

It took a little over an hour to drive the distance to the outskirts of Milo, Oregon. The cabin sat a mile up a dirt road, the entrance of which Kenny now parked the Jeep. He clambered out the side and onto the hard-packed soil. "Wait here," he said to Logan as he walked over to a chain-linked barrier. He fumbled with his key chain, found his brother's key, opened the padlock, and then the barrier dropped.

Minutes later, he was scooting the Jeep up the dirt road, through a shaded canyon of timber and scrub brush. It was a pleasant drive, and when they arrived at the cabin, Kenny's shoulders dropped a bit, and he let out some air. In no time, George was out of the Jeep and sniffing the ground. Logan took his time getting out, but Kenny wasn't far behind the dog.

It'd been a few weeks since he was last here, and he didn't stay long. "Looks nice," he said, turning his direction to Logan. There was movement in the boy's eyes, as this was the first time he'd been to the cabin. "Come on out, son. We'll get set up to stay... You hungry, yet?" he added, walking over and to the porch.

Kenny didn't wait to see his son's reply. He was at the cabin's door, fumbling once again with his key chain. George let out a sudden bark as he tore past Kenny, almost clipping the back of his knees. He turned and watched his dog chase across a field, toward the tree line, hot on the tail of three scrambling does.

The commotion caused Kenny to drop the key chain. He waited a second, watched George run hopelessly after the deer, before stooping to pick up the keys. It was at this juncture, this pause between sudden action and a rippling afterthought, that Kenny spotted the crushed, darkened smear of the cigarette butt lying on the floor of the deck.

CHAPTER 17

Vance was in the kitchen microwaving a burrito when he heard a *thump* at the door. This was followed by what sounded like a muffled curse, and then, "Open up, fucker!" He looked around for a weapon, anything, until he heard the next statement: "Yo! It's me. Your *brah!*"

Rob. He was back, and Vance felt minor relief; but only a little, as his recent imaginings of Rob and his biker gang stabbing him to death over a few pounds of weed still weighed heavily on Vance's mind. Heavy as concrete.

"Hurry, asshole." This time Rob spoke in a low tone, what sounded like a half-assed attempt at discretion, but there was still a wide hint of distress in his voice. "I ain't got all day, man."

The microwave dinged. Vance hesitated, looked at the microwave door, looked at the front door, and looked again for a weapon. He pulled a drawer open, grabbed a steak knife and stashed it in the tube pocket of his sweatshirt. The uncertainty of the last few days put into his head that anything was possible right now. Anything could happen.

"Just a minute, dude," Vance said, stalking out of the kitchen and toward the door. He now had the burrito in one hand—would use that as his weapon-of-first-strike if he had to—and his other hand was hovering near his pocket, ready to grip the steak knife. Both of his hands were sweating.

"Shit's serious," Rob said, "so hurry the fuck up."

Vance turned on the porch light and then peeked through the peephole. He saw Rob's scruffy dome, saw his enlarged lips and bulbous fish eyes—eyes magnified with urgency. Vance opened the door, and then Rob burst into the room like he had many times before—haphazardly, full of crank-induced energy. But this time, he brought with him the presence of fear.

"We've got to go, man," he said, "right now. Shit! Gotta go right now!" Rob moved into the living room, started circling it. He looked frenetic, smelled like piss and booze. He was scratching his head and arms rhythmically, almost desperately, and seemed to Vance like he couldn't decide which section of his body itched more than the other. "Hurry up, man, get your shit together. It's time to go."

Vance scratched his chin and then tucked his hand under his armpit, as if to warm it. He was dumbfounded. "Go where?" he asked.

Rob looked at him, stared right at his face, his eyes wide as Christ's arms. "To the scene, you idiot! Get your shit together and let's go!"

Vance hesitated. He had wanted to go up and check on their crop soon, had even mentioned it to Rob the night before. But *right now?* "What's the hurry, dude? Besides, it's almost midnight." He made a move to sit down, was opening the plastic wrapper over his burrito, then paused. A sudden jolt of terror swept through his heart. "Did your biker friends find out about our shit? You told them, didn't you?"

"No, man," Rob said, then hesitated. "But they might as well." He looked up at the ceiling, rolled his eyes. "Hurry the fuck up, already!"

"What's that supposed to mean?" Vance replied, setting the burrito on the coffee table, his appetite at once abandoned. "*Might as well.* Might as well what?"

"It doesn't fucking matter. Just get your shit together and let's go. Bring your fucking burrito with you." Rob went outside and climbed into his Ford Bronco, then turned the engine on.

Vance sat on the couch, thunderstruck and speechless. He could see his partner staring at him from behind the wheel, an ugly face stamped with condescension and expectancy.

Baffled, Vance made a move to gather his things. He went into the drying room and retrieved his duffle bag full of gear, made a sweep of the room for no particular reason other than to take inventory. Did he have everything he needed to harvest? Was the window locked, the room secure? He took a minute to double check his entire apartment, lock things down, turn things off, until he heard the distinct "honk" come from the Bronco. "Fucking asshole," he muttered, as he then stashed the steak knife into his duffle bag. He threw the bag over his shoulder, stepped outside, and locked the door. He gave Rob the bird as he approached the vehicle. Twice he looked over both shoulders, hoping not to see the eyes of a bystander locked onto them.

"Christ," Vance said, climbing in and slamming the passenger door. "You're a piece of work, you know that? Next time, just yell from the parking lot: *Hey, man! It's time to go pick our weed!*"

Rob simply looked at Vance, said nothing, and then backed the Bronco up before gunning it. Gravel spat into the air and Vance heard it strike parked cars. "Really, dude? Like, what's the fucking hurry?"

Minutes down the road and Rob looked again at Vance. "Leroy... I think my time's running out. Leroy... The old man's got his sights on my ass. Wants to shoot to kill. Fucking, Leroy."

"Who the hell is Leroy?" Vance said.

"Leroy is Hondo's uncle, that's who. Fucking old geezer, don't know shit. Doesn't like me, either, for whatever reason. Can you believe that?" Rob glanced at Vance, slammed his hand on the dashboard. "That's some serious shit, man! Get it? If Leroy doesn't like me, then I ain't getting patched into the club. My ass is a goner."

"Really?" Vance said, laughing to himself. He could give a rat's ass about Rob getting patched into his biker gang. Better yet, Vance would likely prosper from the situation if his partner had nothing to do with those white trash thugs. "Just like that, you're out? Because of this Leroy dude?"

"Well, not exactly. But same difference, I guess. Either way, I need to make things happen with the club. I need that money, man. All of it. It's time."

Vance thought about Rob's words and inwardly shook his head. There really was no limit to the guy's idiocy. What was he going to do, harvest the entire scene? He was definitely talking like that was the plan. And where was the wisdom in that, Vance wondered? What a dumb motherfucker...

They stopped at Rob's place on the way. "Stay here," Rob said, jumping out of the vehicle. "I won't be long. Forgot something, is all."

It struck Vance as uncanny—the scene of less than twenty minutes ago reversing itself. He was in the vehicle now, staring out the window at his partner. He could see Rob's profile through the tiny camper door, could see that the man was apparently rummaging through a bag of some sort. Then he saw Rob drop the bag, turn away, and step toward a counter. Seconds later, Vance watched as Rob lifted his hand up to his face, then throw his head back in one swift motion.

"That fucker's snorting," Vance said in disbelief. The shit had gotten deep, was now a slippery slope, real as quicksand. It was all Vance could do not to get behind the wheel and bail. Common sense told him to act upon this notion. Common sense, the contradictory asshole it's always been, also told him to sit tight and wait for a better opportunity.

But a better opportunity for what?

He glanced at his duffle bag in the back seat, grim scenarios running foul in his mind. Perhaps he could use the steak knife to open Rob's throat, then stage a wreck of some sort. Crash the Bronco into a tree with Rob at the wheel; a scene taken right out of a movie. Then Vance could lie on the side of the road and pretend he had staggered away from the accident. Inevitably, this plan would involve local law enforcement, and that scenario, as Vance quickly deduced, would turn most disagreeable for him.

The other strategy, one which offered the most pristine opportunity for Vance, was to kill Rob somewhere near the scene. But that would mean having to first survive the drive up there. With coke-fiend Rob escorting them along one-lane roads, and up winding canyons, Vance wondered just how plausible his chances of survival would be. Then again, more than once, he'd been in this same situation: a helpless passenger at the whims of a driver operating without his full faculties in play. In all likelihood, every time Vance had ridden as a passenger in a car while living in southern Humboldt, he was at the mercy of a driver presently stoned out of his gourd.

Why Vance even worried about Rob's driving was a mystery to him. At this point, wouldn't death be a not-so-bad alternative? So why then was he worrying?

The paranoia, that's what it was. Had to be. All of Rob's shit for the last several months was finally taking its toll on Vance. Not to mention the reoccurring dilemma of having to commit murder. His mind went back to its homicidal wonderings. He suspected the killing, if it took place up at the scene, would be easy enough to pull off. He'd simply pick up a rock and then brain Rob when the guy wasn't looking. Just knock him out, that was all. And then the rest of the work—caving his skull in... well... Vance assumed the rest would be easy enough.

Suddenly, he felt sick to his stomach. Once again, he was actually considering killing another human being. What in Jah's name was he thinking? Shit, what in Jah's name had become of him? Could it be that he was standing on the edge of having a nervous breakdown? Was he slowly, positively, losing his mind?

Insane or not, with Rob out of the picture...

Vance could almost taste the freedom, a sweetness lingering at the tip of his tongue. Despite the messiness of smashing Rob's head into pulp, from the crime itself, Vance might climb out clean as a whistle. Who, other than Rob's biker friends, would ever go looking for the guy? And who's saying even they'd bother to do that? Vance also knew that by the time anyone grew suspicious of Rob's whereabouts, Vance would be long gone, living somewhere deep in Humboldt County. And with him would be all of that wonderful weed. The entire harvest.

He caught himself staring out the window. Southern Oregon was passing him by like the reel of a comic strip. Pine trees mixed with Manzanita brush were laughing at him, so it seemed, the shadow of their silhouettes an inkblot under the Bronco's headlights. And above, the night sky stressed the gloom he was feeling.

His thoughts took him back to his childhood and the chunks of time spent living in the family car. He'd experienced hopelessness then, he remembered, but never felt dread—the dread he felt now. Still, things had worked out for him in the end. To an absolute degree, he had escaped his depressing life when he moved to Humboldt. Although he could never escape the clutches of financial destitution (and sometimes his level of resources had dropped so low as to approach the point of being critical, even life-threatening), Vance had never lost sight of happiness. Or hope. Not while living in Humboldt. That's what the place offered him. And it always came readily and free. Humboldt was Vance's home...

He blinked his eyes and suddenly realized that the trip was almost over. In the last half hour, Rob had gotten back in the Bronco and driven them out of town and up the canyon leading toward the scene, and—*shit*, Vance was still alive. Perhaps the guy wasn't as wasted as Vance originally assumed. It occurred to him that his partner was strangely quiet, despite being jacked up on coke (along with whatever else was likely coursing through his system). Vance thought the dude was probably still stressing. All the asshole's talk earlier, about some guy named Leroy, and patching into his club. Or *not* patching in, that's what he had said. It was no wonder Rob was on edge.

Fuck him, Vance thought. Let him be silent. Let him stew. Maybe he'll think of something original for once in his life. Maybe he'll catch on to how stupid he was being.

"We ain't worrying about leaving tracks," Rob said, at last shattering the cone of silence between them. "When we get up there, I mean. Got it?"

Vance wasn't surprised. "Yeah," he said, biting a nail. He turned away and looked out the window again. "So what's the plan, then? We just gonna harvest the whole fucking lot before it's ready?"

"Yep," Rob replied. He was staring at the road, his face matter-of-fact. "That's the plan, *Rastaman*."

Half an hour ago, Vance would have objected vehemently to this so-called plan. Christ, fifteen minutes ago. He knew that at least half of the crop wasn't yet ready for an ideal harvest. Waiting a little longer, even a few days, would add more weight to the buds, and that would translate to greater profits. But the fact remained, it was long past the time to get out of this nightmare with Rob. Vance could no longer deny it. Also, he would have to accept whatever consequences came his way. Or would he? He looked sidelong at Rob, wondering what else the wannabe biker had in mind. What other plans had Rob contrived in that paranoid brain of his?

Vance considered an alternate scenario, the one in which *he* was the guy who gets his head smashed in. Of course, he knew it would happen after they'd packed their harvest into the Bronco and were getting ready to leave. With no painful effort, and certainly without remorse, Rob would overpower, and then club Vance with a tire iron, or what have you. He'd dig a shallow grave into which he would then roll Vance's lifeless body. Throw a little dirt back in, maybe a few handfuls of dried leaves—nowhere near enough to keep the various critters at bay. Then, in the night, Vance's body would get violated, dragged through the forest, picked at by crows, dismembered by coyotes and raccoons, strewn about and then deposited into a hundred holes and muddy hollows, caved-out tree roots, burrows, dens, nests. Not a soul alive would come looking for him. Who would even know he was missing? His death would be quieter than Rob's, that's for sure. His death—nay, his *murder*—would become the coldest case known to man. So cold, as to be *case-less*.

There really was no choice, Vance knew that now. He was convinced of the course of action he must take, saw no other way out. His mind was steadfast, a timepiece ticking meticulously through the steps of killing Rob. Admittedly, Vance's thoughts were horrible and sickening, even painful to consider—a cluster of bruises that pulsed within his skull, having the effect of metal gears grinding through sand and rubble. But these thoughts, painful as they were... they were absolutely necessary.

When Rob pulled the Bronco to a dead stop in the forest a hundred yards off the main road, Vance stepped out and turned on his headlamp. He looked around. He took in the trees, the brush, the patches of dried grass—the entire wooded scenery— and for the first time in his life, he felt disgusted with what he saw. He didn't see, or hear, or taste, or *feel* the tranquility he had always grasped while being in nature.

What he saw was a furrowed ditch twenty yards away: a rutted scar upon the earth, an opening that waited, so it seemed, for something—or *someone*—to be placed into it. And Vance saw a crooked tree limb lying on the ground, not too far, just a few paces off. He saw that the piece of wood looked solid and stout, and was probably heavy... Heavy enough to kill, that is.

For the first time in his life Vance looked beyond the trees and the land, saw right through them, and he recognized, with exquisite horror, that he was gazing into the mouth of a crime scene. What Vance observed was nothing short of a graveyard.

CHAPTER 18

Beneath the chilled press of a dim night, the cabin stood as a hollow of comfort. The seasonal weather had changed, its touch a few degrees colder than the last time Kenny had been up here. On the floor beside him, the Coleman lantern sputtered in its effort to push away the darkness, and it gave off an insignificant amount of heat.

Their sleeping bags and pads were more than enough to keep him and Logan warm. They were both lying in the middle of the cabin's main room. Most of the cabin's outer walls had already been framed and sided, and the roof was intact. But in the back, some of the additional rooms still had windows missing, and there was a spot for a back door which had yet to be fitted. These were gaps into the night which opened the cabin's interior to a cold breeze—a breeze that breached the room and threatened the lantern every few minutes or so.

A rudimentary inspection by anyone knowledgeable would reveal that the cabin's structure was but a hodgepodge affair. The lack of a systematic approach to its construction brought a voice that seemed to permeate out from its walls, an echo that mildly irritated Kenny. He hadn't been involved with most of the work already done. More so, several hands had taken part in the raising of this building. Several disconnected minds, from various laborers to the occasional weekend effort by Kenny's brother. Results of this uncoordinated approach had left much to be desired in the way of "cleaning things up." That was Kenny's job now.

Presently, he thought his son was asleep, but wasn't too sure. It was hard to tell with Logan anymore. George, on the other hand, was curled into a ball next to the boy's head, and Kenny had heard the dog's breathing. It was very possible that Kenny was the only one awake, which would not have surprised him. There was a lot on his mind, more than the average load, now that he was up here and prepared to get to work.

Getting to work...

The thought had a nice ring to it. It had been a long time since he had a daily routine to follow. He wondered if his current life was what retirement would look like: each of his days a string of domestic chores, yet lacking any regular order, except for the basic routines consistent to a person's necessities—getting dressed, getting fed, using the bathroom. There were plenty of other things Kenny had been doing, such as raising his kids, but he looked forward to when he could get himself back on some sort of normal regimen. People were creatures of habit, after all, and since Marley had died, the only habit Kenny now had seemed to be waking up, and then suppressing his grief.

He thought about homeschooling his son. There would certainly be a regimen involved with that, but would it be a familiar one? Kenny didn't think so—not for him at least—but it would be a routine and he would get used to it.

There were other things plaguing his mind, though, keeping him from falling asleep. His son's "disability" for one, the ever-present crisis that it was, and one that Kenny had not yet fully accepted. The word itself—disability—seemed impossible to Kenny's tongue, let alone his mind. Was this his habit now—to ponder over this unspoken disability, the mental puzzle he wrestled with every night—before finally falling asleep?

And then, presently, a worry of a completely different sort: that cigarette butt smeared across the front porch. Maybe it wasn't a big deal. Kenny tried to convince himself that it wasn't, that it was probably just from the guy who'd brought the construction materials up for his brother. Something about that theory didn't sit well, though. According to Wayne, that delivery occurred almost two weeks ago. But the cigarette looked as if it had been there only a few days. Who could it have come from then? Trespassers? Or, even worse... poachers?

The thought put an uncomfortable stir into Kenny's stomach. This was private property, with signs that showed as much. Signs that read: NO TRESPASSING, and NO HUNTING. Of course, Kenny was no fool; he understood such signs did little at keeping people out. Even law-abiding citizens might feel tempted to bend a few rules when searching for the perfect hunting grounds.

He tried to push the worry out of his head by thinking about his plan for the next day. He pictured in his mind a morning list. He'd use the Coleman stove to cook sausages and eggs, toast, then some coffee. Sometimes Logan liked to drink coffee. Kenny thought he'd serve the boy a hot mug in the morning, and then let him watch and listen, as Kenny began writing up his "construction plan".

The plan would start with taking inventory of his tools as well as supplies. He'd get the generator going, just to make sure it was functional, before he got too comfortable staging his work. Then... Well, then Kenny would get to it. He knew he would first dig into finishing the cabin's framing, which he presumed would take at least a full day. Maybe less, with his son's help.

These thoughts of putting a plan into action gained in weight and became a dull heaviness inside Kenny's head. They sat like wet sand at the base of his skull, yet were oddly comforting. His thoughts ate away at the minutes and pushed the evening further into its colder depths. They coaxed Kenny into an allayed slumber, and in the morning, he'd reflect with gratitude at being able to get some sleep. But before he finally slept, that nagging worry once again reared its ugly head, as if it had to have the final word. There was something he couldn't quite shake, something about how that cigarette sat on the porch, which left a bitter feeling swimming inside his gut. He thought he could almost see how it happened, see the events that had precluded the formation of the cigarette's fate: a derelict of a man, disheveled and unclean, with a seedy stare bubbling out of his eyes as he looked through the window and into the cabin, just before dropping his smoldering butt onto the ground.

Kenny glanced over at the window, saw only a black pane of darkness that shimmered with gilded fire, the reflection of the lantern's light. It was a cold and dark night, and the lantern seemed to gloat in its brightness, robbing Kenny of that which lay in wait.

"I'll look in the morning," he whispered. Then he thought about doing this and pictured what he would see. He'd see the cabin's unfinished perimeter, and the surrounding thicket of trees. He'd see the rising hillside behind the property, and the open flat of grass spread out before the Jeep. The sloping embankment on the south side. *I'll check it out in the morning*, he thought again—his final thought. Then somewhere, sometime, after these images had diminished inside his head, Kenny slipped across the icy pavement of consciousness and fell headlong into a deep sleep.

• • •

Dawn came in what seemed like a matter of seconds. George's wet tongue awakened Kenny, lapping repeatedly across his face. "Dammit, George," he said, pushing the dog away. He was at once irritated, felt the fierceness of the morning's cold, and had to take a leak; but he just wanted to stay inside his sleeping bag.

He looked over at Logan, worried that his son might be uncomfortably cold. It was too dark to tell, yet Kenny knew that the boy wasn't restless, was perhaps sound asleep. He reached over and put his hand on Logan, checking to make sure he was still encased in his sleeping bag.

George walked circles around Kenny, whimpering. It was the coldness of the morning, putting the urge to piss onto both man and beast. "Christ, George," Kenny said, "you can just go out through the back. It's open, you know." If there were words attached to the look George gave Kenny, they would have said, *But I can't go out there without you.*

Slowly, Kenny climbed out of his sleeping bag. His body was stiff, and his muscles ached. There was a pain in his upper back, tucked deep under a shoulder blade. It was a hard sleep, as Kenny underestimated the effect that the weather would have on his body. He knew the season was yet young, that the days ahead would be colder still, much colder than he and his kids had been used to. Their first Oregon winter was fast approaching.

Immediately, his body was shivering. He quickly got dressed and found his jacket where he'd left it, hanging on a nail by the door. He put it on and zipped it up, and from a pocket in his jacket he pulled out a wool beanie, slipped that over his head. Then he opened the door and George was outside and off the porch and into the darkness, all with a display of urgency that brought a smile to Kenny's face.

Kenny took his time, despite the chill. There was something nice about the dawning of a new day while being up in the mountains. The crisp air held a silence all its own, unlike anything heard or not heard within the breast of society. Despite the cruel sharpness in the air, a bite that Kenny felt on his nose and cheeks, there was something unseen, yet pliable, about this early, mountainous dawn. Something soft and nameless that Kenny couldn't put his finger on—was, in fact, only slightly aware of. Was it something like a primordial nuance? Or perhaps the closeness that came from the caressing breath of Mother Nature?

He walked around the side of the cabin, opposite to where he'd parked the Jeep, and closest to the dirt road that led down through the canyon. He relieved himself there before walking back to the cabin. George had evidently finished with his own business, but the dog was also taking his time. He was presently sniffing the cabin's perimeter, moving back and forth along the outside wall, as if searching in haste for an elusive scent.

Then the dog barked—a single, loud bark, with its attention focused at the ground near the cornice of two walls. Kenny suspected some critter had gotten under the cabin—a raccoon, perhaps, or a badger. Stepping onto the deck, he made a mental note to flush the animal out at some point, then inspect and reinforce the cabin's skirting.

"George, come!" Kenny said with a whistle, before opening the door. Reluctantly, George followed as Kenny went back inside.

CHAPTER 19

"That was a fucking dog," Vance said. "Didn't you hear that?"

Rob hesitated. "Could've been a coyote."

"No way, man. I've heard coyotes. That bark was too deep. That was from a dog—a *big* dog."

Something caught Rob's eye in the distance, beyond the obscuring mantle of the forest. It might have been something walking on the dirt road... Or was that his imagination? Perhaps it was a dying shadow from the sinking moon, some trick of the night. The long night, as he thought about it. The long-*ass* night—which had, as yet, been composed of gathering a truck full of shit, picking up his shithead partner and then dealing with *his* shit, then driving up here—the entire, abysmally long-ass night, was now apparently unfolding into a pre-dawn encapsulated by fear. Fear because of the company of uncertainty.

"A fucking *dog*, brah," Vance repeated.

"Will you shut up already?" Rob replied. He and Vance were standing on an embankment roughly fifty feet from the dirt road. Their view down to the road was partially hidden by an assortment of vegetation, along with the darkness from the small hours of dawn. "I might have seen something," Rob added.

From a rise a hundred feet away, and above, came the hoot of an owl, and then some of the worry released from Rob's shoulders. "Just an owl," he muttered unconvincingly.

"That wasn't an owl that I heard. It was a—"

"Yeah, yeah, a fucking dog. I get it." He could feel as much as hear Vance's breathing behind him. He squeezed his hands into rock-hard fists, the impulse of insanity running like liquid fire through his veins. Sometimes Vance's cowardly ways drove Rob to the point of madness. "So you heard a dog. Big deal."

"Big deal?" Vance said.

"Yeah. Big fucking deal." But it was a big deal, Rob half admitted to himself. It was some kind of deal, at least. Fear had a solid grip on him right now, and he hated that, but for whatever reason was unwilling to accept, let alone reveal his feelings to Vance. Maybe it was the meth he'd snorted earlier, sending his adrenaline and other animalistic hormones into overdrive. He had the shakes, that was for sure—and that too could have been from the drugs.

Rob's hands were sweating, and his stomach was roiling. His scalp was itchy. His fingers tingled. And in his mind... it seemed as if the world itself had taken hold of his body, and then dangled it over a canyon—the Grand Canyon. He could almost taste the long fall waiting for him, the spiral crashing into a post-doped oblivion.

"Dude?" Vance replied. There was an incredulous tone to the guy's voice, which grated wonderfully on Rob's nerves. "I knew this was a bad idea. We shouldn't be here right now. It's getting light out, man. Fucking light out."

"Listen, you twit," Rob said, spinning around and facing Vance. "We're going up there to get our shit. I don't care about no dog, or who the hell might be up here with us. They'll just have to stay out of my way."

Vance laughed absurdly. "Oh yeah? And what if it's a sheriff? What then?"

"Then we fucking deal with it..." The subsequent minute was one long, dramatic pause. Rob pictured his words sink through Vance's thick mound of dreadlocks, through his soft, brotherly love skull, his patchouli-stunk core, and then finally come to rest, like thick bile, at the bottom of the hippie's bowels. There was dread dancing across his partner's eyes now. Rob could see it, almost made him laugh out loud. The silence of the forest took over, and he turned away and crept towards the road. "Now let's go get our weed," he added.

As far as Rob could tell, they were almost at the cabin. They had hiked a different route than the last time they'd been up here, one that Rob figured would be shorter. It kept them off the road, which both men agreed was a good idea. But it also put them in the dark about any vehicle that might drive up the canyon. Not that it mattered too much, considering how there was likely already somebody up here.

Rob didn't think that it was a sheriff, or even a forest ranger. This was private property, so he suspected something worse. In his mind, he pictured a whole gaggle of hunters now up at the cabin, cooking breakfast and drinking coffee. Taking their shits, and cleaning their guns, and getting ready for an early morning hunt... A hunt which would undoubtedly drag their fat asses right through the middle of his marijuana crop.

These thoughts temporarily provoked the anxiety which lived somewhere along Rob's spine, bringing him dangerously close to erupting into sheer panic. The feeling was riveting, and it left Rob's mouth chalky and dry. At once, he felt a pin-pricking sensation run up and down both arms, as if a host of centipedes were trapped inside his sleeves, wriggling desperately to be free. They'd bite him any fucking second now, of this he was sure. Sure as the fact that before he left this mountain, he would put a second dead man three feet into the earth.

That's right... Vance was a dead man. A dead man walking.

Maybe Rob wouldn't stop there. Maybe, when he arrived upon the scene of the cabin and saw those hunters, those men, sitting around a campfire, drinking their coffee, he'd walk right up and get the drop on them. Put a bullet into each of their fat skulls before they knew what hit them. Maybe he'd do it like that, just maybe. Sure, things would become drastically more complex, but at least then he'd be rid of the terrible uncertainty plaguing him at the moment.

And then suddenly, Rob had another thought, a gorgeously pristine thought. One that bloomed with the effect of abrupt violence inside his head, like the bursting of the sky on the fourth of July. He would pin the murders on Vance... his *partner*. Now, wouldn't that be breathtaking? A masterful plan, a fucking work of art. *A goddamned Picasso.*

Rob thought about this new plan of his as he moved cautiously through the forest, step by step, adding one detail to another. And of these details, shit, they were as simple as getting high. So simple, Rob could hardly believe it. The details would go like this: shoot whoever was up there; club Vance to death like the fucking furry mammal that he was; stage some kind of "scuffle scene"; wipe his prints off his gun, press the cold steel into Vance's cold palm. Then, Rob would leave a bag of freshly cut buds somewhere nearby, the criminal glue to his plot. This would give the local authorities something familiar to chew on, would leave a definite, comfortable flavor in their mouths. They'd certainly look around and find the harvest location. And, they'd likely put two-and-two together and conclude that, sure, the dead hippie had himself a partner. But they'd never figure out who his partner was.

Or would they?

Would they...?

Once again, the uncertainty took hold of Rob, was an icy knot in the pit of his stomach. He felt the sudden urge to shit (maybe that was the meth running its course) but his nerves were shot, nonetheless. All of the fucking sudden, the brilliance of his plan seemed to grow smaller in scope, as the seeds of doubt broke through the surface of his thoughts. Confusion struck him with the effect of a ball peen hammer, blunt-force trauma ringing inside his head. The centipedes were once again on the warpath, scrabbling for escape. Rob had no fucking clue what to do.

And so, he was a bit surprised—pleasantly so—when he and Vance at last came upon the cabin and discovered that the place was deathly quiet. Quiet as a graveyard. Cricket-chirping quiet.

"Check it out," Rob said. He could see clearly the outline of a Jeep Wrangler parked at the side, next to the end of the porch. And he could see what appeared to be a person moving around inside the cabin. Only one person, perhaps more—but certainly not a bunch of rowdy hunters with rifles. And certainly no sheriff. He didn't see anybody he couldn't handle, if it came to that. The observation sat well with Rob and seemed to rub away some of that dreaded uncertainty.

"Christ," Vance said. "We're fucked, brah!" The sound of panic coming from Vance's mouth was clear as whiskey to Rob's ear.

"Whatever," Rob whispered, suddenly aware of what he'd forgotten to do. Reaching down to his pack, he unzipped the top pocket and pulled out a shoulder holster containing his Browning High Power. He backed away a few steps, leaving Vance to stare panic-stricken at the cabin. Then Rob wriggled into the holster and took the gun out.

"This shit is fucked," Vance said. "*Dude*—we are fucked!"

Rob pulled the slide on his gun, chambering a round. The sound of the action echoed into the darkness, was coldly hollow, and rang with impending dread. "*Dude*," Rob said, mockingly, "you might be fucked. But I'm not."

CHAPTER 20

He heard the gun before he saw it. The metal clack of the slide, slamming a round into the chamber, put a wet, nauseous feeling straight into Vance's gut. He knew little about guns, wanted nothing to do with them, in fact. But he knew enough to understand what he'd just heard. Anybody would have understood that sound.

Of course, it wasn't the gun itself that summoned absolute dread upon Vance's mindset, as he'd seen many pot-growers toting guns down in Southern Humboldt. It was the uncertainty—or presumed *certainty*, rather—of his partner's intentions.

What Vance didn't know was what he should do now. How should he respond? Should he say something? For once, he didn't think that opening his mouth would lighten up the situation. Perhaps he should run? Maybe his drug-induced partner was at last ready to kill him, like Vance had predicted all along.

In the end, Vance didn't do or say anything. He turned. He stared at Rob. Then he stood in silence. He watched passively, with brittle knees and clammy hands. He observed his partner standing there with a gun in hand, his attention twitching like a bird's head, and with eyes that skipped randomly while bleeding suspicion. Vance watched with rising, tingling hair at the back of his neck as Rob holstered the gun and moved forward.

"Let's go," Rob said, and he brushed past Vance. There was a foul aura that seemed to come off the man, a black, stinking cloud of sorts. Vance felt a chill run down his spine, and down his legs, making his feet feel like blocks of concrete. "Come on!" Rob repeated.

They skirted the outside perimeter of the cabin and made their way to the opposite side, and to the hillside beyond. When they found the tree line and entered it, Vance's pulse slowed, the primal urge of concealment cutting a bit of slack off his tension. It was only the mildest of comforts, however. Nothing about his current situation was even remotely reassuring. Rob had a gun, and he likely had murder on his mind. And Vance knew without a doubt just how foolish their actions were, traipsing out here in the soon-to-be broad daylight. Finally, down there in that cabin was at least one other human being—probably a hunter—who had a dog with him. Of all things, a fucking dog!

Vance paused briefly and studied the cabin. The small building sat on a western slope, was still coated in deep shadow. Yet the promise of another bright day loomed on the horizon. It was in the very air, this very moment—a sense of fullness. A sense of life: the sound of roosted birds whistling out of their sleep; the soft rustle of the earth, with its small things moving through foliage and grounded leaves. The dawning breeze, with its fresh breath hinting at the new day to come.

Vance stood in the dark cover of the forest and heard and felt these things. The entire world was waking up. Unhindered, the world was coming back to life, and this brought for Vance a maddening thought. There was nothing positive he could determine about this day's "promise".

Soon enough, whoever was down there in that cabin would also become fully awake—if they weren't already. The dog bark was still fresh in his memory, was now a warm tremor at the front of his mind, taking shape as he looked at the cabin below. He could almost picture the invisible scene from moments ago:

some guy staggering outside to take a piss, along with his dog. Maybe he then lit a cigarette and smoked it for a while, as he stared out into the woods, wondering what might be out there creeping about. Vance was sure the scene went something along those lines.

Then he wondered if that person, or persons, would be the catalyst for his doom. Or would his doom simply come from the hands of Rob after they finished up with the harvest?

"Hey," Rob whispered, "hurry the fuck up."

Vance turned and followed his partner further into the trees. Half-mindedly, he counted his steps as he went. Only two hundred yards away was their scene—not nearly far enough to conceal any full-weighted sound. Although Vance was sure that he could remain stealthy while harvesting, he was less certain about Rob. But none of that would matter if whoever it was in that cabin came across their harvest. *How are we not doomed?* Vance asked himself. *How am I not doomed?*

Then, if Vance was so doomed—or at least destined to be— what was stopping him from taking corporeal action right now? This very moment, in fact, with Rob in front of him, his back turned toward Vance...

"Just cut and bag," Rob said, turning suddenly, looking Vance square in the eyes. They were now almost upon the scene. Vance could already smell the earthy tang of the ripened buds, their distinct aroma a thin veneer in the morning air. "That's the plan, man," continued Rob. "Cut and bag. And then we high-tail it out of here. Shouldn't take more than an hour."

Vance couldn't help but run the minutes in his head. He knew from experience that an hour was an absurdly short amount of time for the number of plants they had. He also knew that they wouldn't be able to get their entire crop back to the Bronco on a single trip. Furthermore, at such a fast pace, the need for delicacy while harvesting would get tossed—especially from the likes of Rob. And without delicacy, they were bound to damage the precious bud resin—which would translate to a damaged product. That would add one more factor to the diminishment of their profits. Vance felt a warming sensation at the base of his neck, below his ears, at the thought of following Rob's ignorant lead with the flippant harvesting of such wonderful agricultural specimens. But then, conversely, *coldly*, he was also reminded of the fact that, considering being discovered by some hunter, or just plain *dead*, any form of harvesting would be a moot point.

When they broke the line of trees on the south side of the mountain, Vance caught sight of a faint outline on the far horizon, a violet hue fracturing the deepened end of the distant sky. The dawn was on the rise. The cusp of daybreak was yet to reveal itself, but it would soon be here. Too soon.

The air was crisp and cold. Vance tasted dew on his lips, felt the weight of the night's death seep heavily into his dreadlocks. Despite this, he felt like he was burning up, as if there was a fire raging somewhere in his bowels, cooking him from the inside out.

"Cut and bag," Rob said again, just before he dropped his large duffle bag onto the ground. His eyes were roving orbs, scanning and preening the scenery—a motorcade in sync with his body, which was itself in a constant state of senseless gestures. The dude was fucking tweaking, Vance observed. He could even hear the guy breathing. "I'll take the high road," Rob continued, making eye contact with Vance, "and you can start down below."

Vance glanced down the hill, which was still mostly dark, a blanket of shadow. He hesitated, thinking about what to say, how to phrase his words, knowing just how close he was to the precipice of Rob's unpredictable temper.

Or, more precisely, the precipice of uncertainty. "Shouldn't we stick together?" he finally asked.

"Fuck that," Rob said. "I don't want you over my shoulder telling me what to do."

"Well," Vance said, cautiously, "try not to be rough when you cut 'em. The buds are fragile, man."

"See what I mean?" Rob replied. Then, in a tone both humorous and questionable: "Fragile? Yeah, alright, I'll be careful. *Real* fucking careful." He reached down, unzipped the duffle and pulled out a pair of pruning shears.

Vance didn't stick around to watch his partner butcher their crop. He zigzagged down the hillside a good hundred yards below, weaving through their patches, instinctively scrutinizing the state of every plant he passed. It was still hard to see with the lack of daylight, but Vance knew what he was looking for. He'd trained his eyes through countless hours of laboring over and handling the end product of the marijuana plant. This wasn't counting the many hours he'd spent daydreaming over the perfect bud. In passing, and in the dark, he could both analyze and evaluate the many hanging colas. And his appraisal, as he crept down that hill, was enough to have him salivating like Pavlov's dog. Even with the premise of murder—that of his, or Rob's—lying heavy in the air, Vance couldn't help but get excited. Standing amid such ripe greenery always had that effect on him.

Minutes later, he reached the bottom of the scene, then set his duffle bag down. He unzipped the bag. Inside were several plastic trash bags and a pair of shears. He took the shears and stuffed them in his back pocket. Then he opened the trash bags and spread them inside the duffle, to be used as liners between the bud stems—which, sadly, he didn't think was going to help that much.

Behind him, and off to his right, the sky finally cracked open, sending out a trickle of orange fire against the plum horizon. That too, Vance observed with sadness.

He could see most of his surroundings now, albeit vaguely. The hillside above was a charcoal canvas, sketched darker by the piercing caps of their cash crop. This spectacle brought about his final thought—and yes, crazy as it seemed, the saddest of them all—before Vance went to it. The thought was the impending insignificance of all his hard work. It was the irrelevance of his knowledge, and all of his time, soon to be wasted by the loser hacking away up there on the hill above him. Or worse: the sudden interjection of a hunter from the cabin.

Vance's thoughts were sad, and infuriating, and rife with questions both oblique and unanswerable. And there was nothing he could do about them. With a pair of Fiskars in his hand and the lid of the sun behind him, Vance went to work. He jumped right in and started harvesting, as fast as humanly possible, his first marijuana plant of that morning.

CHAPTER 21

In desperate need of a wood-burning stove, the cabin's interior was only a few degrees warmer than outside. Coldness sat everywhere, its ghostlike presence hanging in the air with each breath, clinging to the unfinished walls and on the soft wooden floor. Kenny shivered, then squatted and lit the lantern. He picked it up, its flame sputtering and crackling against the morning chill, and he hung it from a nail he'd put into a ceiling joist the night before. The room blossomed with contradictory light, one that was cold, yet inviting, hinting at a touch of warmth.

Momentarily, Kenny thought about his daughter. Jolie would still be asleep, laying in the bed next to Laney, her cousin. She'd spent the night engaged in exhaustive play, he was sure. Today would be no different. If her three cousins didn't keep the girl busy, her aunt would. It was an amiable thought for Kenny, as he knew his daughter would enjoy both the maternal and feminine qualities that his brother's house always provided.

A sense of guilt writhed inside of Kenny at the reminder of him raising his daughter without a wife—without a mother. It was just one of the many shades of guilt that had plagued him recently, and one that Beth had inherently kept buoyant. Speaking of guilt, Kenny now felt a tinge of regret for snapping at his brother's wife only the day before. He told himself she had it coming, but such a harsh rebuke was so out of character for Kenny, so against the grain of his personality.

Thinking back, he thought he understood the catalyst for his unexpected emotional outburst, other than the immediate, insulting comments from the woman. The catalyst was the steady pressure Beth had been putting against him. Like a sculptor, she had been chipping away at Kenny since he'd first moved up there, cutting into, and shaping the foundation of his person, until at last, he'd cracked. Thinking again of his daughter, he hoped Beth wouldn't take out anything unspent onto the girl. Then, feeling foolish, Kenny dismissed this idea. He knew the woman was beyond such petty backlashes. Once again, and like the contradicting emissions from the lantern above, Kenny felt both guilty and comforted.

Logan rustled slowly in his sleeping bag, evidently coming out of a world of dreams. At once, George was at the boy's side, burrowing himself into the sleeping bag, attempting to get warm, or so it seemed. The result was the complete waking of Logan, who then sat up and rubbed knuckles into his eyes. The boy blinked and looked around, a slim aspect of confusion floating in his stare.

It was moments like these that put an awful dagger into Kenny's ribcage. Here was when any other kid would say something, anything. Give a grunt against mild discomfort; or perhaps squeak amusingly, to the waking inside of a cabin, at the elbow of a mountain, in what was clearly a brand new day. *Say something—anything*, Kenny thought.

Then, with odd amusement, Kenny wondered if, while in his sleep, or in the clutch of silence, as the rest of the world was but a fog of white noise, were things any different for his son? Were they perhaps more real? Did the boy still speak in his mind? Did he replay conversations he'd heard earlier, filling in words left unsaid, answering all those questions asked in silence, or maybe asked with volume, a thousand times over? Also, was it possible for the boy to wake up one day and simply forget that he hadn't said a word in almost six months? Was it? Just wake up into a world that had forgotten about the whole damn nightmare. And then, after what would certainly be such a brilliant maneuver brought on by the dawn, would Logan simply move forward, retrieving the distant past and placing it ahead of him, granting the world around him with the normal provisions of childhood, letting everyone watch in bafflement at this innocence, as it chugged forward, one mile at a time, with all its glorious comments and complaints. With its laughter. Christ, even with its crying.

"We're gonna get started after breakfast." Kenny said. He gathered Logan's clothes and handed them to the boy, who took them without looking, his eyes staring low. "Did you get some good sleep?"

Logan made a slight gesture with his shoulders, a fragile shrug, then started petting George's head.

Kenny sighed, stood up and went to a corner of the room, which contained an ice chest and other supplies. He set up a camp stove and small table, then opened the ice chest and got out the breakfast ingredients—sausage and eggs, and a plastic bag of pre-mixed pancake mix. He put two cast-iron skillets on the grill and warmed his hands from the expanding heat. In the minutes that passed, Logan had gotten dressed, and then went outside with George. They were still out there by the time the food was ready, so Kenny called the boy in after serving their breakfast on paper plates. Then he made coffee.

They ate sitting on the floor. Logan finished one pancake and started another before setting his plate down.

"You should eat some eggs," Kenny said. "Your body needs protein."

Logan put his interest on a far wall, as if deep in study, before peeling away from his dad. He crawled on hands and knees, slow and creature-like, back to his sleeping bag.

"Don't get too comfortable," Kenny said, rising from the floor. He took their plates and went outside, threw them in the fire pit at the side of the house. The sun was beyond the horizon now, a godly orb shedding radiant tears across the void of space and onto the land. There was still little warmth, and Kenny swung his arms side to side, exercising to heat himself, as he remained outside and began the day's work.

He built a crude worktable, using plywood and sawhorses, and on this, he mounted a ten-inch, powered miter saw. He uncoiled a hundred-foot extension cord, ran it from the table to the generator at the back of the house. Then he picked through and gathered two-by-fours for most of twenty minutes, the small perfectionist in him presenting itself for a most pointless endeavor.

When he caught himself belaboring the task at hand and identified its ridiculousness (for he was only preparing to add framing to the cabin, not a finished product), he dropped a board to the ground and went back inside.

He found Logan still in the sleeping bag, George curled beside him. "Come on, Logan," Kenny said, "let's go. Get your shoes back on and come on out. You can help me."

He prodded the boy a few more times while he cleaned up and put away the breakfast ingredients.

Minutes later and they were outside standing on the cold earth, looking at lumber. "Here," Kenny said, "put these on." He gave Logan a pair of leather gloves that engulfed the boy's hands when he slid them on. "Never handle lumber without them, unless you want a splinter, or a good pinch... Now then, grab four boards and lean them against the table." Kenny gestured to a stack of lumber and then watched as his son slowly bent to his instruction.

After the boy had finished, Kenny motioned for him to follow, and they walked over behind the house to the generator presently covered with a brown tarp. Kenny pulled the tarp away, then stepped back, half-expecting a creature of some sort to jump out in protest.

"Fold that up," he said, gesturing at the tarp. He handed Logan a ball of twine and an Exacto knife. "Use this to cut some twine and tie up the tarp after you fold it."

Doubt lingered in Logan's eyes as he looked at Kenny.

"I know, it ain't a big deal," Kenny added, "but it's good practice. Besides, if a wind kicks up, it could damage the tarp."

Kenny checked the gas in the generator before starting it up. The mountain's hollow captured the dull growl of the motor, rolled it like a stone marble around the cabin, against the adjacent hillside and surrounding tree line. The sound was riveting against the quiet morning. George came snooping by, but shortly after, Kenny watched as the dog disappeared down the road leading to the cabin.

Minutes later, Kenny tested a few cuts on a piece of scrapped board. The miter saw howled in the wilderness. He made Logan stand and watch to see how it was done, and when he finished, Kenny said, "You never mess around with this tool, son. It'll cut you before you know what happened." Logan nodded, then turned to see George sprint past, hackles stiff as horsehair.

Kenny watched the dog run across the opposite end of the field, and into the tree line fencing the hillside. It could've been a coyote, or even a deer, but Kenny worried also that it was something much larger, and much more dangerous. He tried to put the thought out of his head and went back to work with Logan at his side. His son had to be learning something, and Kenny focused on this.

They made cuts according to the spec sheet Kenny had written out. Stacks of trimmed two-by-fours had been lined out on the porch, waiting now to be included in the cabin's framing. Logan had been designated as the organizer of this wood, so he placed them in neat rows, matching them to their lengths. He'd been practicing with a measuring tape when Kenny walked up, carrying a portable Skil saw, and dragging the extension cord. "We're gonna be cutting in here now." He handed Logan a pair of earmuffs. "Hang on to these—it'll get loud."

But Kenny didn't make any cuts right away. He got busy with laying out the two-by-fours in the other rooms, sizing them up, and pre-fitting them into place. Then he got busy with taking window measurements, and that got him thinking about windows in particular, and he tried to recall which type his brother had in order.

And it wasn't until after several more thoughts had passed when Kenny observed his son was no longer at his side.

CHAPTER 22

Amazingly, Vance hadn't panicked when they heard the rumble of the generator, followed by the high-pitched whine of the miter saw. Neither had Rob. The Prospect knew what tools sounded like, and he knew the sound of steel shearing through wood. It was a sound that took him back to his high-school days, when he used to smoke weed in the bathroom during wood shop class. Such a simple life back then. He wondered if his hippie partner had a similar history. It would explain why the smelly Rastaman hadn't dropped shit and run once all that racket climbed up into the morning.

Either way, some explanations were now coming together, bringing with them a small sense of relief for Rob. That was no hunter down there, he realized. Just some dude fixing things up. Rob recalled his earlier observations of the cabin, how it still looked raw and incomplete. Vaguely, he remembered seeing the tarps outside, to the rear of the building. Probably set there to cover up lumber, or that generator he now heard. Yes, things *were* making sense to him now, despite the centipedes still crawling under his sleeves, and the raging fire burning under his skin.

Rob had other problems to consider. His duffle bag was full, and he'd only harvested a few plants. Sure, this might be what people call a "good" problem, but he was looking beyond the fact of having too much weed to sell. Rob wanted to get off this mountain, dammit. He wanted to be done with this shit. He wanted to load up the Bronco, drive his K-bar through Vance's spine, and then get the fuck out of Dodge.

But there was no way in hell he was leaving without the entire crop. And that meant one thing: that they would need to make more than one trip back up here. Which meant one more chance to run into whomever it was working down at that cabin. And then one more opportunity for that dog to catch a whiff of him and his stinking partner. One more shot at having this fucked up situation get fucked up beyond all repair.

Rob chewed his lip and scratched his palms, and picked at a scab on his elbow as he stared at the duffle bag on the ground. He couldn't even zip the damn thing up. It was that full. He caught movement in the corner of his eye and looked down the hill. Vance was climbing toward him, his own bag slung heavily over his shoulder.

"I ain't got any more room," Rob said, just as Vance met up with him.

"No shit," Vance replied. He lowered his bag to the ground and reached back to retie his dreadlocks. "I tried telling you. We're fucked if—"

"Yeah, yeah," Rob cut him off. "I get it. We're fucked and all. *Doomed*. Quit your damn preaching already. Let's just haul this shit back to the truck."

Vance gave him an icy look. "Dude, we're gonna get busted if we go down there right now. We need to sit tight and wait it out."

"Wait?" Rob gave his partner an incredible stare. "What the fuck are we gonna wait for?"

"Dude, we need to wait until it gets dark again."

Rob laughed. "You're fucking nuts, *brah*. That's a whole day." He shook his head. "I ain't waiting a whole day to finish this shit."

"Dude, we're nuts if we don't," Vance protested. "Like I've been trying to tell you, man, this whole thing is insane." He turned and pointed across the open hillside to the tree line beyond. "We need to go over there and wait it out. Shit, we can get some sleep, and then finish the job tonight."

Rob was disgusted. "*Shut up*, you damn pussy... I'm done with your bitch talk. And who the hell's gonna bust us, anyway?" He tapped the grip of his gun. "Out here... man, this is the fucking law. The fucking law, and I'm wearing it." He bent down and gripped his bag. "Now help me zip this fucker up so we can get moving."

Rob fought with the zipper for several seconds, closing the bag most of the way. He got little help from Vance, who seemed to move stiffly, as if he was a distant cousin to the trees out here.

"That's good enough," Rob said, and then he slid his arms through the looped handles of the bag, effectively donning it like a backpack. Vance did the same, and then Rob spoke quietly. "We'll go downhill before we cross the cabin. Should be far enough away."

The morning sun had long since crested the horizon. The surrounding air had become less cold by a few degrees. And the waking hour was now on the retreat, cuffing at the heels of twilight's shadow. Rob took in a lungful of air, then suppressed the urge to cough and hack. His body felt weighted down, as if the duffle bag, his clothes, even his skin, were all packed with half a ton of stone. Mr. Rob Boyle was coming off his recent high, and fuck if he didn't want to murder someone right now. He began a slow, angled route that led down the hill and through the tree line. He took ten steps before he heard the growl.

Now both men went stiff. Rob stared at the dog, which he saw to be a large, Golden Retriever. It didn't look particularly menacing. Its growl was perhaps a mild warning. But one could never tell with dogs. And should it bark, well then, things would become more complicated. The dog stood between two trees, not more than twenty feet away, its stare rebounding off the two men.

Slowly, Rob slid his duffle bag off his back and placed it on the ground. He could hear Vance behind him, panic-stricken, his breath laboring for air. "Easy, now," Rob said, squatting down, his words meant for both the dog and his useless partner. He stretched a hand out and affected a mild tone to his voice. "Come here, boy," he said, then clicked his tongue.

"Dude, what the hell are you doing?" Vance said.

"Come here," Rob repeated. He made a slight whistle and watched as the dog's tail gradually wagged. The creature put its nose to the ground but kept narrow eyes on the men, and slowly the retriever paced forward, wary, yet curious.

"*Dude*," Vance squeaked.

By the time the dog met Rob, it was in full spirits, the back half of its body pendulous with motion. There was brightness in the dog's eyes, and its tongue was a shift of violence, lashing wantonly across Rob's fingers.

"That's a good boy," Rob said, taking the dog into his arms, patting its ribcage.

"What the fuck now, brah?" Vance said, impatiently.

Rob wasted no time. As he smoothed the dog's fur with one hand, he retrieved his K-bar with the other. With a violent thrust, he plunged the blade deep into the dog's neck, and pushed the creature to the ground, sat on it, and it fought back for three or four seconds, yipping and biting, licking, before all the air seemed to escape it in one long, agonizing draft.

"Shit!" Vance cried. Panic shrilled in his voice. "I can't believe you just did that. What the fuck, man?" It seemed as if the Rastaman was about to come loose and retaliate. He was grasping at the side of his head, terror rising, then bleeding out of his eyes. But then Vance went mysteriously quiet.

"Now," Rob said, resignation heavy in his voice, "we don't have to worry about this damn dog anymore."

As if in the breast of a dark and sudden storm, the ambient life of the wilderness collapsed. The surrounding forest grew three shades darker, and it pitched itself headlong into a deathlike calm. The trees lost all their life—no birds, and no wind—and they became stone pillars with grim faces and ragged skin.

In the eerie silence, Rob withdrew his knife and wiped it across the dog's fur, cleaning the blade. He sheathed it and stood, situated the duffle bag across his back once again, and resumed his route down the mountain.

He took two steps before he saw the boy.

CHAPTER 23

Rob watched as the child's entire face went flaccid. It was as if the boy had lived through his dog's death. His eyes glazed over, and under his dark shock of hair, his face turned to pure alabaster. His body lurched backward, and then he stumbled against a tree, half his life pouring out of him.

"Hey, get that—little—kid!" Rob said, his words tripping over themselves. He made a move toward the boy, but then the boy snapped out of it. His eyelids blinked, and he turned and ran. "Son of a bitch—get him!"

Rob dropped his duffle bag and took off in pursuit. Everything moved so fast, the world and time at once cohorts against him. The forest clipped past in a state of slow animation, the colors of earth and foliage fusing together. He chased the boy along the side of the hill, through a forest of oak and pine, and in line with a slight, downward grade. Rob felt the run in his knees, which protested with cold fire, and threatened to buckle. He tripped and stumbled, caught himself on a tree branch. The boy was too fast; there was no gaining on him. But there was no choice, either. Rob had to catch up. He *would* catch up.

The boy was a fleeting shadow now, but Rob knew where he was heading. He kept running, his breath heavy as his lungs heaved for air. A few seconds later and the darkness of the forest receded. The light of the imminent meadow was quickly taking over, and Rob spotted one side of the cabin, and then a sliver of the Jeep Wrangler. He slowed to a fast walk, and oddly, this was when he heard the boy's stomping feet slap onto the packed earth of the meadow, just as the kid raced past the tree line. Then Rob heard the man's voice.

"What's the matter, Logan?"

No reply came from the boy, no words spoken, just a muffled sob.

"What is it?" the man repeated.

Rob stepped into the clearing, and both men made eye contact. He knew at once that there would be no friendly discourse between the two of them, and was mildly relieved from this. With a lazy swagger, he walked toward the man, drew his pistol and brought it level to the stranger's eyes.

"Now, now," Rob said, "don't you do anything stupid."

"What's this about?" the man asked, raising his hands.

Rob didn't reply. He studied the man carefully while crossing the distance between them.

"What are you doing here?" the man said. "We don't want any trouble."

"It doesn't matter what you want," Rob replied, looking around. "You got anybody else up here? Or is it just the two of you? And don't you fucking lie to me." He turned his head and made a quick glance over his shoulder, keeping his gun sighted on the man. His finger rested on the trigger, deadly in its position because no one had taught Rob otherwise. His arm, stretched out in front of him and holding the pistol, shook. Where was his damn partner? He hoped Vance hadn't run off, but wouldn't be surprised if the hippie had.

"No, there's nobody else out here," the man said. "Just the two of us—and my dog. But he doesn't bite... So why don't you lower that gun, mister?"

"Why don't you shut your trap?" Rob said. Then he yelled toward the tree line. "Hey, Vance! Get your ass down here, you damn bastard!" He looked again at the man, and what was obviously his son. The boy was tucked close to his father, his body pressed into him, sobbing.

"Now," Rob began, but then stopped. Half a dozen scenes from various movies and television shows replayed in his mind. Scenes where a bad man was imposing his will onto innocents through brute force, or the threat of deadly harm. The images irritated him, and provoked a series of white flashes at the front of his skull, behind his eyes. He told himself he wasn't a bad man. Just a Prospect trying to tie up some loose ends. Something to that effect.

He heard the snap of a branch, turned and spotted Vance slowly creep out of the forest. His partner's face was sickly pale, and it again reminded Rob of the Rastaman's nauseating cowardice. Vance was loaded down, his duffle bag strapped to his back, along with Rob's bag in his hands. He moved with the gait of a small child approaching a drunk and angry father. "Just get the fuck over here," Rob said impatiently.

Vance said nothing as he cleared the meadow, but when he stopped next to Rob, he whispered, "You've gone way too far, man."

"I don't fucking care," Rob snapped. "We're getting our business done with. Then we'll get the fuck out of here. Besides, I'm tired of worrying about who else is up here. Now we know."

"Look, mister," the man said, raising his hands, "like I said, we don't want any trouble. How about you and your friend do whatever it is you're out here for, and then just leave? We'll keep out of your way."

"Don't get any stupid ideas, and maybe that's how it'll work out." Rob turned to Vance. "Put the duffle bags in the Jeep. Then find some more bags—I don't care what, just something to carry our crop with."

Vance hesitated for a moment before walking over to the Jeep. He placed the duffle bags in the back and went into the cabin.

"Logan, where's George?" the man said quietly, looking down at his son.

"What'd you say?" Rob asked.

"George is my dog, that's all. A Golden Retriever."

Rob paused long enough to weigh the man's words. He wondered how the boy would respond. Sometime, on a different day perhaps, in a different situation, Rob suspected he would've felt sorry for killing the dog. Even sorry for the kid. But on this day, things were much too complicated for any such feelings to get in the way. "Go on, kid," Rob said, a bold tone to his voice, "why don't you tell him? Tell your dad where your dog is."

There was a rift of silence that stretched across the meadow for two or three long minutes, broken finally by Vance stumbling out of the cabin. "This'll work," he said, holding a brown canvas tarp and a length of twine.

Rob glanced briefly at his partner, and then looked back at the man with his kid, studying them. He read the man's face and could tell that the man now suspected the worst about his dog. "Go on, tell him," Rob said, smirking.

"He can't talk," the man said.

Rob's smile faded. "What do you mean?"

"I mean, my son doesn't talk. He can't."

Rob heard a challenge in the man's voice, chuckled, and accepted it. "Well then, I guess I'll just have to speak on the boy's behalf." He smiled again, musing over the cleverness of his words. "You're right; your dog doesn't bite... Not anymore, that is." Then he laughed.

At this, the boy visibly clutched closer to his dad, squeezing him. Rob noticed the boy's response and said, "He can hear, though, which is good, since I hate to repeat myself." He motioned toward the cabin with his gun. "So don't make me. Go on, now, let's go see what's inside."

They walked to the deck in front of the cabin. Vance had the tarp laid out, and was using a pocket knife to slice it in half. He still looked as if he'd seen the waking of a ghost. His eyes were full, on the brink of yawning, yawning with terror, so it seemed. He was moving quickly; the implication being that the sooner he finished, the sooner he'd be out of this mess.

"Any more of that string?" Rob said, referring to the length of twine lying next to the tarp.

Vance motioned with his head. "Inside. There's a spool."

"Get it," Rob said. "We'll deal with that tarp in a minute—soon as we deal with these two." Tying up the man and his son was exactly what Rob was thinking of doing—for now. It would be a quick solution to the problem these people posed. But in the back of his head, Rob was still thinking of the other solution—the one he'd concocted earlier, while standing in the dark, staring at the cabin, and thinking it was filled with eager hunters.

And in his mind, Rob played scenes of other movies he'd watched, ones with more drastic scenarios; ones with graphic endings. His thoughts still irritated him, perhaps even more now, since he heard that challenging—and yes, *judging*—tone in the man's voice. In one sentence, Rob realized the man had both challenged and judged him, and nothing pissed Rob off more than being judged by his peers. Sure, it rankled him, thanks to his thoughts. But there was something that trumped these irritating notions. Rob was a Prospect, dammit. And he had loose ends needing to get tied.

CHAPTER 24

Vance folded the knife and put it in his pocket. He stood and followed Rob and their prisoners into the cabin.

Yes... their *prisoners*.

That's exactly what that man and his son were, weren't they? The thought left Vance feeling legitimately sick. His stomach slipped and his mouth watered. He felt a heavy compression deep in his knees and his spine, as if his body were being crushed by a hydraulic press, the kind they used to turn cars into neat little cubes. He honestly felt like he was going to hurl.

"Get in there and get that fucking twine," Rob said. "Leave the damn tarp for later."

Slowly, Vance stepped past the man and his son, and walked into the cabin. He swore he could smell the fear coming off the boy, and he felt another rapid twinge of guilt. In Jah's name, what had he gotten himself into?

The man and his son followed Vance into the cabin, prodded along by Rob and his pistol. Vance retrieved the spool of twine from the tool-bag on the floor. He saw a roll of duct tape inside as well, then, still traumatized with guilt, was struck with an idea. "Why don't we use this instead?" he said, picking up the tape. "Twine will hurt the kid. Besides, this is stronger."

"Hey, I don't need your damn input. Just tie them up. And use what I told you to."

Vance dropped the tape into the bag. He approached the man from behind, then hesitated. "Christ, dude," he said, lifting his hands in exasperation, "I don't know how to tie a person up."

"Just tie them!" Rob snapped. "It ain't that hard. Like tying your damn shoes." He used his gun to motion at the man again. "Go sit over there by the wall—and get your back against it!"

"So we're just going to tie them up and leave them here?" Vance said. "Is that the plan?" The thought that Rob was about to kill these poor people crossed Vance's mind, and a rush of horror flooded his body.

"No, wait," Rob said. "I got a better idea." He reached into his pocket and pulled out a cigarette, clumsily lit it with one hand, his pistol-bearing hand still aiming at the man and his son. "No point in being discreet anymore," he said, referring to his cigarette. "You two get up now. You're coming with us."

Vance looked at Rob. His mind was battling against both fear and confusion. "What for?" he asked. *"Now* what?"

"You're just stupid, aren't you?" Rob said. "We leave them here while we finish our work. Then his friends show up to help him with this place... find him and the boy tied up." He looked again at the man. "Get up, I said. You're coming with us."

"What are we going to do," Vance said, "tie them up at the scene?"

"Damn right we are."

At least he hadn't killed them yet, Vance told himself. But he was certain it was an imminent possibility. Both the man and his son had seen their faces, and Rob had loudly spoken Vance's name, and already that was too much information to let slide. If Rob was smart enough to think about the risks that were now on the table, fully exposed—and Vance suspected his partner *was* smart enough, despite being a full-blown tweaker—then without question, or hesitation, Rob would need to kill these two innocents. It was a possibility—a *certainty*—that Vance simply could not ignore. Now, more than ever, he needed to be done with Rob. He needed to kill the bastard.

The man and his son stood and walked out the door. Rob led them past the meadow and to the tree line, then shouted back at Vance, "Bring the tarp and that twine... and whatever else we need. And hurry the hell up."

Quickly, Vance finished cutting the tarp and then folded the two pieces together, making them smaller to carry. He stuck the spool of twine in his sweatshirt pocket and went back inside the cabin to look for anything else he could use. Despite Rob's objection, he grabbed the roll of duct tape and stuffed it between the two tarps. He scanned the room, searching for something useful, but his mind was too fogged up to concentrate. He was stuck on how he should kill Rob. And what would happen after he did, what he would do with their prisoners. He'd let them go, that's for sure. There was no way in hell Vance would kill these people. Fuck it; he would take his chances on them now, knowing who he was. Perhaps, after he took out Rob, and when he let them go, he could explain to them how this was all one big mistake.

Vance realized his hands were shaking—as he contemplated murder. He'd been thinking about it for a while, but with things now dramatically more complicated, the time to act was obviously now. Or should he wait until they finished up with the harvest?

The sense of guilt came back, rolling through his body like a strong tide. Shit. He was going to string this man and his son out, along with their terror, and let them suffer for the day, while he used Rob to finish the job.

Guilt? Fuck yeah.

But then again, why shouldn't he consider finishing up with the scene? This was his chance, his one and only opportunity, to move back to Humboldt and get a piece of property. A slice of the American pie overlooking the Eel River, and along a southern slope, smack dab in the middle of nowhere. It would be *Vance's* property, with *his* house and *his* piece of land—all for growing. The home of his dreams. And besides, wasn't it also quite possible for this whole damn nightmare to end on a positive note, end happily, with him sticking it to Rob just as soon as that son of a bitch clipped off the last ganja stem? And before Rob exhaled his last breath, Vance would be sure to tell him just how much of an asshole the guy was.

It was all too much to think about. Vance walked out of the cabin, the inside of his head flashing patches of black and white, a lightning storm of hope and guilt and squeamish fear. He still felt like throwing up, but also, his stomach rumbled, as he hadn't eaten a damn thing since that burrito, hours ago. Not that he cared, considering he had no appetite for anything other than being done with this mess.

And Vance *was* going to be done with it.

He stopped at the Jeep and opened up his duffle bag, lying in the back. He wiggled his hand into the bag, careful not to damage the precious buds anymore than they already had been. He found the steak knife and pulled it out, slid it into his sweatshirt pocket. Just a few more hours, he told himself. A few more hours of Rob, and all his bullshit, and his terrorizing of innocent people. A few more hours of hard labor, and the picking of the harvest…

Just a few more hours, that was all, and then Vance would go home.

CHAPTER 25

Kenny wondered what the product of fear and anger were, when multiplied by each other. Whatever it was, that's what he felt now. And that product was running through his veins like a drug, pumping out from somewhere deep in the pit of his stomach.

In minutes, these lowlifes had transformed a quaint morning into a day of horror. They had killed his dog, Kenny was quite certain. Now they had him and Logan held at gunpoint—and haphazardly at that, as Kenny observed. He feared the trigger on that gun would get pulled, with intent—or otherwise.

Kenny assumed the possibility of that trigger getting pulled was high. He knew what the men looked like, even knew one of their names. And Kenny was far from stupid. Alone, this knowledge he had was enough to consider the worst-case scenario, from the perspectives of these assholes. He thought about this, and at once it made him feel both terrified and livid.

Then there was the prospect of the gun going off by accident. The man holding the pistol was obviously on drugs, or had been a short time ago. He looked like a druggie. He looked *bad* in every application of the word. A bad person with bad intentions, pointing a gun while using bad form. It was a minute detail, but somehow Kenny had observed it—how the man kept his finger on the trigger. And how he held his gun at an angle, gangster-style.

These details were both comforting and nerve-wracking. Apparently, the man had never been trained on how to use a gun properly, a fault which Kenny would actively search to exploit. But also, with this lack of training, that gun could errantly fire off at any second.

The other guy wasn't any better than the first. He looked unkempt and ragged, and his dreadlocks only added to the impression. Also, the man looked malnourished in some obscure way. He obviously wasn't calling the shots, which was of no surprise to Kenny. Based on his appearance, the man wasn't a hired thug, either.

Kenny wondered if there were any more of them out here. He didn't think so. He knew now what they were up to—growing weed—and they seemed desperate and skittish, and very much in a hurry.

"Stop over there at that tree," said the man holding the gun, "the big one with the crooked limb coming off it."

Kenny kept moving, his son cemented at his side. They traipsed up the hill, through the forest, and stopped at the big pine tree the man had indicated. Kenny saw the clearing beyond, just a few yards out. He observed the tops of some marijuana plants swaying in the breeze. So close to the cabin, it added chills to his overall horror. But he was angry, and these two emotions went through him in alternating waves. He thought about Logan and Jolie, and all the trauma they'd been dealing with for the past several months. And now this.

"Put your back against the tree," said the man holding the gun. He pointed the pistol between Logan's eyes, only a foot away, and his arm shook awkwardly, in obvious strain from the prolonged weight of steel in his hand.

"You," continued the man, "sit on the ground right here. And just wait." He lowered the gun, sucked his cigarette down to a nub, then squatted and smeared the ember out onto a flat rock. He moved his body with an uncertain purpose, as if he were uncomfortable in his own skin, itching—literally, as he scratched frequently at his hands and cheeks and stomach—to leap out. Then, like before, in clumsy fashion, he maneuvered a fresh cigarette to his mouth with one hand, and then lit it. He looked back into the forest, impatience rippling his brow. "Hurry the fuck up, Vance."

The other guy—Vance—arrived shortly, staggering through the forest like a stick bug, lanky and slow-moving. He dropped the bundle of tarps on the ground and glanced at his partner in crime. There was a brief look that swept across Vance's face. Kenny noticed it, a gesture that didn't sit right. It was as if a vague uncertainty swam behind his eyes. A moment of contemplation, perhaps. Maybe the observation was Kenny's imagination, but he wondered about it, nonetheless. He honed in on it.

"Tie him against the tree," said the man with the gun. "Then tie the boy over there, against the other tree. And make sure they're sitting down."

With lethargic movements, Vance did as he was told. Kenny sat on the ground against the tree, and Vance used the twine to tie his hands back and around. The rope cut into Kenny's wrist, but the pain seemed insignificant when compared to his feelings.

Vance then motioned for Logan to sit against the other tree, and shame shuddered across the man's face. And that was another thing Kenny was quick to notice, despite the torrent of anger rising from the pit of his stomach after watching the violation exercised onto his son.

"I'm using the tape on the boy," Vance said, a tone of defiance in his voice. "I'm not tying him with this shit." He lifted the spool of twine with emphasis. "Besides, his hands are too small. They'll just wriggle out."

"Fine, then!" said the other man. "But hurry, already."

Kenny watched as Vance bound Logan's hands behind the tree. He made eye contact with his son, and Kenny spoke to the boy with his eyes, sending forth a volley of comfort and sympathy, perhaps a sliver of renewal, and the guarantee that things will all work out, somehow. For Kenny, this communication was inherent, unintended—it was how a man comforted his son—and it passed in mere seconds, his mind now focused on the immediate present.

Kenny flexed his hands slowly, working for slack in the twine. To his surprise, Vance had done a good job of tying him up.

"There," Vance said, standing. "That should work."

"Well, alright," said the other man. He holstered his pistol, an action which caused Kenny to let out some air. "Let's get this job finished. Grab the tarps."

Vance stooped and picked up the bundle of tarps, and then he and the other man left the forest and went out into the clearing. Kenny waited until he thought they were far enough, then whispered, "Don't worry, Logan, I'll get us out of this." His boy looked fragile and minute sitting there against the tree, legs folded up to his chest. He looked like a small animal in the forest.

Kenny tested the twine again, trying to get his hands out. He was thinking if he could break loose, he'd free Logan and then they'd sneak off back to the Jeep, cut out of there with the haste of a brushfire on the wind.

He wrenched his hands against the twine, pulled and yanked with his arms. It was no use. All his efforts only worked the twine deeper into his wrists, and his arms heated now with exhaustion.

He looked again at his son. The boy kept trying to turn around and glance behind him. He brought his legs over to his left, then pushed out against the earth, craning his head far to the right, looking at something. Kenny followed the boy's gaze until he saw it, fifty feet away... The bottom half of George's body. The sloping grade of the hill screened the rest of the dog, but Kenny was certain that it was George. And nothing about the dog was moving. He was dead.

A rush of anger bolted down Kenny's spine. He fought again at his bindings, slapped his feet down and tried to leverage himself up, pushing his back against the trunk of the tree, small branch nubs digging sharply into his shoulders and back. He fought for another half a minute before he heard someone coming. Quickly, Kenny dropped back down to a seated position.

The man with the gun came out of the clearing and through the trees, and he carried with him a sense of determination. He approached Kenny and said, "I figured you'd try to get loose. Fucking retarded hippie, forgot to tie up your legs." He was carrying the roll of duct tape, and he bent down and pulled the end loose, and wrapped its length around Kenny's ankles several times.

Kenny glared and sat motionless as the man bound his legs together. "You didn't have to kill my dog," he said.

The man looked at Kenny, hesitated for a moment, as if thinking of what to say. Then he laughed, stood, and sauntered back to the clearing.

Kenny fumed with anger. He slumped heavily, weighted down with deep emotion. "Don't look at him, Logan," he said. "Don't look at George." He paused, and felt his breath push in and out of him like a moving tide, thick, yet rapid. Slowly, Logan turned back and put his stare on the ground. Even now, Kenny wondered if his son would speak. Would this tragic event, their second one of the year, break the boy's silence? Or would it push him further into his hole, drop him at last into the abyss he'd been circling since his mother died?

Kenny feared the latter, and he suddenly felt desperate. "Don't worry about him, Logan. Don't you worry about George, he's in a better place now. He's not in any pain. You know that, don't you?" His mind raced, searching to find the right words—and not the wrong words. The moment felt like a stroll through a minefield, was laced with dread and panic. Kenny chewed his lip, and without thinking, he continued to work away at the twine, rubbing the inside of his wrists against the bark of the tree.

A sudden thought compelled him to stop moving, and the subsequent silence brought with it a sheet of darkness, as if a heavy cloud had dropped into the sky above. "He's with your mom, Logan, you know that? He's up there... keeping her company."

The boy didn't move, didn't take his eyes off the piece of ground he was staring at. He looked lost, and perhaps he was. Perhaps Kenny was too late. Perhaps Logan had fallen already, fallen deep into his black hole of silence, to remain there forever. That's what the doctor had said. Said it was possible the boy could stay like this for the rest of his life, if he didn't get any help.

The dark moment became one of sheer panic. Kenny's heart pounded for a way out, and he went to work on the twine with fierce tenacity. He had to get him and Logan out of there. He had to end the turmoil. And if he couldn't break loose, he had to think, think hard. What were those scumbags' weaknesses? What moment could he capitalize on? What in the hell was he going to do?

The twine wouldn't budge. But in his attempt to break free, Kenny found something. He felt with the tips of his fingers a thick, sharp twig on the ground behind him. He fumbled with it, brought it in closer to his hands. It was maybe five or six inches long, jagged on one end, and with a diameter almost equal to that of a twenty-five-cent piece. Carefully, so as not to lose grip of it, Kenny worked the length of wood up inside the sleeve of his right arm. And once there, tucked away, hidden, he forced himself to relax. He inhaled deeply, exhaled slowly, and he thought about his family. He thought about his wife, Marley. Thought about Logan and Jolie, and he thought about his poor dog. Then Kenny turned his head, looking out past the forest, to the field of drugs, while he contemplated his role as a father—a protector—and he thought about what that meant for those two assholes beyond.

CHAPTER 26

It took Rob and Vance three hours to harvest the entire crop. For Rob, the day had dragged on as slow as the sun's movement across the open sky. After the first hour of their work, the bundle of tarps that Vance had brought with him to the scene was overflowing with ripe ganja—thick green bud stems, still wet and weighted down from the morning's dew. The men had strapped the tarp bundle between two long branches, essentially making a crude gurney, which they used to transport the package of weed. It required both Rob and Vance to carry the heavy load through the forest and to the cabin, with Rob checking on the boy and his dad on the way, making sure their bindings were still secure. It was tiring work, which infused fury into Rob's veins. He was *so* ready to be done with all of this bullshit.

Perhaps it was this eagerness to finish that also gifted Rob with a bolt of inspiration. On the first trip back up the hill from the cabin, he thought more about his "alternate plan." And he apparently discovered another piece of the puzzle he'd been working on. A critical piece.

Rob thought it uncanny, the phrase which had suddenly popped into his head upon this discovery: collateral damage. He did not know where the words had come from, but he knew what they meant... and what they meant at this very moment.

It was the boy and his father. They would be the collateral damage.

If the situation were different, perhaps Rob would have felt a little sorry about all of this. But now just wasn't the time. He let all of his thoughts pertaining to the alternate plan marinate inside his head for the remaining hours, and by the time they were finished, walking now toward the cabin carrying their last load of marijuana, Rob felt he had everything finely tuned, and ready to launch.

"I don't think we should use the Jeep," he announced, greasing up the cogs to the mechanism of his end game. Before he could put some lead into the boy and his father, he needed to get Vance out of the way. Far out of the way; enough to be out of hearing range. And just in case he wasn't far enough, Rob decided he would use one of those sleeping bags in the cabin to muffle the sounds of the gun blast. He'd seen this same technique in a movie, used with a pillow instead, but figured the bags would be good enough. It had to be done like this, Rob reasoned, in order to pin the deadly crime on his partner. Besides, there was the convenience in sending Vance on this errand, as he would return with the Bronco, which Rob would need.

"I don't think we should use it," he repeated, helping to unpack the load of weed onto the cabin's front deck. Vance looked suspicious, Rob could tell... But the hell with him.

An afternoon breeze stirred the grassy field beyond, and high above, a bird of prey cast its shadow down on the men. "Think about it," Rob continued, "if we drive that Jeep, we'll leave behind too much evidence." There was a long stretch to this reasoning, but not enough to alter Rob's course. He was counting on his partner's stupidity for leverage. "Fingerprints and shit. Maybe even hair samples. Too much evidence, man. They'll find us out."

"So what are we supposed to do, then?" asked Vance.

"You need to go down there and get the Bronco. Bring it up here."

Vance stared distantly at Rob, as if he were thinking hard, or not thinking at all.

"Go on down and get the Bronco," Rob repeated. "I'll wait here with them," he gave a nod toward the tree line, "so they don't try anything stupid. Or in case one of their friends shows up."

Vance hesitated. He looked down at the weed, looked at the Jeep, then at Rob. Rob could tell the tree-hugger was contemplating something, which made Rob feel suddenly alarmed and irritated. "Just fucking do it," he said, relying now on the threat behind his authoritative voice.

"Alright," Vance said. "I guess so. But what if the chain is locked? What do I do then?"

"Just drive on through it," Rob replied. "Trust me, it'll break." Briefly, Rob's thoughts centered on the grim event he'd witnessed a few days before—the literal tearing apart of a human body. Despite the strength and apparent lethality of the steel chain, he knew those links wouldn't stand up to the driving force behind a Ford Bronco.

Quietly, Vance meandered around on the deck, as if pondering Rob's proposal. He opened the tarp and absently picked through a few of the buds, seemingly studying their texture and firmness. The odor coming off the piles of weed was thick and staggering, something Rob could tell his partner appreciated. Eager to be done, and most anxious to commit a triple homicide, Rob quickly lost his patience with Vance's meandering attitude. "Fucking go, already!" he shouted.

"Whatever, man," Vance replied, irritably. "Give me the damn keys."

Rob fished his key chain out of his pocket and tossed it to Vance. The Rastaman caught it, then thrust it angrily into his sweatshirt pocket. His demeanor was both abrupt and cautious, and by now Rob was feeling suspicious of his partner.

He noticed Vance's hand stayed inside the pocket and that it looked as if it were taking grip of something else. A lapse of mere seconds passed between the two men, the awkwardness of the need for action hanging dreadfully in the air. Despite his jittery nerves, and his roving thoughts, and the constant itching and screaming of his body for its next high, Rob remained focused on Vance. For those mere seconds, he watched, waited, and considered the very real possibility of having to draw his pistol and put a bullet straight through the hippie's head, right then and there. It would certainly put him at a disadvantage, but maybe he didn't have any choice.

"Well?" Rob said, killing the silence.

"Yeah, I'm going," Vance replied. "Just make sure you get all our shit together. We don't want to leave anything important behind." He took his hand out of his pocket and reached down and re-covered the pile of stems with the tarp. Then he stood erect and looked around, uncertainty still bleeding off him like a bad wound. "I'll go now," he said, turning slowly, walking away from the cabin and toward the direction they had come from when they had first arrived. Toward the Bronco hidden off the road, at the base of the canyon.

"Goodbye," Rob said, in a tone meant to shove his partner along.

Rob watched Vance walk away. He watched him stroll down the dirt road, and through the tree line below the cabin, then into the forest. He watched the last of his partner's body, his mangy dreadlocks, as they disappeared into the green and brown foliage. Then Rob waited some more. He waited and studied the forest beyond the dirt road for a good twenty minutes. Then he turned and walked into the cabin, and gathered up one of the sleeping bags from the floor. He walked out of the cabin, across the open field, and into the tree line, his gait as determined as his thoughts.

And his thoughts told him it was now time to create some of that collateral damage.

CHAPTER 27

Vance and his partner—the man with the gun—hadn't come back yet. They passed Kenny and Logan close to half an hour ago, or so it seemed. They were carrying another load of weed on that crude stretcher one of them had crafted. *Was that their final trip?*

The thought rekindled the black dread currently sitting in the pit of Kenny's stomach. He had yet to break free of his bindings, let alone come up with a solid plan for escape. The only thing he had was that sharp stick he'd found on the ground, still stashed up his sleeve. He was hoping to use it as a weapon once he was released. But now he wondered if that would even happen. For the sake of convenience, Kenny and his son just might get left here to die—if they weren't shot.

For hours they had sat while those bastards harvested their plants on the hill-slope beyond. Now the day was pushing far into its second half, the gloom of a late afternoon sinking shadows into the forest.

The men had passed by occasionally, hauling their precious cargo, huffing with exhaustion, and complaining. And always they would stop so the paranoid one could check on Kenny and Logan's bindings. They never gave up any clue what their plans were for Kenny and his son. But Kenny had a good idea... And his idea was still that of the worst. What criminal would be okay with having their names and faces available to deliver to the authorities?

He wondered what they were up to. They were still down there, somewhere by the cabin. They had planned on using the Jeep to haul their crops out, but there was no way they could fit the amount of marijuana they had into Kenny's vehicle. Not in one trip. Perhaps they were just now figuring that out, and were arguing over what to do next.

The suspense of not knowing what the men were going to do kept the dread in his stomach freshly stirred. If there was ever a time to break free, Kenny was sure this was it. He bit his lip and strained against his bindings, but the damn twine still held.

Then Kenny looked up, noticing the sudden movements coming from his son. Logan was struggling to break free as well. Only the boy seemed more focused on repositioning himself against the tree, pushing his backside closer to the trunk. He eventually got his feet under him and assumed a squatting position. Kenny watched in silence, intrigued by what his son was doing, yet fighting back the urge to ask. A calm breeze stirred through the trees, and from afar, Kenny heard the squawk of a raven, followed by eerie silence.

Suddenly, Logan stood and vaulted forward toward his father. He was free! Duct tape hung loose from his wrists like strips of ragged cloth. In his right hand, he held the box cutter Kenny had given him earlier.

Of course, Kenny thought, suddenly proud of his son, proud to the point of tears. The boy had stashed the tool in his back pocket for later use. And what better use was there than now?

"*Yes!* Good job, Logan," Kenny said, keeping his voice low despite the excitement he felt. His son reached down and cut the twine around Kenny's wrists, and the bindings that he had been fighting with for several hours fell away with the same lightness of the breeze presently moving through the forest. Then Logan cut through the tape around his dad's ankles, and now Kenny was free.

Immediately, Kenny stood and looked through the trees and down the hill, toward the cabin. Instinctively, he placed his hand on Logan's shoulder, and then he took the box cutter, which he shoved in his front pocket. His mind raced for a plan. The first thing he thought about was to take his son and run in the opposite direction, across the mountainside and away from the cabin.

But then he saw the other man—the paranoid, gun-wielding tweaker—coming up the hill. He was alone, and carrying what looked like Logan's red sleeping bag, dragging it loosely behind him. A shot of adrenaline swamped through Kenny's body, causing an electric sensation to spark behind his eyes and temples.

On the verge of panic, Kenny's mind strained for a solution. He could take Logan and go, and they might ditch the druggy without too much effort. But another idea hit him, and with the weight of an eight-pound hammer. As soon as the man walked past them, Kenny would sneak up behind him and take him out.

"Quick, Logan," he said, "get back down—against your tree."

His son stared at Kenny, a confused look crossing his face. "Just do it," Kenny said, guiding his son back toward the spot he'd been sitting at for hours.

With obvious reluctance, Logan did as instructed. He sat on the ground, and Kenny did the same, dropping against the crooked pine tree. Quickly, he slid the sharp stick out of his sleeve and took a grip of it. "Put your hands behind your back," he said. "Make it look like you're still tied up."

Kenny heard his own breathing, which alarmed him. Air heaved in and out of his chest, as if his lungs were the workings of a fire bellows. Then, not far down the hill, he heard the snap of a twig, the crunch of leaves, as the man slowly closed the distance.

Kenny forced himself to gain control of his breathing. He rested his head against the tree and closed his eyes for a second. Then he opened them, glanced at Logan, making sure his son hadn't moved, turned his head and looked back toward the man.

He was closer now, definitely carrying Logan's sleeping bag, and on his face, Kenny saw the stern look of resolve. His blood ran cold, and now the dread swam wantonly in his stomach, and with a stab of self-hatred, Kenny doubted his sudden decision not to take his son and run.

The man stopped less than ten feet away. Kenny watched him, slowly. They made eye contact, and in that moment, Kenny absorbed the man's thoughts. He knew what the man was going to do, what he came here for.

"Well," the man said, "looks like..." he paused, as if at a sudden loss of what to say. "I guess this is the end for you two." He gathered the sleeping bag and rolled it up. He scrunched it together and clenched it in his left hand as he pulled his pistol out from its shoulder harness. He looked at Kenny, then at Logan, at Kenny again, obviously trying to decide whom he should shoot first. Shrugging his shoulders, he grunted and moved decidedly toward Kenny, thrusting the sleeping bag forward while following it with the Browning High Power. Then, remorselessly, he pushed the whole package against Kenny's face.

"NOOOO!!"

Logan's scream sent birds into flight. The rush of emotion that followed—a conglomeration of panic, relief, bewildering terror, and hope—surged like liquid fire through Kenny's veins.

And also—the tweaker froze. He slightly lowered the sleeping bag and gun, and he stood his ground and turned toward Logan, cocking his head in trivial observation. "I thought you said he can't talk."

They were his last coherent words.

Kenny moved with the speed of a linebacker. In one swift motion, he threw his arms out, striking the man's gun away as he stood erect and drove the pointed stick half into the man's eye socket. Their bodies fell together onto the ground into a violent heap of squirming flesh, the man screaming savagely, clawing at Kenny, the air, the piece of wood in his face.

"Look away, Logan," Kenny warned. He untangled himself from the man and stood. "This is for George, you son of a bitch." With sudden force, Kenny slammed his foot into the man's ribcage—three solid blows.

A short, hollow sound escaped the man's lungs as he curled up his body. His hands hung inches from his face, fearful so it seemed to dislodge the piece of wood. His remaining eye, uninjured, was a monstrous orb rolling in its socket, white with terror and wide as the sky.

Kenny backed away. There was blood on his hands and on his shirt. He saw the man's wallet on the ground, obviously fallen out of a pocket in their struggle. Kenny picked it up and opened it, studied the man's identification, then pocketed the wallet. "See you later, Robert James Boyle," he said, triumphantly.

The tweaker's body convulsed on the forest floor, fingers straightened and indecisive, probing at his wound. He was crying—an incessant, laborious shrieking that sounded not entirely human.

"Let's go," Kenny said, out loud. He motioned for Logan to get up, then searched the ground, finding the gun. He picked it up, checked to make sure a bullet was chambered, and shoved it behind his waistline. "Let's get out of here," he repeated, staring as he stepped past the contorted man. Then Kenny grabbed Logan by the elbow and walked him away in the opposite direction.

They hurried across the slope of the hill, where they found George. Kenny lifted the dog into his arms. He was cold and stiff. The sadness and anger Kenny felt at that moment was staggering. He looked at Logan—the boy was staring back at him, at George, perhaps at nothing—and his eyes were swollen with tears.

"Keep an eye out for the other one," Kenny said as he began walking in the cabin's direction. Logan fell in behind. The boy was openly crying now, louder than Kenny had observed since his mother had died. "Hang in there, Logan. Just stay close to me. We'll get through this—I promise you, son."

Kenny slowed his pace as he approached the break in the forest. The cabin sat in dull silence, the late afternoon sun casting shadows from the distant trees across its roof. He couldn't see Vance, and he suspected the guy must have left—perhaps to get their vehicle. Maybe they changed their minds over using the Jeep after all. In any case, it didn't matter. Kenny now had a gun, and he wouldn't hesitate to use it.

Cautiously, he continued forward, crossing the tree line and the field, before stopping at the Jeep. He placed George in the backseat. "Get inside, Logan," he said, motioning to the front seat. "Stay here—I'll just be a second."

Kenny drew the pistol and walked over to the cabin. He scanned the area, searching for Vance. He studied the distant tree line, just opposite the dirt road, in case the hippie guy might be hiding in there, staring back. Kenny watched for a few minutes, but didn't see anything. Then he thought about the other man—Robert Boyle—and wondered if he was up yet. He didn't think so, considering the damage he'd done to the guy. Probably, Mr. Boyle was currently passed out from pain.

Kenny leveled the gun and went into the cabin, prepared to shoot. He wasted no time. He found the other sleeping bag and grabbed it, then ran back out to the Jeep. He covered George with the sleeping bag, securing the corners of it into the crease of the backseat. Then he climbed into the front and started the engine. A minute later, the road up to the cabin was an impenetrable canvas of dust and debris.

CHAPTER 28

Vance was almost at the entrance of the dirt road when he heard the vehicle coming down the canyon. He had taken the same route he and Rob had traversed when they were here a few weeks ago. He thought the chained entrance was just ahead, not more than fifty yards. He was sure to find out soon enough.

He wasn't in a state of full-blown panic—not yet, at least. But damn if he wasn't on the verge. The sense of overwhelming confusion, and of sickening dread, had enough of a grip on him to keep the panic at bay. He heard the grind of a downshift, and the sound came from just behind him now, much closer. His mind raced as fast as his feet, curious who the hell was driving the vehicle. It was either Rob or the man—*their prisoner*.

If it was Rob... well, Vance wondered what had then happened to the man and his son. He had heard no gunshots, but that didn't mean a much. There were plenty of other ways to kill a person. And if Vance was correct, if it was Rob driving the vehicle, then just what was the psycho's plan?

And if it wasn't Rob, what then?

At last, panic set in. Vance picked up his speed, started sprinting through the forest, dodging trees and crashing through bushes like some wild animal on the chase. His dreadlocks swung crazily behind him, whipping across his back, snagging foliage. His arms were pistons driving the air. He closed his eyes and pushed through a giant cluster of manzanita, its scraggly branches raking across his cheeks and forearms, until he finally broke through. And then he was staring at the entrance of the road, less than fifty feet away.

He saw the chain barrier, suspended between two steel poles. He heard the vehicle fast approaching. It was almost on him now, and the sound caused him to duck instinctively behind a nearby tree.

Vance dropped and lay flat on the ground. He concentrated on keeping his body small as he peeked around the tree's trunk. He watched anxiously, his heart a pounding fist inside his chest. Vance saw the vehicle come roaring down the dirt road, dragging a tail of dust and leaves. It was the Jeep, sure enough. But he still couldn't tell who was driving it.

As the vehicle got closer, it slowed down. And as it passed by, Vance tucked his head behind the tree, shifted to the other side, and watched as the Jeep came to a lurching stop at the entrance of the road.

The door opened, and out came a leg, followed by a body. With a shudder, Vance realized immediately that it wasn't Rob.

The man slowly climbed out of the Jeep, his eyes scanning cautiously at the trees, a pistol extending from a double grip. And shit, it looked like he knew how to use the gun, as he was holding it like some military man.

Vance's breathing increased by what seemed like a power of ten. He watched the man's movements. Also, he noticed the kid sitting in the front seat, saw the boy's head pivoting back and forth, searching for Vance, likely, and worried to shit, undoubtedly. It seemed their prisoners were prisoners no more.

Briefly, Vance wondered what that meant for his partner. Where *was* his partner, and what was he up to? Then, almost surprisingly, Vance realized he didn't care. Because, frankly, Rob's location had no bearing on the here and now. What mattered was for Vance to keep his fucking head down.

He bit his lower lip; he thought the man couldn't move any slower. Gradually, he went over to the gate and unlocked it. And when the length of chain fell to the ground, causing a dull thud that kicked up a pillow of dust, the man still didn't hurry. Like some Ranger or fucking Green Beret, he took his goddamn time, gun poised evenly toward the woods. He crept back to the Jeep, his attention razor-sharp on his surroundings.

Vance kept his head behind the tree, peeking out with one eye only, praying the man didn't see him, hoping he would hurry the fuck up and get in his vehicle. Hoping he would just take his kid and leave.

Eventually, the man did leave, and that's when he moved fast. Seconds after he climbed into the Jeep, they were gone, and only then did Vance realize he'd been holding his breath.

Instinctively, Vance stood and stared. A cloud of hazel-colored dust rose into the forest before him, billowing outward and beyond, reaching Vance at about the same time as the seemingly unnatural silence. The silence was eerie, and ghostlike, and it drove a cold shiver through the pit of his stomach. He tasted dirt on his tongue, and he smelled the rawness of the land as it enveloped him.

He waited a long minute to make sure the Jeep was truly gone. Then he turned and looked up the canyon. *Now what?* he thought. But it wasn't a thought, so much as a feeling. A nauseating sense of despair—*more dread*—climbing through the rungs of his spine like some burrowing, alien larvae, tunneling toward, and *for*, the meat between Vance's ears.

Rob was still up there at the cabin. And so was their weed. And time, along with Vance's churning stomach, was slipping further into the realms of uncertainty. *Now-the-fuck-what?*

He went for the Bronco. Whatever the situation was—and he really was at a loss to what was going on—he figured he should get back up to the cabin and find out, find out quickly.

He turned and started running toward the direction of the Bronco, thinking about what his next moves were going to be. Horribly, he still considered the possibility of killing Rob. But now that the lives of innocent people were no longer on the line, the feeling—*the urge to become a murderer*—wasn't as intense.

Nevertheless...

When he made it to the Bronco, Vance's eyes skimmed the surrounding forest until landing on the furrowed ditch he'd observed earlier—his imaginary gravesite. Then he spotted the crooked tree branch on the ground, the one he'd pictured Rob using to cave his head in. Almost without thought, Vance went to the branch, picked it up and tossed it into a stand of trees. No use making things easy for the wannabe biker.

Then he climbed into the Bronco, turned the engine over, and drove off. Not so absently, he checked for the steak knife hidden in the pocket of his sweatshirt, worried that it might have fallen out during his panicked fracas through the forest only moments ago. Thankfully, the knife was still there. But would he use it? The desire to resolve this day was a never-ending ache for Vance, and it became the influence for him to "gun-it" once he cleared the forest and hit the road. He peeled rubber, accelerated to forty miles an hour for half a mile, then slammed the brakes as he came to the canyon's entrance. The Bronco went perpendicular, screeched to a violent halt, and then Vance punched the gas again, speeding through the entrance, onto the dirt road, and then up the canyon.

CHAPTER 29

The act of breathing was an abysmal strain. With each shortened breath, Rob felt the solid slam of a steel-toed boot all over again. There were fissures beneath the surface of his skin, and they hurt like hell, but they still had nothing on the pain coming from his other wound.

The pain coming from his eye—or what was left of it—now that was something grand. Excruciatingly horrible; overwhelmingly terrifying; the pain could only be described exactly as it was: a sharp stick gouged inches deep into one's eyeball. This was the worst pain Rob had felt in his life.

He found the piece of wood, inspected it lightly with his fingers. For some ungodly reason, he thought it to be a rib bone sticking out of him.

There was blood everywhere. He found its sticky wetness clinging to his fingers, smelled its tangy metallic odor assaulting his nostrils. And he tasted the blood—on his lips and tongue. Tasted it as it slid down his gullet, pooling in his stomach.

He bent over and retched, his mouth a cracked faucet spraying liquid onto the ground. His upper chest cavity lurched as he heaved, and he was sure someone was driving an iron spear into him.

He struggled to stand back up, tried to stand fully erect. The forest spun in a state of surreal oddness. It looked like a vintage photo. Everything appeared in black and white, nothing in between. Rob tried to turn his head, but the pain in his eye threatened to become worse, a pain beyond his imagination, so he turned with his shoulders instead.

He took in the world around him, took it in with his good eye, and he tried to see the forest from the trees. He tried to see something bright and colorful, something beyond a sea of milk and shadow. Something beyond a universe of colossal agony.

He felt the pull of gravity and went with it. Rob stumbled forward, stumbled *downward*, one hand dangling limp at his side, the other probing gently at the branch in his face, a voice telling him loudly not to pull it out, to just leave it there. The branch had pierced something inside his skull, brain matter perhaps, and as Rob realized this, he imagined with clarity what the face of stark terror looked like.

He tried to speak, tried to form words, but nothing worked like it should. Words were as elusive as ghosts, and for reasons which Rob couldn't pin down. Perhaps he was in shock. He *hoped* he was in shock.

For a second, he wondered where he was. The following second, he knew exactly where he was, and what had happened to him. And the second after that, another hazy blur fogging his mind. This overwhelming confusion went on for what seemed like an imprecise amount of time—it could've been going on forever, for all that Rob could ascertain—until he trained his thoughts and vision on the path ahead. The direction in which he'd been slowly traveling, all because of gravity.

Rob stumbled out of the shadowed forest and into the clearing, lost his balance and fell to his knees. He looked around, was vastly confused. He saw the little house ahead, some sort of building made of weathered pine, slightly out of order, slightly incomplete. His gaze followed the building's pitched roof, broke upward across the horizon until landing high above, craning his neck and sending bolts of electricity through his damaged ribs.

The sky above was battleship gray. He heard the warble of birds, but then thought the sound wasn't coming from birds at all. That perhaps it was the sound of little forest people squabbling in the bushes. Something from out of a dream, because yes, Rob was dreaming. He *had* to be dreaming.

The pain was unrelenting. A force of nature pressing its heel onto Rob's body, setting up for the final grind. He fought back. He got to his feet and carried on, staggering forward toward the house, every inch a bastard's mile, arms and legs and spine dragging ball and chain alike, through sand dunes, and mud. It seemed gravity was no longer Rob's friend. It seemed gravity had abandoned him, left him cold and helpless on the battlefield, a deserter to the cause, the most unworthy of partners...

Then Rob suddenly remembered.

Vance.

His *partner*, that tree hugging piece of shit. He too had abandoned Rob, left him here to die. Or had he? More confusion, swimming through Rob's skull, sending his entire world into a catastrophic spin. The vertigo came on fast, was absolute. Rob was back on the ground, on hands and knees, face down, strings of clotted blood leaking from his head. He gave up and fell to his side. His breath—it grew thin, became shallow and raspy, and sounded moist. He laid there for an indeterminable amount of time. The sky he could still see, a slate of gray, and Rob had an odd memory then, something some person had told him once, many eons ago.

All people had goodness inside them. That people were born as selfless blank slates, without guilt or ambition. Without sin. Without the inflection of that god-awful weight incurred from the act of living.

Rob stared at the enormous gray sky, and he laughed, and then cried. Despite the wretched pain, and the fogbank clouding his thoughts, and the staggering sense of utter hopelessness, Rob found it in him to just cry. And not for want of anything, but because of the memory that kept flashing inside his head.

The day seemed to draw forward. Had it actually vanished? Was this a new day, in fact? A new week? Perhaps he had finally died, and this was his afterlife... An afterlife wrought with misery.

Hell, Rob thought, *I have died and gone to Hell.* Then he heard something, something that sounded very real, something mechanical. Something non-organic. The workings of metal, gears and chains, the combustible sputtering of blocked steel— *an engine.*

Rob pushed with his arms, and pulled with his legs, and he raised his body. He fought against gravity, his enemy now, and he fought against pain and stood erect, facing the little building. He saw movement over there, a vehicle of some sort. His vehicle—*the Bronco!*

He moved forward, one foot, then the other, an agonizing shuffle bringing him closer to what, he couldn't tell. His partner? Something about a crop. A vision of men branding leather, riding motorcycles...

Rob heard the distinct slap of metal, and at once knew it to be the closing of a car door. Knew it without a doubt. He saw the man walking toward him, saw him suddenly stop, as if frozen in ice. Then Rob recognized this man... Vance... and he watched as Vance slowly backed away and disappeared into the haze of distance.

Rob took another step, shuffled one foot after the other. He did it again, then stopped and stared. Things were bigger now— the house, the vehicle, the trees with their looming shadows—but still, nothing seemed bigger than the sky.

Except for when Vance came back.

He looked bigger, somehow. Was closer, much closer. Rob stared at him, thought to say something, but knew he couldn't. He tried anyway, and what came out was a sickening, incomprehensible gurgle.

Vance smiled. Then he laughed. And then Rob heard the words in his head once again... *I have died and gone to Hell...*

"Fuck you, you fucking asshole!" Vance said, and he smiled as he said that, and Rob immediately felt the riveting pang of anger. He felt a boiling inside his head and washed away were all those other thoughts—the bullshit of feeling guilty; the remorsefulness of this day, and of many others; the candy-ass crying; the fucking "without sin" nonsense whispering inside his skull; and the hollowed-out existence of his sorry life, judged and sneered at by the monstrous and almighty, gloating sky.

In his fury, Rob remembered what he had kept at his side. He remembered he had a gun, and he went for it. His hand reached and grasped, but dammit, it couldn't find a fucking thing.

He kept reaching though, even as he saw Vance raise something high and to his back, saw the bastard winding up. Rob kept grasping, and he formed the cursing retaliation in his mind because his throat had gone to shit, and he did this even as Vance's expression grew rigid, and mean-like. And Rob drew anyway, because fuck it, maybe the gun *was* in his hand, and he just didn't know it. He drew, and he aimed, aimed with his one remaining eye, and he fired—even as Vance swung a home run with whatever that was in his hand—and the bullet that came out, Rob swore, was the blackest piece of steel ever crafted by the hands of a human.

CHAPTER 30

Vance's hands shook like paper in the wind. They seemed fine as long as he kept them gripped to the steering wheel, but as soon as he let one of them go, to brush away his dreadlocks, or wipe the cold sweat from his lips, the hand jittered fiercely, as if the thing was having its own petite seizure.

He'd been driving for close to an hour, and still, his hands wouldn't stop. He told himself he had the right to kill Rob, that the man had it coming... and that, perhaps, if Vance hadn't intervened, Rob might've died, anyway. All Vance did was toss a little salt onto a wound that might already have been fatal. Vance told himself these things, was sure he'd convinced himself it was true, but it seemed even this did nothing to ease his nerves.

He was slightly confused. True, he hadn't drawn first blood out of Rob, but what he did do... Well, wasn't that what they called being an accomplice to a murder?

Vance wasn't so sure. He thought there was no way Rob would've come back, seeing how much blood had streaked down his face. No way in hell—that dude was too far gone. So what then was the difference? Would the same crime apply if Vance were to walk into a mortuary and smack a dead guy upside the head, full force with a shovel?

Like brittle leaves in the fall, his hands shook.

He kept his eyes on the road. Daylight had finally subsided, and now dusk was settling over the land, making things difficult to see. This just might be the worst time of day to drive—he considered—when the encroaching shadows of the night began their dancing trickery upon the eyes. Just a little more anxiety to add to a smorgasbord of mental strain. *Fuck it, why not have a full-blown nervous breakdown?*

He kept his eyes ahead, watching for anything that could stamp a fucked-up ending on a situation that was just now becoming something worth living for. Some enormous animal in the road, perhaps. The out of control swerve from a drunk driver. *That's how shit happens,* Vance thought. Get so close to the finish line, and then *bam!*, something like a fucking flat tire to send you off the road and down the ravine (one-thousand-foot drop, nothing less), and into a hurtling tumble of twisting metal and raging fire...

Vance tried to think of something positive. He considered that the events in his life were finally shaping up to a somewhat decent ending. In fact, the situation wasn't all that terrible, despite the whole "accomplice to a murder" incident looming over his shoulders.

For what might have been the tenth time since he left the cabin, Vance replayed the recent events in his mind. He remembered seeing Rob standing there in the field as he drove up. And at that moment he remembered thinking that shit, things were back on some kind of remotely sane track, and that he even felt a touch of relief, figuring that in a sudden case of profound guilt, Rob had evidently released the man and his kid.

But this relief Vance felt lasted for only a second and was quickly devoured by his long-standing problem—just how and when he was going to put an end to his partner? Yes, how again was he planning on doing that? With the steak knife, perhaps, if Vance could ever summon the balls to do such a thing.

He remembered slamming the Bronco into "park," and remembered stepping out. Then he walked around the front of the vehicle to meet up with his partner, his mind furiously whittling away at an attempt to craft a homicidal plot, until he looked up...

And that's when he *really* saw Rob.

At that precise moment, when Vance saw Rob, his emotions had entered a strange foray, accompanied by a completely different and unfamiliar realm. He felt an inexplicable rush of exhilaration, as if being injected with an extraordinarily fast-acting drug, a spirit-lifting elixir that brought him close, if not equal, to the altitude of heaven. At once, he knew that all his deepest troubles were now a thing of the past. But, at the same time, Vance felt a sense of terse horror, a gut-wrenching blast of hot air that brought to mind people being thrown face down onto some ancient, primordial slab of stone. In all his life, Vance had never seen so much blood. He had never seen the human body violated in such a state—the state in which Rob was. Streaking bands of wet blackness stained the entire upper half of his partner. Vaguely, Vance recognized something foreign projecting out of Rob's eye, insinuating damage that was both certain, and final.

Vance's memory went a little foggy after that. He remembered feeling anxious, overwhelmed even, with the need to finish the business at hand—and whether that business was to put an end to Rob's life, or simply grab his weed and go, Vance was uncertain. He just had to get things done.

He remembered walking away, in search of something—a tool of some kind, preferably large and stout. He remembered seeing the shovel leaning against the side of the cabin; remembered thinking "perfect," as he grabbed it and returned to Rob.

And Vance remembered the broken look on Rob's face—would never forget that look, in fact, for as long as he lived—as he brought the shovel high, and to his back.

Vance remembered saying something. And he remembered his feelings at that moment, just prior to, and slightly after, the swing of the shovel. It was a host of feelings, each with seemingly unlimited capacities—guilt, finality, queasiness—and all of which were underscored by a note of subtle triumph.

Strangely, as soon as Vance clobbered Rob over the head, his world became one of muted clarity—at least for the time it took him to deal with Rob's body, pack up his weed, and then get the fuck out of there.

Vance wasn't sure why he wanted to "deal" with Rob's body, why he didn't just leave the guy there, dead in that field. But he remembered Rob's warnings of evidence being left behind, when he'd said to go get the Bronco. That was a concern for Vance; but also, he kept thinking back to that story Rob had told him about the butchered man he had recently buried. It seemed as if the wannabe biker had taken a little too much pride in his actions. Then there was the killing of that dog, and the poor boy who had to witness that. It seemed as if this perverted pride of Rob's, and his actions as a whole, had affected Vance in a profoundly negative way. In any case, Vance had a shovel, and he decided to use it.

The hardest part was getting Rob's body into the front seat of the Bronco. Vance struggled for minutes on end with that chore, but he eventually got it done.

The rest of the chores were only slightly easier: A frantic rush to pack the entire crop of weed into the back of the Bronco, and then spitting up gravel as Vance tore out of there and down the canyon. Then the quick pit-stop to deal with Rob. Vance had pulled into the forest clearing off the side of the main road, where they had parked the Bronco earlier. He dragged Rob out of the vehicle and into the rutted ditch—the one Vance had previously imagined would be his own grave. He used the shovel and opened up the ditch much wider. Vance was amazed at how precise the fit was—how Rob's body simply rolled into place. He also remembered feeling impressed at how the small, ragged berms hugged the tweaker's corpse so closely, as if to suggest a queer scene of intimateness.

He had used the shovel and scooped dirt over Rob's body, just enough to cover up most of the man. And then, in an assured manner that approached a level of extravagance, Vance made a primordial grunting noise from the pit of his stomach as he laid down the final scoop, a scoop that completely covered Rob's face. *Now you're the one getting buried, fucker!* he'd announced.

Then it was the drive homebound, with the elusive shadows of dusk settling in, the shaky hands, the very nerve-wracking present.

Vance noticed the muskiness coming off his body, a mixture of fresh soil and ripe herb, sweat and grime, the stink of vomit, and possibly fear. His own smell seemed to have filled the Bronco's cabin, despite the reigning odor of the harvest coming from the back. Vance rolled the windows down and said a prayer to the mighty *Selassie-I* that no lawman should pull him over right now, for any reason. Said officer wouldn't get two feet from his vehicle before catching a whiff of what Vance was hauling.

He focused his thoughts ahead, considering what the next step was to this impromptu plan he'd inherited. He hoped to take a shower once he got home, then maybe get a few hours of sleep before packing up and splitting town. But he was also worried about running into Rob's associates. They were still an enormous threat. And if any of them discovered what Vance and Rob had been up to, if they discovered any of the weed—in his apartment, or right here in the Bronco—then the results would be beyond fucked.

He thought about the possibilities. He pictured that one biker—Cecil, that was his name, the guy he'd gotten stoned—showing up and catching Vance in the middle of transferring the many pounds of weed from the Bronco to his car. Vance's thoughts instantly turned into a stream of horrible images, a collage containing the sights and sounds associated with abrupt violence, and where his body ultimately ended up looking like that of Rob's. Like a small lamb being thrown into a pack of hungry wolves. Vance was certain that he would be the lamb, and just as sure that's exactly how things would materialize, if any of those bikers found his shit out. Shivering, he rolled the windows halfway up.

So what then was the plan?

He stared at the road ahead. Dusk had finally given way to night, and the surrounding shadows, the obscurity of a world cast in a half-light, half-darkness, had fallen behind a black curtain. The road ahead was less confusing, easier to see. He was tired and hungry, in definite need of a shower and a good night's rest. In *dire* need of smoking a fat joint...

But he had to have a plan.

Without a doubt, he had to get rid of the Bronco. That was his priority. The vehicle was too much of a beacon to those bikers. Not to mention it would soon be on the lookout for the police once they found Rob's body. If they found Rob's body...

On that note, Vance wasn't so sure anyone would ever find Rob—which was fine by him.

Still, he needed to get rid of the vehicle. He decided to do that soon, and that he should avoid driving it to his place, for fear of drawing unwanted attention to himself. What he should do, he thought, is park it somewhere off the road, in some bushes, or behind a stand of trees. Someplace obscure and out of sight. Something in the vein of where he and Rob had parked it earlier, back there up on the mountain. And he would only need to do this for a few hours, no more. But did he know of such a place?

Vance concentrated...

He remembered seeing something of an old warehouse of sorts, just outside of town, down the dirt road, and only a few miles past his apartment. *Were there any trees there?* He couldn't remember. But he decided to check it out, as it may work, and he wouldn't leave the vehicle for long. Sadly, he considered forgoing the shower and sleep, maybe even the joint as well (probably not the joint) and simply packing up his car and bailing.

It was well into the evening when he finally made it into town. At his first red light, he paused with his mental machinations and just listened. Everything seemed deathly quiet, despite the low rumble of the Bronco's engine. Vance waited, listening, then thinking...

The night was peaceful, that's what it was. A small town nestled in the groves of wood and grass, the Southern Oregon wilderness, with its small town pride, and small town secrets. Vance chuckled... *Fuck this fucking place.* He couldn't get out of here soon enough. And little did these white trash fuckers know what *his* secrets were. He chuckled again, the first measure of pride over his actions now coursing through his veins, pushing back at the guilt, the fear.

The time was almost ten o'clock. Vance listened for the sounds of motorcycles—and watched for cops—knowing that it was mostly cops and robbers who roamed the streets at night, neither of which he could afford a run in with.

When the light turned green, he took his time getting through the intersection. He passed the liquor store on his right, noticed a group of teenagers hanging out, dudes propped up against their 4X4's, girls sitting in back and on the cabin top, the lot of them drinking beer and smoking cigarettes. Vance broke eye contact and kept going, actively scanning the streets for motorcycles. He was paranoid... But he had damn good reason to be.

He made a left at the next light, and this was the road, his road. He took his time, not one tick past the speed limit, and he even slowed down for good measure as soon as the asphalt gave way to dirt and gravel. A mile later and he was approaching his apartments—a row of duplexes, to be exact—and Vance eased back on the gas. The Bronco crawled past. He stared... nothing. Nothing to be seen from the light of the single street lamp, other than the ragged, rust-colored siding, and the drooping roofs made of black tar shingles. Vance shuddered; the sight of the buildings and the colors contained within instantly reminded him of the stains running down Rob's face and chest.

Everything was so quiet, so dead, that Vance was tempted to pull up and get to work right then. He thought about how long it would take him to clear out his house. An hour, perhaps. Two at the most. Certainly no more. All he needed were his clothes and records, stereo system, an assortment of tools and paraphernalia, and, of course, most of all, the buds currently drying in the spare bedroom. Two hours at the most, that was it. And Vance knew he could squeeze it all into his VW, with room to spare. With room for the rest of the weed currently in the back of the Bronco.

But then he thought about what time it was, and what time it would be, in those two hours of packing... The middle of the night. And the middle of the night for shitheads like those bikers was just the same as mid-day for normal folks. The chance for a run-in with them now was at an all-time high, and Vance was doomed if they saw the Bronco, knowing—or suspecting, for they knew nothing of what went on this night—that Rob was present.

Vance stuck with his original plan and resisted stopping at his place. He put a little more pressure on the gas and the Bronco puttered past. He checked the odometer and made a mental note, wanting to know just how far he'd have to be hoofing it, when he came back.

He drove further down the road, which was confined on both sides by wide expanses of grass, sparsely dotted with trees, and the occasional cutoff towards some private, unseen residence. It wasn't until two miles past that Vance spotted the place he'd been thinking about.

Slowly, he drove up to it, then recognized it as some long abandoned industrial complex, perhaps used by the logging industry, or a sand and gravel company. He didn't know—and he didn't care. To the back of the property stood a thicket of eucalyptus trees, not meant for access from the road, but easily accomplished all the same.

Vance drove up and parked the Bronco behind the trees. He double checked the windows, killed the engine, then got out and shut and locked the doors. He looked around, peering into the all-encompassing darkness, on the lookout for something, anything... yet suspecting he'd discover nothing, in the solitude of this night.

He reached down and slapped at his legs, dusting himself off, and dropped the keys into his pocket. Only two miles to go; forty minutes of walking, and Vance would be there.

He started off down the road, and within a hundred yards, his mind was running full speed through its obstacle course of thoughts, pinging with each step between the past, the present, and the future. And this train of thoughts kept up with Vance for the interim that it took him to walk most of those two miles.

In broad detail, his reflections reminded him of the miserable partnership formed, and thus endured, with Rob, and all the agony contained therein. They reminded him of the grim finality that became of his partner. Vance reminisced on the fusion of feelings surrounding that incident. And of those feelings, he focused on the best of them—the glorious triumph—which, of course, swung his mind toward the future. And of the future, well, those were the greatest thoughts of all.

He began to calculate, preparing to spend the money he would soon make. Maybe, with a bit of luck, he'd get enough to buy an acre of land, perhaps more. An acre was all he needed to run a second crop. He could build on that, turn future profits over to buy more land, do it all over again, and then shit, the sky was the limit. All in southern Humboldt, his home away from home. Vance's proper home, not this sorry excuse for a town. *This fucking backwoods, hick town...*

Then Vance's mind was back to the present, verging on slipping into his recent, horrific past before he realized he was close to his destination. Forty minutes had walked on by, and on its small journey, those minutes had brought with them a dense, mental fog, a fog that obscured the surrounding night, with its hushed assembly of shadows, its assurance of invisible critters, sleeping or otherwise, and the unbroken sounds of Vance's footsteps crunching over gravel. A sound that had quickly become invisible in its own sense. Becoming that of white noise— yet overbearing all the same, omniscient and treacherous with its perverse ostinato, smothering all the other sounds—the sounds which should have signaled a three-alarm fire in Vance's dense skull.

He finally heard them, though, before it was too late: the distinct growl of the wolves; the deep reverberation of such machines, sending acoustic chaos into the night, killing the silence.

A violent flash of heat swamped through Vance's body, and he shivered in response, every muscle and joint mimicking the actions of his hands earlier in the night. Here he was, the trembling lamb hiding in the forest, peering through the darkness at the pack of meat eaters dangerously close in the distance.

Vance heard them.

And he observed them, these bikers on bikes presently bathed in the pale radiance of a gasping street lamp, dangling leather-clad legs over their machines, or swaggering brazenly through the parking lot, crying out sounds incomprehensible to thought, yet quite clear as to emotion. And these men, these bikers, as Vance so horridly understood, were no different from wolves howling in the moonlight.

CHAPTER 31

Vance watched as they banged on his door. He hid off the road behind a tree and listened as they called for Rob, and then for him. He felt the sluggish liquid of fear tingle through his veins, as the bikers made their ruckus and cursed obscenely in the parking lot for ten minutes before abandoning their project. But before they did, one of them slammed something into Vance's door, then mounted his bike and took off. Their retreat was a blasting cacophony of thunderous roars cracking through the night air.

Vance waited another ten minutes before crawling out of the shadows. He walked slowly toward his place, eyes peeled on the distant blackness of the road beyond, watching for headlamps. He got halfway there, twenty yards from his front door, before pausing. Vance listened to the night, listened for their potential return, but after several more minutes, was convinced enough of his own safety to keep moving.

There was a note on his door, slammed and stuck in place by a K-bar knife. The note was meant for Rob, who, of course, would never read its order. And the order comprised two simple words: *Check in.*

Vance reached to pull the note and knife out, but then stopped, thinking otherwise. He pulled his keys out of his pocket instead and opened the door.

He moved quickly. He checked his watch, and banked on getting everything packed, and then out of there in *way* less than two hours. Shit, an hour tops, as he moved like a private's first day in boot camp.

The first thing he did was take a speed-shower and change his clothes. Then he put his stereo system and records into the van. He stashed them in the back and piled his sleeping bag and pillow on top. Then he took a trash bag from the kitchen pantry and gathered up all of his clothes, stretching the bag thin as he jammed in both clean and soiled. He hefted the bag onto his shoulder and hauled it to the van, where he slung it into the front seat. He shut the passenger door and went back inside, briefly checking his surroundings.

The time was almost midnight, and those bikers just might come back. Or, his neighbors might do something supremely stupid, such as call the police. Vance was sure some of them were awake by now, spying his movements through cracks in their curtains. But he was also sure that many of them—for reasons which he could easily guess—were less than eager to have the cops out here. He could tell many of the tenants were burn-outs of one kind or another. Section eights and broken-up divorcees. Fearful old geezers living on tight incomes with one foot in the grave, hacking from wet lungs in the night. Vance had seen and heard these people, all of them. And despite having nothing common with his neighbors, as he wanted nothing to do with any of them, he now felt confident and appreciative of their unkempt, distant lives. No, none of these people would call the police. And that meant a world of gratitude for Vance right now.

As soon as he had all his personal items, the entire lot of his life, crammed into his VW, Vance started with the marijuana from the back bedroom. He plucked the branches off the strung wire and stacked them gingerly onto a bedsheet. He got all of it there, all the remaining weed from his and Rob's first harvest. Vance guessed there to be about three or four pounds' worth—

which amounted to several thousand dollars once it was good and ready. And that was just a fraction when compared to what waited for him back in the Bronco.

Carefully, he rolled the sheet up burrito style, and cinched the corners with twine. While he worked the twine, he thought about that kid and his dad. He couldn't help it. Vance wondered what kind of horror they must have felt, and he tried to put himself into that man's shoes. He tried to imagine what it would be like to be a parent, a father, but had nothing to relate to other than what his imagination could conjure up.

All the same, Vance felt a moment of dread quiver in his chest when he thought hard about it—when he thought about that man, and his son, and what they went through. Then the feeling—no, the *instinct*—which must have weighed heavily onto that man's shoulders, and inside his guts, until finally, it gave way and drove piston-like through his hands.

It wasn't hard for Vance to picture how the ending must have played out up there on that mountain. That father got himself loose, then caught Rob by surprise and rammed a sharp stick into his fucking eye. And well, Vance assumed that father took care of business the way any decent parent would have done. Shit, he saved his boy, his family. And wasn't that the prime directive of his job? To protect his family.

Vance imagined as much.

Apparently, his imagination worked better than he could have predicted. He felt a tear bubble in his eye. A father like that, taking care of such business... That was something Vance had never known. He never had a father, in fact, at least not one that would have been around when he needed it most.

Vance smiled, despite the sudden welling of tears. *Taking care of business*. Shit, that son of a bitch partner of his had often preached those same words. It was another one of his stupid-ass phrases he'd picked up from his stupid-ass biker pals.

Yes, Vance smiled—smiled proudly. Then he broke out from his reverie and got back to work, which was quick work at that. He stashed the rolled sheet of weed in the van, and grabbed the last of everything—the cardboard box of clipped buds from the living room, along with his trimming tools, and placed them on the floor of the passenger seat. He took a last run through of his apartment before climbing into the van. At the wheel, he checked his watch, which read one-oh-five, and then he fired up the engine and drove away.

Less than thirty minutes later, he was driving back past his apartment, his vehicle crammed ceiling high with all the weed from the Bronco. The blood in his veins ran cold as ice from anxiety. He stared with huge bug eyes, on constant alert for all that would damn him: cops or robbers, and not much else, but one never knew.

He was hauling hundreds of pounds of marijuana, which would undoubtedly put him away for the rest of his life if he got pulled over. Perhaps it was because he was driving his own vehicle now, but Vance felt more paranoid and more panic-stricken than when he'd come down the mountain in the Bronco. His hands shook more intensely. But eventually, he drove on by, and nothing became of it.

Then he was on a paved road and in town, but the terror never once let up. It seemed his was the only vehicle in movement, an impossible sight not to notice. He felt like a duck in a shooting gallery, just waiting for that crack of sound and then that punch of load right between the eyes. The intensity of his fear sat heavy on his back, and it hung there as he made his way through town. Throughout Main Street, and then the outskirts, heading southwest, towards his real home, away from all of this, before the intensity finally subsided.

But eventually, nothing happened. Fifty miles down the road, the cooling of Vance's fear fused itself into an even lesser version of the emotion. When this occurred, it gave room for the sacred reign of excitement. Half a dozen scenarios roped Vance's mind then, each one of them bringing an outlook of favorable design. With an almost casual deliverance of the mind, he pondered the minor details in his future: where he would set up for the following weeks to dry and process his weed (some patch of desolation up in the hills, of course, away from all human contact) and Vance knew of at least three spots which would satisfy that criteria. Then there would be the process of offloading his product to a buyer, and getting a good deal—yet again, another simple-as-pie scenario for the likes of Vance, once he landed himself back at home.

And then, at that thought, the thought of his home...

Vance broke into a sudden burst of blubber and tears. His chest heaved for air and he cried out loudly, his eyes blurring against the rush of relief and hope, against the glorious prospect of his future. He rolled the window down and screamed a babble of laughter into the Oregon night. He was driving toward Humboldt, goddammit, Humboldt at last, and from this moment forward, Vance figured everything would be okay, because that's what Humboldt had always ever offered him—the sense of knowing that things *would* be okay.

Crying for joy, and for sorrow, and for everything in between, Vance glanced at his side mirror. He saw nothing but the trust of the night. He saw its black void, there in the mirror, and it was vacant of every facet of humanity, peaceful or otherwise—no lights from houses, or from cars, or, god forbid, from motorcycles.

And the sight was the most reassuring thing Vance had seen, or experienced, since he'd been away from his home.

His hands... Yes, they still trembled. But Vance used them anyway, to wipe away the tears from his face. Then he said a prayer of gratitude to the almighty King of Zion for just such a blessing—the blessing of his trembling hands—as he was now damn sure that trembling was the best thing he'd felt in a long, long time.

CHAPTER 32

Jolie was a wreck, and it broke everyone's heart. She wailed at the sight of George, and cried about how she couldn't understand how anyone—even a bad man—could kill such a wonderful, loving dog.

"I hope George bit that man," she had finally said, while buried in Kenny's embrace. "I hope George bit him real hard, Daddy."

Kenny hurt for his daughter. He knew at that moment her innocent, childish trust in humanity had been fractured forever. There would be no choice but for her to join those other sad juveniles who lingered in the gray area between childhood and adulthood.

The pain he felt from this knowledge was both surprising and unexpected. Kenny was beside himself, torn at how many details he should let his daughter hear about the incident, and just what to keep her sheltered from. But it was hard to keep anything quiet, and for the next day and a half, for once, Kenny envied Logan's skill at not speaking.

The boy hadn't said another word, not since his scream of protest in the forest, but Kenny didn't care. In his mind, his son had said enough—enough to save both their lives. How much more could any sane person expect from the kid?

A lot had happened in that day and a half, there at Wayne's house. They wrapped George in a plastic trash bag and stuck him in Wayne's freezer in the garage. Kenny had a place in mind to bury his dog, back home in his yard, out by the black cottonwoods, where George used to chase the squirrels. It would be the first thing he'd do once he got back home.

When he'd arrived at his brother's house that first night, and told them what had happened, it wasn't fifteen minutes later before three sheriff cars were in the driveway. Each of those officers was a friend, and client, of Wayne's. They took Kenny's statement with a mixture of duty-bound professionalism; and then a subtle, caustic level of righteous pride after hearing how Kenny ultimately handled the situation.

The sheriffs assured him that his actions of self-defense were warranted and justified, and that he'd ultimately have little to worry about stabbing a man in the eye—regarding getting in trouble with the law, that is.

"I don't really give a shit," Kenny had said. "I'd do it all over again."

Nobody argued with him, or said anything otherwise. The sheriffs warned Kenny that he might have to be more involved with this mess than he'd care to be, in the unlikely event that Mr. Robert Boyle showed up, wanting to press assault charges against Kenny; and assuming he was even alive. An official search of the remote property the next morning would ultimately yield little in evidence, so the question as to whatever happened to Rob would be left unanswered.

Kenny still held zero reservations or concerns about Mr. Boyle, as he knew he would likely never see the man again. He was glad he took the man's wallet, which he'd promptly handed over to the sheriffs. But he didn't think or care about repercussions beyond that. His thoughts now revolved around helping his kids cope with just one more tragedy in their small lives. At least now they were safe and sound. But even more so, they were surrounded by family, which Kenny not once took for granted.

There was one thing Kenny found of interest, though, that night at his brother's house. He had noticed an abrupt change in Beth's attitude. After all the crying, and all the commotion stirred up by his arrival; after his short, tamed version of what had happened up there; and after the children all fell into a vanquished heap of swollen-eyed slumber, Kenny sat back with a beer and told the longer version of the story.

He told the details of how Logan had cut him loose, how the bad man climbed up the hill and put a gun to Kenny's face, almost got that trigger pulled. And how Logan finally spoke—and boy, did he ever. Then, the blur of motion and memory as Kenny simply reacted to his opportunity. The influx of adrenaline, the spark of instinct, and then the flush of fire, as discovered through bloody violence.

After he told his story, Beth's attitude had turned altogether. She'd become a different woman, so it seemed. Her mannerisms had changed. At one point, she brought Kenny another beer, and she rested her hand on his shoulder then, a touch of affection that offered kindness and affirmation. As Wayne beamed, and bragged garishly about his little brother's actions, Kenny thought he noticed a veneer of pride coat his sister-in-law, who, for once, seemed speechless.

Whatever her thoughts were, that night at his brother's house saw the end of Kenny's domestic squabbles with Beth. From then onward, he would sense the woman's quiet, yet proud acceptance of him—as if she had now garnered hope for him and his kids.

On the light of the second morning, Kenny put George into the back of Wayne's truck. His brother had offered to make the trip with them, said he'd drive his own vehicle, just him and George, so the kids wouldn't have to share a seat with their dead dog. Kenny didn't think too hard on that before agreeing.

"I cleared my calendar for the next couple of days," Wayne said. "And I made a few calls. We'll get this mess cleared up as quickly as possible."

His brother followed him home, and the passing of that familiar drive for Kenny stood in massive contrast, as it was both like, and unlike, any other time he'd made it.

In its entirety, the drive resided in a bubble of gray haze and confusion. But Kenny remembered, with stark clarity, his feelings about his children, and what they were now going through—once again—and the impact of loss, which was sadly all too recognizable to this family.

But also, his thoughts now carried the fresh weight of severely damaging another human being—something he hadn't expected to deal with at this point in his life. He had no regrets about his actions, as he had stated earlier. But Kenny couldn't help but wonder about the guy—about Rob—and if he had, or ultimately *would*, die from his wound. The weight of this thought proved for Kenny to be heavier than he would've expected.

When he got home, he went on auto-pilot. The first thing he did was get a shovel from the garage, wanting with an intense desire to bury this chapter of his life, and to move forward onto newer chapters, despite the overwhelming bitterness clinging to such transition. He dug a deep hole just near those cottonwoods, and the soil was damp, healthy of smell, black in its richness. They gathered around the hole, Kenny and the kids, along with Wayne. And Kenny placed George into the hole with care and precision, keeping in mind the importance of his dog's comfort, all the while understanding the silliness of such a notion.

Jolie wept openly, as most kids do. But on her face Kenny observed a hint of resolution, and he saw that she now knew with absolute confidence, the confidence found only in that of a child's mind, that George was up in Heaven, spending his time between guarding the Lord's gates, licking angels, and chasing legions of squirrels. And of course, being with Marley.

Logan stood beside his sister, stoic as ever, statue ready. He was as quiet as a cloud and had unbroken tears running down his cheeks.

Kenny said a brief prayer, and then they each took time and turns, shoveling dirt onto George, bringing the grave to near completion. "I'll make a sign for him," Kenny said after they finished. And they all knew that would be later. Perhaps in the morning, when they were all ready to come back to revisit this place.

CHAPTER 33

One morning, several days later, the cobalt sky was blanketed in brass. There wasn't a cloud in sight. Kenny stood outside, third cup of coffee in hand, as he skipped glances between the house, the sky, Jolie playing in the yard, and the humble garage before him.

The garage.

Logan was in there—*had* been in there for an hour already. This was the third day in a row that the boy had begun work before his dad. Kenny figured his son had seen a light at the end of the tunnel. And quietly, Kenny hoped that tunnel led to something more than the simple end to the sorting of nuts and bolts. Regardless, he had come outside prepared. He slipped a hand in his coat pocket and absently rubbed between his fingers the ten-dollar bill from the fridge. If nothing else came of it, today would be Logan's payday.

His son still hadn't said a single word since that tragic day in the forest. And Kenny still didn't mind. He had now found peace with the boy, or so he liked to think. At any rate, he no longer felt the agonizing need for his son to transition beyond his code of silence. The satisfaction of Logan's safety was plenty enough for Kenny. Everything else seemed trivial. And also, Kenny now believed that in time, everything else would eventually work itself out.

As he walked into the garage, he heard clinking sounds coming from the worktable. Logan had his back turned and was presently sorting through an assortment of machine screws. He had his favorite sweatshirt on, with the hood pulled over his head. Alone, and in the gloom of the garage, the boy was but a frail shadow.

Kenny walked over and turned on the lamp mounted on the wall. A pocket of bright light swamped the table, and Logan suddenly froze in place. The boy turned toward his dad, just a fraction of an inch was all, before nodding—a subtle expression addressing Kenny's presence. Then he went back to sorting.

It was their last pile of fasteners. A bulk of metal screws consisting of various lengths and thread sizes, as well as different heads and alloy types. There were pan heads and flat heads, round, oval, and hexagonal heads. Some were stainless steel, others were not. It was their last pile, and they were almost done, and damn if Kenny didn't feel something pull inside his chest.

He looked at the table, and then he smiled and looked at the back wall, with its shelves of coffee cans resembling rows of tin soldiers standing in formation. Approaching the completion of a job often left Kenny feeling warm and satisfied. He felt that way now, and he wondered if it was the same for his son.

The non-stop effort to organize the cans had begun on their first full day back from the cabin. Moments after they had posted the marker over George's grave, in fact.

It was Logan who had been the catalyst to the maelstrom, which would later consume almost a week's worth of waking hours. At first, Kenny wasn't sure what to make of his son's abrupt activity. But it wasn't long before he gave up thinking about it and simply joined in with the boy's momentum. Soon they were working with the speed of a pit crew, two sets of hands gliding quickly and effortlessly over the various mounds of hardware spread out across the table. Everything was done in silence, not a word spoken. At one point, Kenny brought out a radio and put on some music, but less than a minute into the first song, Logan walked over and turned it off. Kenny responded with a smile.

It was their last pile, and it would take them an hour at most to complete. With a brief jolt of panic, Kenny considered the very real consequences that awaited him at the end of this job. At the end of his own tunnel.

He wondered what they were going to do next. What would be the next forest fire to come along and devour up all the impending silence? Would there be one? Perhaps Logan could help him tear down the dilapidated shed out back. Then maybe they could build a new shed, a great big one. A clubhouse even— something for the kids to play in. Then again, maybe they'd take a break from work all together, and just go fishing.

One thing they wouldn't do was go back up to the cabin. Not Logan, anyway. And not anytime soon. But eventually, Kenny would make it back up there to finish his job.

The last pile—it had grown thinner, even before Kenny was ready. He set his cup down on the windowsill and rolled up his sleeves. Then he joined his son and began sifting through the fasteners...

She hit him then, five minutes into it. Marley. Bold as brass, bold as the sun's rays outside, the image of her face a sudden beacon to his thoughts, a one light burning in his mind. There was no reason for it. She was just there. And she was smiling, smiling fiercely. For all the good, and all the ill, and all the godforsaken tragedy that passed for their family, the woman was still there—smiling.

"I'm sorry, son," Kenny said.

The boy went still.

"I'm sorry, Logan. Sorry for what you've had to deal with." Kenny brushed a hand across his face. "Sorry for everything... everything I should have been doing for you, and for your sister, long before your mother died. I'm sorry—"

Logan's unexpected movement halted Kenny's speech. The boy pulled his hood down and looked up at his dad. His eyes were a storm of emotion. "It's not your fault," he said coldly.

A confusing mixture of fear and hope took root in the pit of Kenny's stomach. He said nothing—he didn't know *what* to say.

Logan picked up a handful of bolts and squeezed them tightly. "It's hers," he said. "It's her fault that she died, Dad... not yours. *She* did this to us." Logan squeezed his hand harder, and he raised it, the knuckles parched and tense, and he suddenly threw the bolts against the wall, and was then in his dad's arms, shouting and crying. "She did this to us, and it's not fair... I *hate her*!"

Those last words came out long and hollow—a deep anguish that resonated with exhaustion and pain, with grief and finality. But not with malice.

At last, Kenny now knew what his son had been feeling. Finally, he knew. And finally, Logan had spoken. And what the boy felt, and what he said, there wasn't an ounce of hate lying in there. Not even the smallest trace.

"She loves you too, Logan," Kenny said. "And she always will."

For five minutes, Kenny held his son as Logan cried. The boy cried long and loud, and at one point Jolie appeared from outside and joined them in their hug. Her presence was both quiet and reassuring.

For five minutes they embraced each other like that, in the garage, just the three of them—strong as pine trees—as they endured a storm of pain and sorrow. And for those five minutes, it killed Kenny not to break down and cry along with his son... for his son... *because* of his son.

Jolie cried though, and the sounds of her tears were soft and sweet, and made up for the bitterness Kenny still felt lingering inside his heart. This same bitterness forced him to realize then that as a parent, the hardest, cruelest, most terrifying thing he had ever faced was his children's sadness.

He saw her again, Marley, only this time she wasn't smiling.

For five minutes, they held one another. And then for ten. And then, for perhaps an hour, or for maybe half a day, or for what seemed like half his life, time tumbled its path into the distance, surreal and stream-like. But when this healing time had finally passed, Kenny blinked reality back into existence, and he saw his family—him and his kids—huddled together on the floor of their garage. *It was finally over*, he thought. *They could finally move on.*

Gently, he stood. Jolie was a split second behind, as she reached up and climbed up, and then she became a small burden to his arms and waist. He held her with both arms, while she rested her crying eyes on his shoulder.

Logan finally stood as well, manlike and proud, wiping tears from his face matter-of-factly. The boy took his time, but he moved over to the table and went back to work. Kenny held Jolie, and he made soft, rhythmic steps in the garage, pacing the shadowed room for a time. Eventually, he heard the dull clink of metal as bolts got tossed one by one into the can. It was a soothing sound to Kenny. The sound of steady persistence. The sound of something getting fixed.

But then, oddly, he heard another sound. A sound that began as a pinpoint in the far distance, but one that approached rapidly, and that came with a constant speed and punctuation. It was a thunderous, yet mechanical, sound. And it was coming up on them.

Kenny set Jolie down and walked outside. His eyes momentarily squinted against the brightness of the morning. And his ears momentarily rang from the cacophony, as produced by the many motorcycles now in his driveway.

There were roughly a dozen of them, men clad in black leather or weathered denim. Hard-looking men, adorned with tattoos and an assortment of metal hardware—rings, wallet chains, necklaces. One man even had on a spiked collar, Kenny noticed, and it was then that he wished he'd brought with him something from the garage. A hammer or screwdriver—a weapon of some sort. It would be a pointless endeavor, of course, as there were way too many of them.

Slowly, Kenny approached the cadre of bikers, but stopped as soon as one of them climbed off his bike. The man smiled, and his smile showed an ease of charisma. Kenny assumed this was the leader, so he fixed his stare on the man's eyes, and he watched him carefully.

"Well, good morning," the man said. "Name's Hondo." He peeled gloves off his hands as he approached Kenny. He was still smiling, and something about his smile struck Kenny as being forced and deliberate, despite the charismatic appeal. "You must be Kenny," the man said, reaching out for a handshake, "Kenny Shelton."

"What do you want?" Kenny said, keeping his hands at his side.

Hondo dropped his own hand and then chuckled. "Yeah, well," he said, an apologetic tone to his voice, "I don't blame you. I guess I wouldn't want to shake my hand either."

"Look, mister, I don't know you, and I don't know what this is about. But I've got my family here, so if you wouldn't mind..."

"Well," Hondo said, "you see, that's exactly why I'm out here." He glanced over his shoulder at the other bikers. "Family's exactly what this *is* about. It's why we're all out here."

Kenny squeezed his hands into fists, and he heard his breath quicken.

Hondo seemed to notice Kenny's reaction. He took a step back and said, "Relax, friend. That's not where this is going." Briefly, he crossed his arms over his chest, then dropped them and casually paced the driveway. "I'll get to the point," he said. "It seems you had a run-in with an associate of ours a few days back. An ugly dude—" he glanced at the others again, smiling, "—not that any of us are worth writing home about, in the way of looks—but this guy was really ugly, if you know what I mean."

Kenny now knew what this visit was about, and the knowledge had his stomach in an instant knot.

"Anyway," Hondo continued, "I heard you ran into this associate—mister Robert J. Boyle—and that, according to my sources, Rob wasn't all that polite to you and your family." Hondo waited, and then said, "And I also heard that you weren't all that nice to him."

"He tried to kill me," Kenny said, wondering just who this man's sources were. "And how'd you find all this out? How'd you find out about me, and where I live?"

"Now, now, don't go asking questions you don't want answers to," Hondo replied. "Let's just settle with the fact that I know people in certain places."

Kenny felt the tension in his hands loosen up. He still felt ill about this man called Hondo and his "associates" being here at his house. But it now seemed to Kenny that violence wasn't on the immediate agenda.

"Another thing," Hondo said, "I also heard Rob killed your dog." His face shifted suddenly, to an exaggerated look of disgust. "Is that true?"

Kenny replied with a nod.

"Did you boys see that?" Hondo said, turning to the other bikers. "Just like what I thought. What ol' Leroy thought, for that matter." He walked over to his bike and then turned back around. He stared at Kenny for several honest seconds, then motioned to one biker and said, "Cecil—bring it over."

Kenny felt the tension shoot back into his hands, not stopping there as it scrambled up his arms and into his shoulders.

The man named Cecil climbed off his bike and reached into a leather saddlebag. It immediately struck Kenny with shock when he saw what the man had pulled out. And he immediately felt and heard the echo of his shock as it blew past, realizing then that his kids were standing not five feet behind him, watching.

It was a puppy. A Shorthaired Pointer, in fact, and Cecil smiled tenderly at the dog as he brought it to them.

"Friend," Hondo said, "there are some lines people just don't cross. And a man's family... well, that's one of them."

They spoke no words after that. Hondo pulled his gloves back on. Then he straddled his bike, and Cecil did the same, and both men grinned and exchanged approving nods with Kenny, before they all turned their machines around and rode away.

In the ensuing silence, Kenny watched as Jolie and Logan took turns cuddling with their new pet. He saw the dog's excitement, saw how it beamed with happiness, as if it had finally found its way back home from a very long and arduous journey. And Kenny hardly missed the depth of his reflection, and the analogy lying therein.

He looked at his son and smiled. Then he held his breath and said, "So, what shall we call her?"

Without a moment's hesitation, Logan replied with, "Marley."

THE END

ABOUT THE AUTHOR

Chris Riley lives near Sacramento, California, vowing one day to move back to the Pacific Northwest. Until then, he continues to enjoy life as a husband, father, special education teacher, and writer.

In addition to *The Broken Pines*, he is the author of the suspense novel, *The Sinking of the Angie Piper*, as well as over 100 published short stories and essays.

NOTE FROM THE AUTHOR

Word-of-mouth is crucial for any author to succeed. If you enjoyed *The Broken Pines*, please leave a review online—anywhere you are able. Even if it's just a sentence or two. It would make all the difference and would be very much appreciated.

Thanks!
Chris Riley

We hope you enjoyed reading this title from:

BLACK ROSE
writing™

www.blackrosewriting.com

Subscribe to our mailing list – *The Rosevine* – and receive **FREE** books, daily deals, and stay current with news about upcoming releases and our hottest authors.
Scan the QR code below to sign up.

Already a subscriber? Please accept a sincere thank you for being a fan of Black Rose Writing authors.

View other Black Rose Writing titles at
www.blackrosewriting.com/books and use promo code
PRINT to receive a **20% discount** when purchasing.

Printed in the USA
CPSIA information can be obtained
at www.ICGtesting.com
BVHW031035220823
668788BV00004B/218